PAN

God of The Woods

BY

LAWRENCE R. SPENCER

Pan - God of the Woods

by Lawrence R. Spencer

Copyright © 2012 - 2017 by Lawrence R. Spencer

All Rights Reserved

ISBN: 978-1-4116-5390-0

Printed in USA

Original Artwork and Cover Designed by *Slavo*

ACKNOWLEDGEMENTS

Gratitude, eternal and unlimited, is deserved by all of the beings who have carried and passed the torch of spiritual enlightenment through the eons down to this present day. Each of us has benefited both spiritually and materially, from their vigilance and perseverance. It is the spiritual foundation of existence which enables one to endure and civilizations to prosper, whether that spirituality is manifested through philosophy, the arts, sciences, religion, humanitarian groups, or simply through being.

The accumulated application of spiritual understandings in our daily lives as individuals, as a family unit, through groups and nations, as part of the physical universe, through other life forms, and as an eternal spirit, is the source of existence and the motivating force of life.

It is my purpose to further the awareness of communication between ourselves and other spiritual beings, whether they are in a body or without. May we all become more able to live our lives effectively and in greater harmony with all beings.

- Lawrence R. Spencer

Disclaimer

    Many of the characters and events in this story are based on documented mythological and historical events. A partial bibliography of reference sources used for writing this book is included as proof that this story is not entirely contrived from the imagination of the author. Any references or resemblance to persons, living or dead, gods, mythological beings, ideas, superstitions, opinions, places, events or blatant lies which have been recorded as historical fact, are purely intentional.

    This novel is a work of fiction and satire. The author and publisher assume no responsibility of any kind whatsoever for any *negative* influence or effect of any kind which the material in this book may have upon the reader. The purpose of this book is to entertain and educate. The author and publisher shall have neither liability nor responsibility to any person or entity with respect to loss or damage caused, or alleged to be caused, directly or indirectly by the information contained in this book. If you do not wish to be bound by the above, you may return the book to the publisher for a full refund.

    The author accepts full responsibility for any *positive* effect the material in the book may have on the reader, no matter how insignificant or remote.

INTRODUCTION

When Zeus still ruled Olympus, the face of Mother Nature was puerile, the bright blue sea and sky shined brightly in Her eyes. Life, abundantly renewed, abounded from Her virgin womb. The myriad creatures flourished, safe and suckling on Her verdant breasts while fishes filled the pristine waters of Her world.

In those primal days, gods of ancient Sumeria, Egypt, Greece, China, India, and many other civilizations of Earth, commanded extraordinary power over men. Spirits were conceived to permeate all matter and space in the ancient world. The gods, however, were not much different than each of us as spiritual beings, except to the degree they were immortal, that is, free from having to inhabit a body. Mortals were condemned to repeat the cycle of birth and death and rebirth into carnal form. Release of the spirits of men from the endless cycle of reincarnation remains the ultimate goal of many world religions to this day.

Gods actively intervened in the affairs of Mankind. Some made their presence known in the form of an animal, as an aura of light or scent, or as an apparition in nature. More often, the gods pervaded the body and mind of a man or woman, either in a dream or simply by taking over their thoughts to carry out their plans.

Since the gods were seen to cause events, both natural and supernatural, they were intimately personified, widely idolized, and artfully glorified by men. Aristocracy, citizens and slaves alike, sought the blessing or advice of the gods regarding marriage, travel, war, purchases, planting, harvesting, building, birth and death. Every village, district and nation had its own retinue of gods. A discreet traveler was wise to observe the rites accorded to the local deities and religious tolerance was widespread.

A vast number of myths or stories about the exploits of the gods have passed down to us through the generations of Mankind from nearly every society of antiquity. Culturally, we have inherited tremendous works of art, poetry, literature, and tradition derived from human interaction with the immortals. The pagan cultural tradition, religious beliefs, and practices associated with the gods still permeate our language, social and religious customs today.

With the advent of the Christian church 2,000 years ago, communication with the pagan gods was very heavily suppressed in Western civilization. Priests had a vested interest in eliminating religious competition, by any means required, including, but not limited to lying, stealing, cheating, murder, mayhem, extortion, torture and blackmail. This included outlawing all pagan religions and the destruction of all pagan temples and schools throughout the Roman Empire by the decree of Emperor Justinian in the third century AD. As a result, general public attention to the pagan gods disappeared.

The premise of PAN – God of the Woods, is that the pagan gods, as active, living beings, may only appear to have disappeared! If any of the ancient gods are still around in the 21st century, what are they doing now? If they are here now -- still watching, still powerful, still immortal -- where or how might we contact them?

Pan, the Greek god of forests, shepherds and fertility, has long represented the pagan gods in general. Although the material in this novel is fictional, it is firmly based in a study of the 10,000 year old tradition of mythology, as well as world history, eastern spiritual philosophy, past lives and out-of-body, extrasensory experiences.

The 19th century poet, Oscar Wilde, beseeched the god Pan in his verse:

"O goat-foot God of Arcady!

This modern world is gray and old,

And what remains to us of thee?

Then blow some trumpet loud and free

And give thine oaten pipe away,

Ah, leave the hills of Arcady!

This modern world hath need of thee!"

Which of us mortals could not use the helping hand of a friendly god once in awhile?

-- Lawrence R. Spencer

- AN INVOCATION OF THE GODS -

Where upon Olympus stand the gods who once ruled over Man? Fallen from the Lofty Land to dwell on Earth as mortal men?

Who remembers how to fly as freeborn spirits through the sky? What powers can be exercised while trapped within a mortal guise?

The gods once caused themselves to bring The Breath of Life itself to being. Their very thoughts made every thing: the sea, a sigh, the sky, the spring!

The Gods of Old like you & me, created everything we see. Have they lost causality? Abandoned their abilities?

Where are the gods of history? What happened to their memory? If we are them and they are we, who will cause our destiny?

Merchant Lords now rule the fold. They want us all to fit their mold: "Be a Man! Do as you're told! The only god there is, is gold!"

How did we ever sink so low, pretending we don't really know that we're the spark that makes life grow, like springtime flowers through the snow?

Infinity is passing by, but time is really just a lie. Are we immortal, you and I? A question states its own reply...

We never really know we're blind until we search around to find a simple way to leave behind the suffering that is Mankind.

Can godly powers be regained, like oceans fall to Earth as rain? Can we go back from whence we came, to greater heights and bigger games?

Lead us homeward once again, to realms beyond the dreams of men. We've gone astray, we've lost our ken*. We need your help, Immortal Friends!

*ken = perception; understanding, range of vision, view; sight.

-- Lawrence R. Spencer

- PAN'S INTRODUCTION -

I, Pan, God of the Woods, God of Fertility and of Shepherds, narrate this partially fictional account, through a mortal, for translation into a written text. It is my decision to communicate directly with you now so that you may receive the true, unaltered knowledge of My Existence, as I have been and always shall be, forever and ever.

I care not for your debased sense of human drama, limited as it is to purely physical perception, which requires that you be bludgeoned in every sentence with murder, mayhem, sexual tension and other such drivel. If these you require to maintain sufficient attention to receive the priceless information contained within My Words, read no further!

However, in order to compensate for the possibility that even I may have misestimated the abysmal depths to which you may have descended, I will structure the narrative in the most simplistic theatrical form – that of the daytime television drama or "soap opera" -- so that even you, mere mortal, (if you pay diligent attention and do not drift and daze, as you are often wont to do) may comprehend the subtle profundities woven within the tale.

My Intention is not to help you pass away the moments of your fruitless and purposeless existence with an entertaining divergence, but rather to impart a small part of the wisdom I have accumulated during my brief visitation as a god to the planet Earth. If you seek to know what lies beyond the perceptions of your mortal flesh, read on.

This is a story of how one human, Derek Adapa, departed his body and I salvaged him, through My Power and Benevolence, from an oblivious return to inhabit yet another body in the endless cycle of birth, death and re-birth -- the common affliction of Lost Souls on Earth, such as Yourself.

These words are made available to you, My Old Friend, on behalf of the gods that are no more. It is for Their sake, the Great Souls, now lost, that I am concerned. You, yourself, may have been among my former Friends, the gods who once ruled and roamed the Earth – from India and Babylon, from KMT, as Egypt once was called, to Olympus Mount, and beyond the bounds defined by men.

May My Story arouse you to remember who you really are. If so, attend! Come, play with Me once again!

Cast of Players

PAN - The Greek/Roman God of the Woods, of Shepherds and Fertility. Creator of the 'Pan pipes'. National God of Arcadia.

AKA – The god Ea of Sumeria and Babylon, AKA – The god Min of Egypt, AKA – Shiva of India

DEREK ADAPA - Founder, CEO of Nimbus Software, Incorporated, makers of "ThunderCalc". *("Adapa" in Babylonian mythology (dating from 14th century B.C.E.) was a god who lost the gift of immortality for Mankind due to the treachery of his 'father', the god Ea.*

JENNIFER ADAPA - Derek's Wife, AKA - Ast (Isis) of Egypt

LAO TZU - Chinese philosopher, legendary author of the *Tao-Te-Ching*

PAULA CADMUS - Derek's secretary/mistress/mother *(Cadmus = "from the east" was a hero in Greek myth, the King of Thebes. His sister Europa was abducted and raped by Zeus.)*

    AKA – Bast or Bastet, Cat goddess of Egypt

AKA - Parvati, wife of Shiva

PENELOPE - Former Greek mortal elevated to the status of a god by Zeus.

PYTHAGORAS - Greek philosopher, mathematician and musician.

HOMOSAPUS – Hero of the 'Myth of Homosapus *(euphemism for Homo sapiens or humankind)*

SHAMANUS - Priest of the Creators in "The Myth of Homo Sapus" *(a shaman, priest)*

PSYCHLES – Wife of Shamanus *(psychles, the witch doctor, the psychiatrist)*

DONNABELLA – Daughter of Shamanus (euphemism for Belladonna, a deadly herb)

BILLY JOE & VIRGIL JARAS - (In mythology 'Jaras' is Old Age, Slayer of Vishnu)

MELVIN "BUBBA" GUMSHOE - Sheriff of Sasquatch County, along with his deputies, Johnlaw and Peeler.

P.R. PROCTOR - Derek's attorney

PETER PLEADER, of the law firm, Pleader, Kryor & Saub - Billy & Virgil's attorney

BARRY BARRISTER - Paula's attorney

FATHER PRYOR FLAMEN – Priest (Pryor and Flamen are both archaic names for 'priest')

DR. SETH "MOUNTEY" MOUNTEBANK* – Psychiatrist (*a mountebank is 'quack' doctor)

Chapter I

"Attribute all to the gods. They pick a man up, stretched on the black loam and set him on his two feet firm. Then again, (they) shake solid men until they fall backward into the worst of luck, wandering hungry, wild of mind."

-- Archilochus of Paros (c. 648 BC)

Derek hated his life. He hated what he had become. He was a tremendous success in the eyes of others but a failure to himself. He didn't even like computers anymore. They hadn't become what he dreamed they might when he got into the personal computer industry in the late 1970's. They had become nothing more than a glorified typewriter/filing cabinet/calculator/pin-ball machine shrouded in a lot of flashy jargon, technical bells and whistles, and big price tags.

Of course he'd become very, very rich selling software to businessmen whose entire purpose for living was chasing the dollar to maintain a lifestyle of buying all the completely useless junk that Madison Avenue copy writers could cram down their already glutted throats through slick glossy magazine copy and boob-tube advertising - the American Dream.

Derek had become a member of this herd without realizing it. He owned a new BMW convertible, a Mercedes for his wife, and a 4-wheel drive monster all-terrain vehicle for weekends. They had a big house in the valley, took vacations abroad, and three day weekend 'business' trips. His investments, meetings, and social life were all politically correct. His life was an endless run on the economic treadmill.

It's not that he needed any more money. Derek's company, Nimbus Software, had become a mega-success in the first ten years. He had been in the right place, at the right time, with the right product, in the right industry. In 1979 the virgin personal computer industry was just emerging into a marketplace hungry for new technology.

His minor in business administration at Cabrillo J.C. and major in the still new and mysterious computer 'sciences' had paid off. He wrote the first successful business accounting software for PCs. He called it *ThunderCalc*.

The company logo was a small cloud with a bolt of lightning descending from it. Little arithmetic signs hung in the cloud like the positive and negative ions in real clouds which soon became the most recognizable symbol in the software business.

Nimbus had just released the newest revision of *ThunderCalc,* version 7.0. When it was first released, it was the only accounting software available. Every businessman in the country, who needed an excuse to buy a computer so they could play "asteroids" without having to put a quarter in an arcade machine, bought *ThunderCalc*. Since then the Nimbus Research and Development team released a plethora of software programs – spreadsheets, word processor, database management, communications, corporate planning, etc. – all the essential programs for American business.

That was a long time ago, Derek thought lethargically. He was tired. Tired of 'corporate culture', decisions about which shade of carpeting would be most suitable for an Assistance VP's office. He was tired of the endless circus of trade shows and hospitality suite cocktail parties, sales meetings, market-share strategies, board meetings, profit and loss statements, tax shelters, hot-and-cold-running attorneys and in recent years, press interviews.

It seemed like every magazine writer he talked to wanted to know the same things: "To what did he attribute the success of Nimbus Software? What about the competitor's new product enhancements? What do you think will be the future of the PC industry?" The whole business and industry seemed so automatic now. It had all become a sales and marketing game with just enough R & D revisions to keep up with the latest technology.

Beginning in 1980 new consumer computer technology was released in carefully spoon-fed portions to the buying public to ensure that every dollar could be squeezed out of existing inventories before unveiling the next "technical breakthrough" to be hyped dramatically in over-priced, four-color glossy trade magazine and television ads.

The profits kept coming in at 100% or more above the previous year. That made the stockholders happy. But Derek wasn't happy. He was tired of playing the game now. Been there, done that, burned out.

Derek built Nimbus Software by riding the enthusiasm of his early success in a new and booming industry. There had been a few dramatic moments along the way: big sales deals, new releases, overcoming the threat of neophyte competitors with increasingly elaborate marketing campaigns and distribution deals. The licensing agreement with the federal government that put Nimbus Software programs on every PC the federal government bought for the next ten years had been the crowning sales coup which ensured perpetual income for Nimbus Software, Inc.

But money wasn't everything. When he first started out in the business he had dreams for the computer. His humanitarian dreams had gradually evaporated from the barren landscape of real world marketing and finance. He had envisioned a vast horizon of technical innovation whose power could be an immense civilizing influence across the entire planet. The technology of computers, he thought, would be the promise and fulfillment of man's dream to rise out of the mud of cultural and technical barbarism into a new golden age of communication and understanding.

Recently, he'd read in some industry magazine about the unprecedented growth in technology over the past twenty years versus cost of a computer. If the airline industry had made similar advances we would all be able to fly around the world in 12 minutes, eat a seven course gourmet meal, choose from one of several thousand in-flight movies, and be delivered to your own front door, all for a cost of only $3.12. Something like that anyway. Used intelligently, a computer could be made to operate all of the mundane mechanical functions of an entire planet. Not just serve as a personal plaything or part-time business tool.

All of the technology already existed to supply everyone in the world with a pocket-sized computer capable of nearly magical power: a combination of telephone, TV, video camera, personal information center, library and fax machine. Each person could have a personal telephone number assigned to him or her for life which they could use anywhere: home, car, abroad, in airplanes, at sea. By punching in a number on a hand-held, cordless keyboard one could access all of the information held in the Library of Congress, every book ever written: indexed and cross referenced. Everyone would have access to photographs of all of the art objects in the Louvre and all the other great art museums available for instant view. You could dial every phone number in the world. Instant shopping, bill paying, news, music, instruction and information services could be available 24 hours a day, 365 days a year. The world could truly become a global society of individuals connected and in communication with each other regardless of artificial boundaries imposed by political bureaucrats.

Over the years Derek had grown up in the real world he learned the realities of the business and economics of myopic, individuated, selfish people. Too many agreements existed to monitor the civilizing process of mankind based on the whim of financial expediency in a culture bent on surviving from one paycheck to the next. There were no long range plans, no unifying philosophy of survival, no purposes or goals for nations or individuals beyond the next buck. It was just a soulless, mindless stampede from one expedient vested interest deal to the next. It was depressing...

"Brrrrrrrik!" Derek was jolted out of his reverie by the intercom on his desk. He pushed the speaker button and said, "Yes?"

"Your wife is on line 7, Mr. Adapa," said the voice of his secretary.

Over the past year and a half Paula had proven to be indispensable: a very effective, efficient, personal secretary.

"Hello Jenny. What's up?" he said, leaning slightly toward the speaker.

"Dear, I wish you wouldn't talk to me on that awful conference call box. It makes you sound like you're inside a tin can. Anyway, listen. Don't forget you must be home by 5:00 tonight. The guests will here for dinner at 7:30 and I have a million things to do to get ready. The caterer will be at the house by 6:00. I need you to be dressed and help me get the drinks ready. I have an appointment with Antonio to get my hair done at 3:30 and God only knows how long it will take."

"OK. OK, Jenny. I'll be there as soon as I can. Don't worry about it. Everything will be fine" said Derek, trying not to sound bored or impatient.

"Oh, and dear, if the caterers get there before I get back, please don't eat any of the hors d'oeuvres. Those are for the guests. I'll see you as soon as I get home. Bye."

Derek switched off the speaker and leaned back into his high-back leather executive chair, absently stirring his half cold cup of coffee, melancholically returning to his reflection.

He and Jennifer were married right after college graduation. They started living together during college to share expenses and sex. They fell in love gradually, like most people do. She was a bright, well organized, athletic sort, a wholesome, pretty, and perfect wife for him. She was his lover, best friend, personal manager, and social coordinator.

Their life together had been a good one he thought, though in recent years their marriage had been consumed by his business life and her charity work. The dinner party they were having tonight was a business/social get together with a few couples from Silicon Valley computer circles.

Derek needed time away from the office to get with Vern Sampson, his VP Marketing, to plan an upcoming trade show. They could discuss it after dinner at his home with fewer distractions than at the office. Their wives could handle all the other guests with gossip about local society news, kids, schools, politics, interior decorating. The usual dinner-party talk. Derek needed excuses to get out of the office more often during the past few years it seemed.

He and Jenny always got along well. They were both too busy to not get along really. They had learned to play the game well together. They still had sex once or twice a week, but that was pretty automatic now too. No magic, no mystery, like when they were younger.

Derek wondered if this had something to do with the incident with Paula one night after hours at the office. They often worked together after hours in his office to catch up on overloads. Their work gradually developed into a close friendship, but they had always maintained a professional relationship

Paula was young, sleek, and cat-like, with long, straight dark brown hair, nearly oriental eyes and full, pouting lips. That evening she seemed to almost purr when near him, unintentionally enticing his attention to her svelte feline form. She leaned over his shoulder to read a document. Her firm young breasts brushed against him. Instantly, he felt like a horny teenager again.

What started as flirting horse-play quickly became kissing and passionate petting. He put his hands under her skirt, pulled down her panties and bent her over his desk. She was filled with hot, wet passion. They made love standing up, then in his chair and finally on the floor. Their lovemaking was frantic and uncontrollable. Their orgasms were simultaneously explosive and all-consuming. Afterward they lay together on the carpet exhausted by the effort. They slept for half an hour in a blissful, semi-naked embrace. The scent of cedar hung lightly in the office air.

They awoke suddenly, alarmed and embarrassed by the realization of what had happened. In retrospect, their lovemaking seemed unintended by either of them and beyond their control. Although they shared a deep affinity for each other, they had a business relationship and friendship which were far too important to risk ruining with an affair. They were both intelligent and worldly: wise enough to know that sex had no place between professionals, especially with a married partner who loved his wife.

Derek and Paula sat for some time talking about what happened. They finally agreed on a reasonable sounding explanation: spiritual attraction between people can be misinterpreted as sexual love. They decided that they must be careful to control their hormones in the future.

Without saying so, she was a very special person to him. He felt he had known her forever, though they had met only two years ago. Although Paula would always be discreet, he was concerned that Jenny have no suspicions of the incident with Paula. He had always been faithful to her till now and loved her deeply, although he found it difficult to express to her in words. It was a knowing feeling, a spiritual bond they shared. He had no intention of losing her.

Derek didn't think he really knew much about Paula's personal life. He had never been to her apartment or met her friends. He knew that she had an uncanny affinity for cats though. He remembered when he interviewed her for the job as his secretary she seemed skittish about his office, examining him, the space, and objects in it, like a cat in a new home, confident, but cautious.

Paula decorated her office with all sorts of cat pictures, knick-knacks and cards. Since she started working for him, Derek had given her presents of several stuffed toy cats, porcelain and bronze statues and cat jewelry. She kept several cats in her apartment and talked about them by name as though they were people. Oh well, it wasn't important. Business is business. And her business was hers.

Derek looked at his watch: 1:35. He didn't feel like working today. He knew the evening would be tied up with "homework". He punched the intercom. "Paula?" he said.

"Yes, Mr. Adapa?"

"Send all my calls to my voice mail today. I'm going to the club this afternoon."

"Can I come too?" Paula teased.

"No. I've got a headache." he whispered. "I'm just going to go for a swim and a rubdown and go home. You know I have to be home by 5:00."

Derek knew that Paula always listened in on calls from Jenny, and God knows who else, even though she would never admit it. Sometimes he thought Paula knew more about what was happening in his life than he did.

"I'll see you tomorrow. We can have lunch together" he said pushing away from his desk.

He drove to the health club he'd been a member of for over seven years now: *GOODBODYS*. Not *great* bodies, just good. But it was only ten minutes away from the office so he could sneak away for a long lunch to swim or jog a little. Sometimes he had a meeting at the club over a game of racquetball. Derek tried to stay in shape though the years were starting to show around his waist. Every year it was a little harder to get up from the dinner table and get it up in bed. "Well, what the hell", he thought. "We can't stay young forever." The idea depressed him further.

Derek looked at his fortyish body in a full-length mirror in the locker room. His "love handles" were lounging along the tops of his swimming trunks. He pulled them up a bit and sucked in his gut a little more.

"Maybe I should get a personal trainer," he thought disconsolately. "Ah, what the hell. Who cares?"

Nobody at work cared. Paula didn't seem to care. Jenny didn't seem to care either. In bed the lights were always out when they made love, so she couldn't really see him anyway. Derek was jolted out of his self-abasing funk by the chill water of the pool. The swim did make him feel better for awhile.

Derek left the gym after a lack-luster workout. He just couldn't get into it. His drive home in the afternoon freeway traffic was a lot faster than the usual commuter crawl. No one was home. Jenny was still out and the caterers hadn't arrived yet.

Derek trudged upstairs to the master bedroom. He flopped down in the overstuffed chair that had been his favorite for years. So many times he had sat there dosing while he waited for Jenny to finish dressing and primping for some dinner or charity ball or art opening or musical they had attended.

He absently flicked on the TV with the remote control. A white-haired, chisel-faced news anchorman appeared in mid-sentence:

"...and the President, attending the 43rd annual secret Summit Conference of Unilateral Money Manipulators (S.C.U.M.M.) in Geneva, Switzerland today. He is expected to deliver a prepared statement appealing for lower interest rates and increased import duty tariffs on raw materials which have been exported by US Corporations to supply Third World factories, who in turn ship finished goods back into the U.S. at prices higher than the same goods could have been manufactured by American workers. The Secretary of State, in a related statement, said that no significant changes in the declining world economy and decaying trade relations were expected from the conference.

In Congress today..."

Derek picked up the TV program guide which lay on an antique end-table next to his chair. He flipped past the first 30 or 40 pages of advertising to get to the daily listings as he sauntered into the bathroom. He dropped his shorts and sat down heavily on the toilet as he read through the 5:00 programs.

"Whew!" he said out loud as he grunted. The stink wafted up from the bowl.
"I better cut back on the cheeseburgers" he thought to himself.

He flushed and read the TV program guide:

Channel 5 (KCOP)	"Cops-R-Us" - Grown men playing cops and robbers at taxpayer expense.
Channel 6 (KFBI)	"Justice Behind Closed Doors" - Courtroom cases are decided with a Federal prosecutor in Judge Harold Harlequin's private chambers.
Channel 7 (KDRG)	"Your Favorite Busts" - Video highlights of heavily armed Law Enforcement Agents busting political activists and small-time drug dealers.
Channel 8 (KFBI)	Movie: "The FBI in Peace and War" - 1938. Jeff Chandler plays an embattled FBI agent during the McCarthy Era fighting movie stars and communists.
Channel 9 (KLAW)	"Lawyers in Love" - Daytime drama. Brad subpoenas his lover, Jeff, to appear before a jury to testify that he had no knowledge of his affair with the D.A.'s wife in her paternity suit against him.
Channel 10 (KDUH)	Really Big Time Wrestling Live! (Pre-recorded) Today's tag-team match-up: The Bataglia Brothers from the Bronx take on the Tiny Titans from Trenton, NJ in this continuing cross-town grudge match. Real sweat! Real fake fights! Real fans! (repeat)
Channel 11 (KDUM)	The Phil O'Donnell Show - Phil's guests today are members of the

	"Children of Lesbian Transsexual Hemophiliacs". Phil discusses the alarming neglect of government welfare agencies of these unfortunate victims of social disease.
Channel 12 (KCUM)	"The Young and Randy" – (Daytime drama) Susan and Sally make love in Brad's bed while Brad secretly video tapes the fun by remote control while he makes love with Sally's mother and younger brother in the next room.
Channel 13 (KSIK)	Kiddie Kartoon Karnival - Space Cyborgs slaughter each other. Starring: Soldier Sam.
Channel 14 (KWAR)	The WAR MOVIE CHANNEL - Movie: "John Wayne Kicks Gook Butt" An anthology of clips from John's 10 best films of 1956. John defends the American Way for U.S. oil companies abroad.
Channel 15 (KCON)	Fake-Book News – Jewish comedians posing as "reporters" drone non-stop drivel about politicians pretending to be "serving" the American people while making themselves and their Zionist owners rich and powerful.
Channel 16 (KDDT)	CIA News Network (CNN) – The latest in zany politics, false flag wars, environmental mayhem, financial con games, cultural chaos, psychotic agendas and cute kittens gathered

	from random social media sources. (Sponsored by Big Pharma)
Channel 17 (KS&M)	Horror Movie Theatre: (1989) "Eat My Guts Baby". Robert Ghoul and Sheila Smut star in a remake of this classic pain and sex thriller.
Channel 18 (KGOD)	Rev. Jerry Fallenangel. Today's sermon topic: "*Is There Life Without Lust?*"

Derek started to feel nauseated. Now he remembered why he stopped watching TV about five years ago. TV programming was bullshit. He finished in the bathroom, returned to the bedroom, flicked the TV off and got dressed for dinner.

Dinner was the typical catered California health food fare: white wine, stuffed cauliflower kabobs with tofu chunks, sautéed in seaweed sauce, avocado salad sandwiches on stone ground seven grain bread, mahi-mahi sushi, and spinach hors d'ouvres and for desert, non-fat red raspberry swirl tofu ice cream.

After the other guests were settled in the living room, chatting over herb tea, Derek and Vern Samson excused themselves and disappeared into the recreation room. At about 9:30 they slipped out the side door and drove to a local *Burger Barn* drive-thru for a chili-cheese burger, Cajun fries and Diet Coke. They talked about the upcoming fall trade show in Las Vegas for awhile, but Derek just couldn't get into it.

"Just go with the same basic booth set-up we always use", Derek burped up some chili which burned his throat a bit.

He farted and rolled down the windows of his BMW and sighed.

"What's up boss?" asked Vern, slouching in his bucket seat and turning away from the window toward his boss in spite of the lingering odor.

"You don't seem to have the same old spark lately. Is everything OK at home?" Vern asked consolingly.

"Oh, I don't know, man. I'm just tired I think. Jenny's OK. I think I've just been working too much. You know these trade shows and new releases just aren't as exciting to me as they were when we were getting started back in the old days. You know what I mean?"

Derek knew he could confide anything in Vern. They'd been together a long time. Derek switched off the headlights and cut the engine as they coasted into the driveway back at the house. He and Vern returned unnoticed into the side entrance to the recreation room. All the guests were still in the living room.

"I'm getting older. I'm not a kid anymore, you know? Jenny and I have been married for almost 17 years now. Everything seems like the same old rehash these days."

Derek plopped down on a leather sofa against the redwood paneled wall at the far end of a spacious, deeply carpeted room. An antique pool table, which he rarely used anymore, stood at the other end of the room adjacent to several arcade-size video games and pin-ball machines.

Vern ventured, "Well, why not diversify? Develop a new product. Build up a new R & D unit. Maybe do a new hardware…"

Derek cut in, "No, I'm not really interested in that either. We've been over all this before. I don't want to reinvent the wheel and start all over again from scratch with another product. I just don't have it in me anymore. I guess I'm just not hungry enough."

Derek slumped back into the overstuffed cushions of the sofa which creaked softly as only leather upholstery can do.

"You know, just between you and me I've been thinking about selling my stock. Maybe retirement. I need something..." he said, running his hand through his thinning black hair and closing his eyes.

"Jeez boss, that's a little drastic isn't it? I mean, who could replace you? What would you do? What would happen to Nimbus without you?" said Vern with astonishment.

"Nobody's irreplaceable Vern. Not even me", sighed Derek.

"Oh" said Vern casting his eyes to the floor and fidgeting with a cocktail napkin.

"Don't worry about it. Forget I said anything. I guess I'm just tired. You know." Derek groaned as he kicked off his Italian loafers onto the carpet. Vern relaxed visibly. After a pause he furrowed his brow, stroked his chin with his fingers, and said "Maybe you should just get away for a bit. Take a vacation. Take Jenny to Maui for a few weeks or something. Take a cruise. Get your mind off things."

"I don't know Vern. Maybe. I'll think about it," yawned Derek pushing himself up wearily as he said, "Let's go see how the others are doing".

*   *   *   *   *   *   *   *   *

At 5:00 AM the sun wouldn't be up for another hour but Derek was already on Interstate 5 on his way north to Whiskeytown National Recreation Area. He figured if he drove straight through with just gas stops he could make it there around noon time, get settled in his rented cabin at the north end of the lake and be set to start his back-packing trip early the next morning.

As the miles droned on under the mild roar of his tires Derek thought back to Friday night. Vern and his wife left about midnight after spending a compulsory half-hour in the living room talking with their wives to exchange the usual social pleasantries and thank you's and "Gee, I guess it's getting lates" and "Gotta get up early tomorrow" chit-chat that seemed interminable to everyone, yet none-the-less essential to socially acceptable existence.

The next morning, over brunch at the country club, for which they paid a huge annual fee to be seen eating a meal once a month or so, he asked, "Why don't we go away together for a while? I need a rest".

Jenny insisted that she would simply not be able to get away from her commitments to the L.O.F.T.Y. (League of Feminine Traditions and Yearning) Benefit Concert with the Palo Alto Philharmonic Virtuosi. She suggested that perhaps he could go camping with the boys for a few days to get his mind off work. He thought this a good idea but couldn't find anyone who could get away for more than a day as they had already had their lives planned for them by their wives weeks in advance and couldn't make it on only a few days' notice. So he decided to go by himself.

Derek hadn't been backpacking for more than four years, but still had all his equipment stored in the loft of the garage. He went to the Army-Navy store to replenish his supply of freeze-dried foods. When he got it all home he realized it was enough to feed three men for a month. But he packed as much as he could in his $375.00 light weight nylon, magnesium-framed pack along with his $450.00 all- temperature sleeping bag, $175.00 hiking boots, his $750.00 automatic 35 mm camera and all the other boy scout type paraphernalia he could think of that he could stuff in between a couple of changes of clothing.

His father took the family camping in the mountains nearly every summer while he was growing up in California.

Derek remembered how much he'd always enjoyed the mountains. The clean, crisp fragrance of pine trees and the fine brown dust that seemed to get everyone so gloriously dirty. Bacon and eggs and burnt pancakes cooked on a cast-iron griddle over an open fire in the chill of the early morning mountain altitude. The smell of campfire smoke in his clothes. The gentle roar of wind in the trees and the always amazing magnificence of the night sky splattered with billions of blinking stars above the towering pines. The precious warmth of lying scrunched down fully clothed, in his sleeping bag near the embers of a dying campfire. There was a serenity and simplicity about it that he had almost forgotten. Now he was off to enjoy it again. To renew old pleasurable moments, relax and take a new look at his life for a few precious days alone.

On the map Derek had chosen a range of forest in the Trinity Mountains for his hiking excursion. He knew that amid that virgin timber in the shadow of Mt. Shasta there were still places to hike where no man had ever stepped. Remote and pristine, primeval pine forests.

The drive north was uneventful and pleasant. The broad base and flat volcanic top of Mt. Shasta grew on the horizon with mysterious majesty. Interstate 5 was one of the finest highways in the world, as were most of the freeways in California. It stretched smooth and straight through the center of the richest agricultural lands on earth which were now being steadily covered with high-priced, single-family housing, fast food franchises and shopping malls. The entire countryside was being transformed into a continuous homogeneous stretch of asphalt, billboards, storefronts and parking lots filled with late-model Japanese cars, driven by lower middle-class consumers of non-biodegradable plastic goods.

It had been years since Derek had driven this route. He was more than a little shocked by the sprawling jumble of human habitation marked by freeway exit signs to towns that he'd never heard of and which didn't exist the last time he'd driven this way.

Derek bought a campfire permit at the ranger station and got directions to the cabin his travel agent had rented for him. Derek had waited his turn in line amid other late season vacationers and early season deer hunters who bought hunting, camping and camp fire permits. Derek had never cared for the idea of killing wild game for sport. Somehow the notion that shooting a beautiful animal in it's natural environment through a high magnification scope mounted on a semi-automatic rifle was not "sport", but legalized murder of innocent life forms whose flesh was not needed for food -- not in a country overflowing with enough food to feed the entire population of Earth. The table scraps thrown into the garbage every day by restaurants and military dining halls alone could feed millions of starving Africans. Hunting was necessary only to satisfy the primordial, Neanderthal blood-lust of a bunch of red-neck pickup truck jockeys with the I.Q. of an empty beer can.

Derek arrived at his cabin in the late afternoon. The cabin would serve as a base from which his hiking excursion would begin. He wanted to have a bed and shower after being on the trail for a couple of days. He unpacked his stuff and settled himself for a one night stay. He'd go to bed early and get up about 6:00 AM to begin his 3-day wilderness trek.

While he ate a frozen pizza heated in the cabin microwave, and cream-filled chocolate cupcakes washed down by diet soda, he began to relax. He didn't want to watch TV, he hadn't brought any books, and there really weren't any other amusements. So he opened the front door of the cabin and sat in a wooden chair on the front porch and just did nothing. As he sat in the calm of the surrounding forest, the affairs of men and life began to ebb from his mind.

He became aware of the smell of pine needles, earth and brush. He heard the rush of breezes high in the trees, the twitter and chirp of birds and the occasional buzz of a passing bug. They soothed him. The soft evening sunlight filtering through the pine boughs and animated tiny dust specks drifting in the air. He sighed and tilted his chair back against the cabin wall. This is what he'd come for. The purifying solitude and natural aesthetic of the mountain forest drained his thoughts into a universe of serene carelessness. There was a pure, pristine pleasantness about it. He sat.

Darkness drank the forest. The evening chill cleansed the air. Stars twinkled in silence. Calm. Sleep. A subtle scent of cedar lingered, though there were no cedar trees. Through the woodland rushed a winsome, whispered sigh.

CHAPTER II

"O goat-foot God of *Arcady!
This modern world is gray and old,
And what remains to us of thee? ...

Then blow some trumpet loud and free,
And give thine oaten pipe away,
Ah, leave the hills of Arcady*!
This modern world hath need of thee!"

-- Oscar Wilde, (c. 1854-1900)

(*Arcady = Arcadia, the southern region of Greece, for which Pan is the national god.)

Derek was on the trail at 6:00 AM as planned. By 8:00 he reached the first landmark shown on the map he'd picked up at the ranger station. It was a small lake around which the trail led as it crawled over a rise on the opposite shore and disappeared into a dense forest. He was invigorated by the clean, oxygen-rich morning air. The crunching scuff of gravel and earth under foot gave substance to his stride. Pine trees scattered the path with brown needles. Their perfume pervaded the air. Occasionally the more acrid odor of sage brush, Manzanita bushes, and milk weed filled his nose. A pair of chattering chipmunks scampered across his path and skittered up a nearby tree, turning to see him pass in arrogant safety high up among the branches, their cheek pouches puffed with pine nuts. Blue jays squawked and scolded him from their tree top sanctuaries. Derek was in the native lands of nature now. An intruder.

About 10:00 A.M. Derek stopped to rest and eat and drink something. He had kept a leisurely but steady pace along the trail. He estimated by the map that he'd come about 9 or 10 miles, having paused only to drink from his canteen briefly and remove his sweatshirt which had become too hot to wear. He propped his pack against a fallen log and sitting there, spread his food beside him. His appetite was keen, invigorated by the exercise and fresh air at this altitude. His body seemed eager and at home here, alive with sensation sharpened by the surroundings and the ever-present sloping grandeur of Mt. Shasta on his left hand vista.

As Derek ate he realized how foreign he seemed to this place. The cellophane wrappers, printed paper labels, plastic forks, and the processed foods he had brought. Dried figs, sharp cheddar cheese, soda crackers and salami. Even the fabrics of his clothes and shoes seemed peculiar here. They were a phony fabrication by man of unnatural nature.

Derek sighed, stuffed the leftovers back into his pack, stood and stretched. He was about half way to his destination for the day, 'Crescent Lake', about 8 miles northeast. That is where the trail would end and he would start out on his own into untrammeled regions. One day out and one day back from the lake. It was to be his real wilderness adventure.

He hadn't seen any other hikers since about 9:00 when he'd passed a young couple coming down from the lake. It was very late in the season for hiking and camping now. By 4:00 Derek had arrived at Crescent Lake, rested, set up his overnight campsite and gathered some firewood. He was alone here, much to his relief and delight. The afternoon sun was still above the hills, casting chilly shadows onto the lake shore through the trees.

Crescent Lake was small, perhaps 100 yards across, set against the side of a hill sloping 500 feet above the far shore. It was fed by several trickling rivulets, nearly dry since the snows had long since receded from the mountain peak except for a few patches of dirt inlaid ice.

Derek did not think about his life, his work, Jenny or Paula. His worries about his frustrating, mid-life confusions dissolved into the trees, the azure sky, and the crisp, fresh air. He felt cleansed and refreshed by an impish, childish wonder and delight, absorbed in fascination for this invigorating environment.

Derek took off his dusty hiking boots and sweaty white gym socks. He crept to the edge of the lake, gingerly dodging the rocks and pebbles along the shore. He found a fallen tree trunk overhanging the water. He sat and dangled his feet in the coolness of the clear water. He breathed deeply at the chilling sensation on his feet and ankles. The lake was mostly in the shadow of the mountain now. A gentle, rhythmic splash lapped the shore on either side of him. Water skippers cruised the surface between his legs like a tiny catamaran, oblivious to his unmoving presence. Tiny minnows nipped curiously at his toes.

Derek caught his breath in excited wonder as a granddaddy-sized brown trout snaked leisurely from beneath the log he sat on. The fish was about 14 inches long, a veteran survivor at dodging fishing lures which had done their best to trick him into becoming somebody's supper. The fish wagged his competent tail and flashed into the shadows toward the center of the lake in search of an evening meal of flies too slow and stupid to avoid becoming food for fish: a silent, submerged hunter who was himself hunted. He was part of the weirdly inverted food chain of planet earth, where in order for one life form to live, another must die -- an absurd pyramid of eating and being eaten at the top of which stands Man: the ultimate eater, the consumer of all consumers.

Derek stared at the distorted slant of his bare feet beneath the rippling water. He shuddered as a sudden chilling breeze wrinkled the lake. The glow of setting sun above the hills around the lake dimmed to gray. A nearly full moon appeared, suspended like a china dish on a blue-gray wall.

That night Derek lay on his back in his sleeping bag listening to the gentle hiss and snap of his nearly spent camp fire. The mighty, silent canopy of night sky splendor consumed him, as it always did when sleeping outdoors in the mountains. Derek thought the same existentially overwhelming thoughts that had pervaded him as a child. Confronted by the unfathomable, infinite vastness of macrocosmic space brought into focus the microscopically inconsequential nonentity of Earth by comparison. He felt the awesome eschatological apathy that always occasioned the experience.

Derek wondered how astronomers ever managed to get over the feeling of their own utter insignificance; a majestic humiliation brought on by this clashing contrast of magnitudes. The microcosm within the macrocosm; a flea on a flea on a flea on a flea, ad infinitum. The 'was', the 'is', and the 'will be' of infinite space and time and matter and the inestimable magnitude and power of twinkling stellar energy: the face of God.

There was nothing to save him from these thoughts except to sleep; to not be -- until the chariot of dawn was driven by the sun to slay the dark illusion of the night and restore myopic sight to those who need eyes to see.

Towering trees seemed to touch the stars above him. Through the boughs a breeze whispered a hushed and haunting hymn.

In sleep he dreamed he heard the simple piping of a flute. There were words he would not remember in the morning -- words without a voice to sing them, as though a child were humming a rhyme to himself:

"I hide in the fuzz on a butterfly wing.

I ride the on waves of electron rings.

I hear the songs that a ladybug sings.

I can be small, like the tiniest things.

I like to play leapfrog over the sun,

Run around Venus and Mars just for fun.

Jogging to Pluto is just a short run.

Heavenly hopscotch is easily done.

By changing my viewpoint I'm smaller than small

I fly with my thoughts! I'll never fall!

I decide to be none! I decide to be all!

I am immortal -- immeasurably tall.

You're just a man! You're weak and small!

I dare you to find me! I dare each and all!

You'll never see me. You'll never get near.

I am a god! I don't have your fears!

I'm here, then I'm there. I'm free to be free.

I don't need to eat or breathe or pee!

I am who I am. It's fun being me!

The same Pan I've been, and always will be!"

*   *   *   *   *   *   *   *   *

     The morning was cloudy and cool but it cleared by 10:00am when he stopped to rest. Derek removed his lightweight jacket, wearing only jeans and a dark green tee-shirt with his company logo on the back; a cloud of arithmetic symbols and a lighting bolt. It was a remnant of the Nimbus Software summer softball team. He wanted to be the pitcher but could never master the proper slow, high-arch, back-spin needed to make batters pop-up or ground out, so he played second base instead.

     Climbing a steadily sloping ridge was hot work as he tramped through the thinning pine trees across the volcanic lava rocks strewn on the hillside. Finally mounting the summit of a ridge Derek paused to regain his breath. From this vantage he could clearly survey a broad panorama of forest rolling across the Trinity mountain range to the eastern horizon.

     Before him a steep decent of about 1,000 feet would bring him to a narrow meadow of tall grass which lay about 2 miles from a river. He plodded stiff-legged, sliding and zigzagging sideways down the slope to ease the speed of his descent. In places he slid in finely powdered dirt and loose gravel, dodging sagebrush, Manzanita branches, boulders and an occasional tree. He sneezed at the dusty, musk scent of the tinder-dry brush. He grabbed at red-barked branches for support. There had been no rain here for three months. He had been warned about the dry conditions and the threat of forest fires, usually caused by careless campers and hunters.

About 11:30 Derek finally slid and staggered to the bottom of the ridge, half crawling beneath a dense stand of tall brush at the edge of the meadow. Dusty, sweating, thirsty and scratched he eased the pack from his back and sat on a rock to dump the dirt out of his boots. The harder than expected climb down to the meadow, gave Derek a sense of boyish exhilaration.

After some canteen water, cheddar cheese and crackers, Derek shouldered his pack to begin the final leg of his hike to the river which lay across the meadow. He'd walked no more than one hundred yards along the edge of the meadow when he stopped and stood breathlessly still.

There, near the middle of the meadow stood two mule deer, not more than fifty yards from him. They had both their heads bent to the ground, intent on grazing. What a delightful sight, he thought. Though he knew he might see wild animals in the woods he was still surprised to see what was, for a city dweller, a rare sight.

The deer were moving slowly away from him as they fed, flicking at flies with long ears and short tails. Derek squatted to remain unseen by the pair. The buck was the larger of the two and had a fine set of antlers. Derek marveled at the sleek grace of their form and large, soft, nearly oriental eyes. Their smooth tan fur and silent steps blended with the tall dry grass of the meadow.

As the deer advanced further from him Derek decided to circle around them through the trees surrounding the meadow to take a position in front of them at the edge of the meadow.

From there he could take some pictures. This was the first time on his trip he's seen anything he wanted to photograph.

When he arrived at the spot Derek stood slowly from his crouch, being careful to stay out of view and to move noiselessly. He raised his camera, stepped forward "Indian style", one foot in front of the other, and then snapped the shutter. The auto-wind motor whirred forward to advance the film. On hearing the sound, the buck raised his head, ears perked up, followed by the doe, they stood still but intensely alert.

Derek was not quite aware of a hint of oddly misplaced of cedar scent in the meadow.

From among a shadowy stand of trees on the opposite side of the meadow, perhaps 75 yards away, Derek saw a tiny puff of white smoke. Both deer started forward. In this same timeless moment Derek felt the sensation of being at the center of an explosion. There was a shattering crash, though he didn't hear it with his ears; an incandescent flash, not seen by his eyes; no pain, only a terrifically violent shock. He thought dimly, "This was the feeling of being struck by lightning".

A sense of utter shriveling weakness overcame him as the meadow, trees, sky and mountains receded into a great, vague distance. Derek saw his body slump to the ground as though he was high above it, looking down like some hovering bird. He sensed that he was very badly hurt but could not imagine how or why. In alarm he swooped back down to his body with the simultaneous realization that he had been shot. In less than a second, he felt numb and dazed, but no pain.

For what seemed an eternity Derek lay stunned, yet intensely aware, as shouting voices and footsteps approached. There were faces above him. Someone lifted his helpless form to tear away his pack and shirt.

"God damn Billy, he's hit! Shit! Oh, shit! Oh, Lord Jesus, man...get his shirt open!"

Billy Joe Jaras and his brother Virgil had been deer hunting together every year since they were in school together in Valdosta, Georgia, more than 15 years ago. They played varsity football at Valdosta High. In Valdosta everybody played football and everybody hunted. Just something everybody did growin' up. After high school they joined the Army and went to 'Nam like most everybody else, 'cept for Yankee, pinko draft-dodgers.

Virgil Jaras met his wife while he was stationed at Fort Ord. After the Army, he stayed in northern California so he and his wife could be near her kin people. He got a job in the hydroelectric plant at Whiskeytown Dam. Billy Joe followed him 6 months later and settled too. It wasn't like down home in Georgia, but the work paid real good and there were plenty of forests for huntin' and fishin'.

They bought double-wide mobile homes on lots right next to each other, just like they lived in when they was growin' up. Just the night before they was sittin' by their campfire, tellin' stories about the old days back home. About stuff they used to do in school and about girls they had screwed and about drinkin' and fightin' and about their old huntin' dog, Sparky. They each drank a six-pack of Coors and threw the empties into the ashes.

But right now Virgil and Billy Joe were just trying to stop the blood from bubbling out of Derek's body. The bullet had gone all the way through his chest and passed out the shoulder blade.

Derek tried to speak. He wanted to find out what was happening. He still couldn't feel any pain. He found he had no voice. He tried to move but the body did not respond. Then he realized he was not "in" his body. He was looking down at it from above. He could perceive Virgil and Billy Joe, but not with the same vision which he saw things through his body's eyeballs. He "knew" they were struggling with makeshift bandages made from torn strips from their t-shirts. He saw them lifting his body but he couldn't feel the motion. His body's head lolled to one side, the arms drooped limply, dragging on the ground as they carried him, almost running, across the meadow.

Derek panicked.

"Oh my God! I must be dead!"

He thought of Jenny, his beautiful wife. He had always loved her. He thought of his business. How could they manage without him? - the major accounts that he personally dealt with, the meetings, the decisions needing to be made.

"This isn't fair! I can't die now! This is totally stupid!"

Derek felt a violent resentment at having to leave his body and life behind. Life suited him. He had been very good at living. He wasn't ready to leave it yet!

"Oh My God!" he thought in desperate horror.

"Yes? You called?" Derek felt a voice say to him.

CHAPTER III

"Ghosts do exist. Death does not finish all.

The colorless shade escapes the burnt-out pyre."

-- Sextus Propertius - *The Elegies* (c 50 BC - 16 BC)

Derek didn't actually *hear* a voice. He *felt* the voice, as though he were thinking to himself, except he knew it wasn't his own thought. "This must be what happens when you die...you start hearing voices," he thought.

"No, not really", said the voice. "You just happened to be in my forest. I saw your body get shot. I made the hunters miss hitting my deer. They hit you instead. Sorry."

"What the hell is going on here?" he thought to himself. "I must be going totally nuts! First I'm dead and now I'm hearing voices! Jesus Christ!" he thought hysterically.

"No, Jesus Christ is not here. Have no fear, I am Pan, Guardian of the Forest and all creatures therein", said Pan.

"Huh?" Derek struggled with his heavily overwrought thoughts. After a moment or two of confusion he thought, "You mean, like the Greek god, from mythology?"

"The same" said Pan.

Derek fainted. He came to. "Oh, Jesus..."

"No, not Jesus. Pan", said Pan. "Once beloved and worshipped by men and thought to symbolize all of the gods and all of the nature spirits of fields and forest, I was hailed as the feeder of flocks and herds. In Egypt I was called Min. The Romans praised me as Faunus, Lord of Fertility. In Sumeria all men shouted my name to celebrate victory in battle: Enlil, Father of Life. The ancient Maya carved my name in stone: Hurakan, of the erect phallus, god of fertility, rain and corn. I have been worshipped at the great feasts of planting and harvest. I am invoked by caravan masters before the journey to ensure safe passage through my domain. My music is the all-purifying gentle wind in the reeds and tree tops, beloved by shepherds whose flocks I have soothed with song throughout the ages. I made love to wood-nymphs and angered my Father Zeus, once upon a time."

In the time of a cat's breath, almost as a single thought without words, he *knew* these things about Pan. Although he was still reeling with overwhelming confusion, Derek thought shakily, "Am I dead?"

"Well, you're not in that body at the moment. Do you feel dead?" asked Pan.

"...ah...I don't know...I've never been dead before...I feel like I'm still here. But my body's down there. Am I like a ghost or something? Oh, shit! This is really weird!"

Derek was even more exasperated than before. He'd read about "out-of-the-body" or "near-death" experiences but none of them ever said anything about having a telepathic conversation with a mythical Greek god. He thought he must be hallucinating.

"Don't believe everything you've read in Earth books. They are nearly all lies and nonsense. I am who I am. You are who you are: an immortal spiritual being", Pan said matter-of-factly.

Derek thought, "Huh, immortal? You mean I'm going to live forever now? Are you going to take me to heaven...or hell? Are you like an angel or something?"

"I am not an angel. I am Pan, Lord of the Wood", answered Pan with a glint of grave amusement in his thought. "You are full of false notions and confusions and you suffer from amnesia, like all men. You have already lived forever and will continue to do so. You have lost your memory of who you really are. This may return to you, provided you do not continue to inhabit one of those bodies.

There is no heaven or hell as you have been taught to think of it. Those are lies told by priests to make people obey them. Although I have often thought that if one were to search for Hell and found Earth, it would fit the purpose very well.

"Oh", thought Derek with a bewildered, breathless sigh. "I should have figured...this sure isn't what they taught me in Sunday school and college".

"Of course not" replied Pan. "There are a few men of wisdom on Earth, but they do not teach Sunday school or college, nor would truth be allowed in such institutions".

It occurred to Derek that he didn't have a clue what was really happening. He was aware of being in communication with someone, that he'd been shot by hunters, that he was apparently dead, but not really dead. Or was he? He had seen his wounded body being carried away off across the meadow by the guys who shot him and that he couldn't do anything about it.

A dark hopelessness crashed over him; a feeling of utter inability to move, to sense, to operate, to see. An empty, cold, black nothingness.

*   *   *   *   *   *   *   *   *   *

Virgil and Billy Joe were drenched with sweat. Panting, their lungs and muscles shrieked with the agony of over-exertion, as they carried Derek's 175 lb. body at a dead run across the meadow, up a steep embankment to a dirt logging road and another 200 yards to Virgil's pickup truck. They pushed and dragged Derek's still breathing body onto the seat of the cab between them.

In a single motion Virgil started the engine, spun the wheel and sprayed dust and gravel in a 180 degree arc behind the oversized tires, speeding toward the main highway which would take them to a hospital 20 miles away.

"Damn, Virg!" Billy Joe panted, "Step on it son! If this guy croaks on us, we're in deep shit!"

Virgil skidded onto the asphalt of the main highway. The tires screamed burning rubber as he floored the gas pedal.

"Get the police on the CB and tell 'em to lay off us man. We're comin' through" he said, handing the mike to Billy Joe. Billy hit the switch, twisted the dial to the police frequency and yelled, "attention all highway patrol cars southbound on highway 239: Code three, code three. We are ten-eight in a red Ford pickup truck, license number...uh..." "J32743!" Virgil shouted for him, "headed to the nearest hospital with a serious gunshot wound. Please assist! Repeat. Please assist. Come back."

Derek's body slumped limply against Billy Joe, who propped it up on the seat next to him with his shoulder. The wound was still bleeding. The CB speaker crackled with an official sounding voice of a dispatcher from the Sasquatch

County Sheriff department, "Uh, ten-four, J32743. We will intercept and assist. What's your twenty? You copy?"

As Virgil kept the pedal to the metal, a Sasquatch County Sheriff patrol car fish-tailed and screeched into pursuit of them from his hiding place behind a roadside billboard. He passed them with siren wailing and lights flashing, leading the way to the emergency entrance of Mother of Mary Memorial Hospital.

*   *   *   *   *   *   *   *   *   *

"Do not despair my friend", soothed Pan. "Do not succumb to your desire for oblivion. I will help you".

Derek had never known an emotion of such utterly empty, senseless devastation before. He felt that his entire existence was lost. Even if he were not dead he could not hope to operate without his body. He was nothing without it.

"You are not your body my friend. All you have ever been or will be is you: your memory, your knowledge, and ability. You are not dead. You are the spark and essence of life itself."

Pan's words were clear, cleansing, and certain. Just as rain rinses away dust from a window, Derek felt reassured. A rush of relief raced through him. He sighed deeply, and then thought, "How can I be sighing?"

Pan, as usual, answered instantly in a matter-of-fact tone, "*You* are the source of breath. Not the body. You are the Cause of Life."

"If you say so..." thought Derek gloomily.

Although he felt better, Derek was still abashed and not a little confused by his current situation.

"I do say so! Therefore, it is", was Pan's robust response.

Derek pondered his new predicament for a moment. "Well, if I'm not really dead and what you say is true, what do I do now?"

"Whatever you decide to do".

"Oh, right...so now I'll just magically reappear on Earth as my old self and pick up where I left off? I'm sure my wife will really like sleeping with a spirit and all my employees will get a big kick out of working for a ghost", Derek fumed.

"There is no reason to be sarcastic with me. If you wish I will leave you here to solve your own problems", scolded Pan.

"Sorry. I'm a little upset, I guess. I mean, I just died didn't I?" Derek moped.

"I understand. Many lesser beings would have already succumbed to the automatic impulse to forget, to lose themselves in the oblivion of death. You are a tougher being than most. I remember you as you once were and will help you regain your former self, if you wish it", instructed Pan.

"Huh?... You remember me?... From where?" Derek sputtered.

"Not long ago you were a free spirit, as I am. But you were overcome by the desire for sensation: for sex, for food, for companionship, for a game to play. You agreed too much with men and became trapped in the body of a man. These things caused you to diminish your own ability. Because of your contact with bodies you, and other gods, lost your power, your freedom, and your memory" concluded Pan.

"Oh, I see", Derek replied vaguely without really understanding at all.

"Dead men are always less lamented by others than by themselves." Pan paused, considering and continued. "However, death is only an illusion, as you have learned. The living, who no longer sees your body, considers that *you* are dead. But only bodies perish. You will live on forever."

"Do you have something philosophical to say about everything?" grumped Derek.

"Yes. Always. Unless of course I choose not to say anything..." There was a long, still, vacuous silence in which Derek started to feel very uncomfortable indeed. And very, very alone...then afraid, and then panicky.

"Pan...?" he ventured a thought. Nothing. "Pan?" again, more urgently. Silence. "Pan? Where are you?!" thought Derek hysterically. "Oh, My God!"

"I am here", replied a thought as though inside of Derek's head...well, not head actually. Startled, but relieved Derek shouted, without a voice, "Don't do that! Christ! Where'd you go anyway?"

"I've been here the whole time. I just chose not to communicate, as you seemed to want not to hear what I had to say. Typical of Earth men: like pigs rutting in a diamond mine looking for truffles are annoyed at having to push aside the glittering gems to feed a body", mused Pan.

"Yeah, I guess you're right. I'm sorry. I guess I'm still too upset to be very understanding at the moment."

Derek was contritely exasperated at realizing that he had felt so utterly helpless during that brief silence. For the first time he could remember, he felt like there was nothing he could do for himself. He was blind, he couldn't feel anything, he couldn't move and the only thing he could hear were Pan's thoughts and only then if Pan intended to be heard.

"God, this is worse than being a baby! I can't do anything without a body!"

"There is a story told by the native people who once lived in this forest, about how the Eagle learned to fly," said Pan. "A very long time ago in the forest there lived a pitiable creature called Shitalkme. All he ever did was talk and talk and talk to himself while he hopped around on the forest floor looking for bugs and seeds which had fallen from the treetops. He never listened, not even to hear his own talking. One day Shitalkme asked a wise old Owl sitting up in the branches of a tree, 'How can I get off the ground and reach the treetops, like you?' The Old Owl answered Shitalkme, 'If you stop talking long enough, you will learn how to reach the treetops'. Shitalkme stopped talking and soon he began to hear the deer and the wolf and the beaver and the other creatures of the forest. After a long time of listening, he heard the wind. When he listened to the wind, Shitalkme began to soar. When he soared, Shitalkme became the Eagle. After that, his soaring said everything the Eagle needed to say."

* * * * * * * * *

After leaving the hospital, Virgil and Billy Joe spent several hours at the Sasquatch County Sheriff office telling their story to Sheriff Melvin "Bubba" Gumshoe, an unpleasantly plump, balding and slightly greasy cop.

Bubba got his nick-name when he started kindergarten. It just seemed to fit. He majored in Heavy Equipment Operation at the local vocational school after high school. But he lasted only three days on his first job as a backhoe operator due to a chronic sinus condition. Everything outdoors -- dust, dirt, pollen, grass, trees -- made Bubba sneeze and it made his nose run. Although police work didn't require much outdoor work, the handkerchief he kept in his pocket was usually wet with constant use in spite of the eight antihistamine tablets he took faithfully each day.

"OK (sniff), so let me get this straight" said Bubba in his usual mechanically nasal monotone. "You state that Billy shot at an alleged deer with a hunting rifle, at a distance of not more than 75 yards, (sniff) sighting through a high-magnification rifle scope aimed directly at the heart of the alleged deer, (sniff) and that the rifle, to use your words, 'just sort of jumped to the right', when you fired the weapon. (sniff) And that you missed the alleged deer and hit this, er... (sniff), Mr. Adapa, who you claim not to have seen until you started running (sniff) after the deer and discovered the victim. Is that the story you're going to have me put in my report?" (sniff)

"Yeah, yeah, yeah! That's exactly what happened!" said Virgil in exasperation. He looked across at Billy Joe shaking his head and rolling his eyes to the ceiling.

"We've been through this 50 times already! That's what happened!"

Virgil was really gettin' peeved but suppressed his temper with a white-knuckled grip on the arms of the straight-backed wooden chair he'd been sitting in all afternoon.

*　　*　　*　　*　　*　　*　　*　　*　　*

"I am a god, not a 'ghost' as the human conception of an active spirit would have it." Pan said to the quiet and attentive Derek who had been given the opportunity to spend a few minutes in calm contemplation of his situation. "However, though I am a god, I am yet, indeed, vulnerable to the same spiritual perils faced by a being with a body. If you have read any of the stories about my past deeds in your 'mythical' history, you will recall that I have had more than my share of escapades with bodies. I have lusted after women, had sex with many, caroused, cavorted, and sullied myself with every imaginable bodily sensation and desire, on this planet and many others. I have intervened in the personal, political and military affairs of men and women and nations. I have often set a very unholy and less-than-venerable example for other spirits to follow – for both men and gods.

However, I have overcome many of these spiritually degrading activities with self-discipline and by maintaining a safe distance from too much association with bodies, especially these last 2,000 years or so. Because I have learned from my own inept experiences of the past, I will pass on what I can of my own observations to you in much the same way the master craftsman of Europe used to train an apprentice during the 16th century through a combination of theory, combined with daily practice at duplicating the actions and techniques of the master. "I understand your pain and confusion. I have been there myself many times", Pan instructed his new apprentice.

"The central purpose of my desire to tutor you that is you may learn to operate effectively while outside the body, and remain free from the cycle of birth and death. Further, in order to maintain this most sought after state of being, I will teach you to be ever vigilant against external distractions and as well as the self-made doubts which can diminish your power as a being.

There is one point of vulnerability... I can impart only as much wisdom as I have gained through the trials and errors of my own experience, much of which I myself understand analytically, but have not necessarily applied with success to others. There are no mystical secrets; there are no hidden meanings in what I have to teach you. There is only a strict adherence to those ideas and actions which have proven to work successfully and consistently, combined with your own hard work to apply this knowledge. It is therefore, possible that you may someday learn to exceed my own abilities, provided that you are diligent and persistent. After all, we're all gods to the degree that we allow ourselves to be" Pan concluded.

Derek didn't really know what to say or think. If the word 'dumbfounded' were ever appropriate to an occasion, this was certainly one of those occasions, he thought to himself.

"Yes, I suppose you must feel quite overwhelmed by all this" thought Pan back to Derek, having perceived his thought. "The key question I have for you is this: Do you have a desire to increase your personal power and ability?

Derek was sure that he did, but not sure that he had any other alternative.

"The alternative", Pan replied to Derek's unknowing question, "is that I can leave you to do as most other beings do -- drift blindly, dumbly and silently into oblivion. You may eventually return to your old body, or to a new one or perhaps none. Without direction, I am sure that you will have no control over your own destiny. However, with my help, you have great potential power."

*   *   *   *   *   *   *   *   *

So, it came to pass that Pan started to train his new student. The next step was to rid Derek of his dependency on a body in order to move and perceive on his own. Pan instructed Derek how to *look*, to reach out with his feelings to permeate space.

To begin, Pan spent some time getting Derek used to the

idea that he was not an object, but truly a spiritual "no-thing". Of course, Derek was accustomed to having a body, being an object, bumping into walls, skinning its knees, and so forth. It took quite a while to get Derek to discover that he could move through objects. It was a very strange experience at first, but one which proved more effortless with practice.

Then, he showed Derek how to feel an object by imagining himself to *be* the object; to flow through it, sensing it through thought, using every perception he could muster: texture, density, weight, gravity, temperature, mass and even to feel the emotion the object was feeling.

Pan made him practice and practice and practice. All of this seemed very strange to Derek at first. It was extremely frustrating. There were many fits and stops and objections and "I can't" and "this is ridiculous".

Pan was compassionately unwavering, unreasonable and insisted that Derek continue to do the drills again and again and again and again.

Derek cascaded by degrees through an emotional roller-coaster ride of anger, grief, apathy, then soaring in a moment of success to enthusiasm, explosive laughter and exhilaration, then crashing down again, and up once more.

Each time Pan made the drill gradually a bit more complex than the last. After many, many repetitions Derek began to have some victories, small at first, then bigger.

Derek relearned, with coaching, how to perceive light particles reflecting from the surface of objects without the use of optic nerves. He learned to just *be there* and *look*, to be the object and experience it and then how to move by considering that he was changing his location in space and *thinking* himself from one location to another.

As himself, he really wasn't located anywhere at all in

particular. He and Pan were just *there*. The more he imagined that he *owned* space, the easier it became. At first he had to pretend to attach himself to a tree or a rock by an imaginary rope and drag himself along. And then, using the ground or a hill as a bracing point, to push himself away. It was a lot like doing push-ups without gravity. He was in a truly weightless condition now.

Derek even learned to smell apples on the trees in a nearby orchard by imagining the taste, putting the imagined taste into the fruit and then *feeling* it back again into himself as though it had come from the fruit itself. As he practiced he realized that the smell didn't really come from apples as much as it came from his own imagination of what an apple smelled like. He didn't have a body's nose telling him how an apple is supposed to smell anymore. It was all up to him now. Perhaps it always had been. He just hadn't realized it before.

A simple thing like smelling an apple or just moving from one location to another was no longer automatic. Derek really had to *think* about it every single, minute aspect of it. The effort was very trying, but at the same time, more gratifying than anything he had ever done before.

"Wow! This is fantastic! I'm me, you know? I'm really not a body! I'm *me*!" Derek enthused at his newly found awareness of himself.

"Very good!" replied Pan with equal enthusiasm.

       *   *   *   *   *   *   *   *

"And you, Mr. Jaras...ah...Billy", Bubba motioned to Billy with his handkerchief, then blew his nose before continuing, "Is that your final statement too?"

"You got it man." Billy sighed heavily. "Can we get goin' now? We been here all day. I ain't had nothin' to eat since first light this mornin'. Give us a break will ya'?" he moaned.

"Yes, OK. You can go now. You will (sniff) be contacted if there is any change in Mr. Adapas condition. Be sure that you are available at all times in case we need further information from you" droned Bubba, sniffing.

As they scuffed outside to the truck Virgil said, "Jesus, where'd they ever dig up that guy? What a sorry-ass son-of-a-bitch! I thought we'd never get out of that place!"
"Yeah. Well, I just hope this guy don't give up and die on us or this sheriff is gonna be on us like stink on shit for murder or manslaughter or somethin'."

"Hey, lighten up Billy! He's gonna be OK. The doc at the hospital said the guy's supposed to live, right?"

"Yeah, but he was hit pretty bad..." Billy moped, fumbling through his keys to unlock the door to this pickup.

"Shit! There's blood all over the seat. We gotta stop by a car wash on the way home. Damn!"

*   *   *   *   *   *   *   *

"So far, so good Derek. You're doing very well. You will get it with more practice", Pan encouraged.

Derek already felt light-years better than he could ever remember feeling. He felt confident, able, powerful and very, very alive. "Quite a feeling for a dead man", he thought.

"There is still much more to learn and remember", Pan continued. "One thing at a time. The abilities that separate men from the gods are the abilities to assume viewpoints. And from these viewpoints, one must then be able to make things happen."

More drilling. Practice, practice, practice. Be a tree. Be a rock. Be a leaf. Be inside a cloud. Be above the forest. Under the water. Three feet above the water. On and on and on. It seemed an interminable, yet timeless lesson to Derek. Pan was always patient, yet insistent that Derek learn.

Derek tried a combination of newly acquired skills on a chipmunk in the forest. He went into the chipmunk's head by thinking of himself as the chipmunk. He *became* the chipmunk. He thought the thought, "stop". The chipmunk, which had been bounding across the pine-needle carpeted floor of the forest suddenly stopped. Derek thought, "sit up" and then "turn your head from left to right". He did exactly as Derek intended.

"Wow! I did it!" Derek spouted. "He did just what I wanted him to. Nothing to it." he continued confidently.

"Of course. Very good. You're getting the idea of it very nicely", Pan acknowledged.

"Now that you're getting some of your own power back, let's go take a look around. We'll do a little sight-seeing. Come on!" Pan disappeared.

Derek waited for several moments before beginning to feel puzzled about where Pan had gone. He felt like scratching his head, but he didn't have one, so he just waited, trying to feel Pan anywhere near him. Nothing.

"Oh my god..." sighed Derek.

"Yes?" answered Pan.

"Jesus!" Derek jumped, half startled out of his wits. "Don't leave me alone like that! Where'd you go anyway?"

"Where did *you* go? I've been down in The Bahamas playing with the dolphins", laughed Pan. "What happened to you anyway?"

Derek just stood there...well, sat..., that is, kind of floated, not really knowing what to say or think.

"You're in worse shape that I thought" Pan lamented. "Oh well, I'll pull you along with me then, until you get your 'wings' back. OK. So, here we go. Hang on!"

In that instant Derek experienced a rush of feelings too many and varied to describe. He found himself hovering inches above gently bobbing ocean waves.

"Isn't this great?" blurted Pan with frisky gusto.

A sleek, shiny gray dolphin squeaked with delight, exploding from beneath the surface as it leaped directly up and through Derek. It soared high into the air, trailing beads of water and splashed with effortless grace back into the blue-green waves.

"What the...what was that?! Where..." spluttered Derek.

"Bahamas. Dolphins", Pan enthused. "I told you. I was playing with friends. Come on!"

Derek was under the water, speeding through a trail of burbling bubbles behind a quartet of sleek gray dolphins. They thrashed their tails rhythmically, gaining speed, turned up and with a surge of playful power burst through the surface, arching and stretching a dozen feet above the spray, straightened and plunged below again. He rode on with them, pulled along by a force he could not feel or resist, but he knew that he was connected to Pan.

The dolphins continued swimming, leaping, diving, splashing gleefully. Derek could feel their immense energy, the exhilaration of their play; the crystal wet sparkle of sunlight reflected from beaded water droplets, the pressure of rushing water. He felt the slippery odor of passing kelp and the scurrying scare of smaller fishes fleeing from them.

Derek was permeated with joy and ecstatic motion. Warm sunlight awash with surf-scented air and sparkling, squealing giggles of dolphins at play.

Derek was immersed, enthralled, consumed, amazed. With a thousand sensations, nothing like he ever experienced in a body: too many to be differentiated. He was thoroughly, completely exhilarated and simultaneously suffused with comprehension. As he and Pan broke above the surface, high into the air above the azure waters he looked down on a teaming stampede of dozens of speeding, splashing dolphins.

"This is what it's like to be a god...this is who I really am" thought Derek. "I'm me! Oh my god!"

"You called?" replied Pan instantly.

"This is completely, totally amazing!" beamed Derek,

"Indeed!" Laughed Pan.

CHAPTER IV

"The soul of man can never be enslaved save by its own infirmities, nor freed save by its very strength and own resolve and constant vision and supreme endeavor!

You will be free? Then, courage, o my brother! O let the soul stand in the open door of life and death and knowledge and desire and see the peaks of thought kindle with sunrise!

Then shall the soul return to rest no more, nor harvest dreams in the dark field of sleep – rather the soul shall go with great resolve to dwell at last upon the shining mountains in liberal converse with the eternal stars."

-- *"Herakles"* – George Cabot Lodge (c. 1873 – 1909)

"And in business news today, the Founder and CEO of Nimbus Software, Derek Adapa, was seriously wounded in what was reported to have been a hunting accident in the mountains of northern California early this morning. Mrs. Adapa was not available for comment. Sheriff Bubba Gumshoe of Sasquatch County, California told our correspondent that a continuing investigation is under way but that no arrests have been made in connection with the shooting. Mr. Adapa remains in critical condition at Mercy of Mother Mary hospital at this hour.

In sports, the San Diego Padres today announced the signing of 16 year-old rookie pitcher, Spike Goodarm, to a record 325 million dollar..."

Jenny flicked off the TV set. The smiling, too well-groomed news anchor person blinked to blackness. Jenny's thoughts were a twisted frenzy of anguished emotion. Trembling, she tried to steady her hands around a glass of whiskey from the limousine bar. She never drank liquor, but the driver insisted that it would help calm her nerves.

Paula ordered a limousine to pick Jenny up and take her to the airport to meet a private helicopter that would fly her directly to the hospital in less than an hour. Although the office would stay closed for the rest of the day, Paula would be there to handle all important messages and to coordinate communications for Jenny.

Jenny was very glad that Paula was so efficient, but wished she weren't so pretty. As the limousine pulled onto the runway to meet the waiting jet, she gulped down the drink, shuddered and prayed, "Please god, let Derek be alright".

*   *   *   *   *   *   *   *

"Hey, see you guys! That was great!" Derek called to the dolphins as Pan dragged him away by the scruff of his ghostly neck. The dolphins replied with a raucous concatenation of squeaks and squeals which Derek clearly understood to mean "sure, come back any time!", as they continued their non-stop swimming party.

"Wow, what amazing creatures they are. Real party animals!" Derek chuckled childishly. "Hey, where are we going now?"

"I must return to my forest to look after my animals for the night. I perceive that you may be needed as well. Your body still lives. Although you are welcome to stay with me if you wish" said Pan as the forest reappeared beneath them.

"My body's still alive?! How can it be alive without me? I'm not even in it!" screeched Derek. "Where is it?"

In that instant Pan and Derek hovered above a hospital bed. A nurse sat next to the bed adjusting an I.V. tube dripping fluid into the right arm. Derek's body looked a little gray, but well enough, considering. It wore a greenish gown covered by a sheet to the waist. The chest had been heavily bandaged after the operation.

The bullets Virgil used were "hollow points". The bullet entered the body cleanly, but once inside it fragmented and spread out. The left lung had disintegrated and the scapula was shattered. The muscle tissue was shredded where the bullet left the body.

"Derek, your body has some motive force of its own. It may survive for some time without you, although it will remain "unconscious". At some point you must decide if you want to re-inhabit it or not" Pan instructed solemnly.

"Well, of course, I have to go back. I have a whole life left to live...but how do I do it? How do I get back into it?"

"Just think yourself into the body. Just be it, as you learned in the drills", Pan directed.

Derek reached out to permeate his body. Terrible, agony seared through his being. He recoiled as the body convulsed and the face grimaced briefly with pain. The nurse stood up quickly and pressed a button at the head of the bed.

"Aaaaauugh!" screamed Derek, retreating from the body. "I can't! There's too much pain!"

A doctor bustled through the door. "What is it nurse?" he asked urgently.

"The patient seemed to regain consciousness doctor, just for a moment. But he's gone again now. His vital signs are still stable though."

After a brief examination of the bandages, and checking the readings of the various instruments monitoring the body the doctor turned to leave.

"The bullet didn't do as much damage as it could have. It didn't sever an artery or he would have bled to death before he ever got here. The fast action of those hunters probably saved his life. He's lucky to be alive. Let me know if anything changes."

As he opened the door he turned to the nurse again, "That cedar air freshener the cleaning people use in here smells good, doesn't it?" he said, closing the door behind himself.

"But I'm *not* alive!" protested Derek. "I mean I'm here and my body is there. I can't even get near it! Oh god, what am I going to do?"

"Well", replied Pan, "it seems the best thing to do might be to just let the body rest and heal itself until the pain subsides. It will be alright without you for awhile. Use this time to your advantage."

"I don't have much choice right now. It's too painful" Derek though gloomily.

Grief rose within him as he confronted the sober reality of his situation and the potential loss of his body and a lifetime associated with it.

"Do not grieve my friend" soothed Pan. "Let it rest. We will return to see how the body is doing later".

"OK. I guess you're right" Derek thought, resigning himself to his currently unsolvable situation.

*   *   *   *   *   *   *   *

Derek had a headache. "Huh?" he thought dully. "How can I have a headache? I don't even have a damned head ".

"It is a psychosomatic illness. The source of pain is in the mind, not the body".

"The mind?" Derek objected grumpily. "How can I have a mind if I don't have a brain either?"

"Do not confuse the brain with the mind, my friend. They are not the same. The brain is merely a spongy mass of nerve tissue which serves the body like a computer circuit board. The mind, however, is made up of mental pictures you carry with you. Some pictures contain memory of pain which can be reactivated in situations similar to the original picture. So you have a headache, without need of a head".

"Do you remember the first time you had a headache?" coaxed Pan.

Derek remembered, dimly at first: during a too-long business meeting. A hangover the morning after a party. The time he had flu in high school.

And then with more clarity: when he got hit in the head by a flying baseball bat. He was sitting on the bench. It was the fifth grade. Recess. The playground at Oak Ridge School. Johnny Harris, the smallest kid in the class, took a clumsy swing at the ball and hit a limp grounder toward third. The next thing Derek remembered was laying on a gurney in the hospital emergency room. Unconscious. Hospital. Pain. His head hurt like hell for two days after that.

"Hmmm. I'd forgotten all about that. It was a long time ago. It reminds me...it's just like...seeing my body in the hospital bed. It was like that time.... Oh, I see!"

Derek's headache subsided with the recollection of having been in the hospital before.

"I feel better" said Derek, relieved.

"You're welcome" said Pan. "You have been through a great deal today" Pan said as they reappeared above the forest, now softly lighted by the moon.

"God, you can say that again" agreed Derek without enthusiasm.

"That will not be necessary" replied Pan.

Behind the silver halo of moonlight a multitude of stars blinked minutely. Shadowy shapes stretched against the earth, cast by the rising moon. A breeze swished through the pine tree tops which, oddly, carried the scent of cedar.

A lumbering black bear, too eager for a bedtime snack of honey, upset a hive of bees housed in a rotting tree trunk. From the cloudless, moonlit sky he was severely cuffed by a carefully placed lance of lightning. Stunned, but unharmed, the bear scampered away thinking dimly that the he should bet back to his cave before the storm came.

* * * * * * * * * *

"Awaken!" commanded Pan.

"What the..." Derek started blearily. "Oh, I guess I drifted off for a minute there."

"Yes. Five hundred and thirty-seven minutes, actually", replied Pan precisely.

"Really? How'd you know that?"

"There are many ways of knowing time. Time is an illusion based on a measurement of the movement of objects through space. Earth, moon, sun. However, the easiest way to measure time is to use your innate sense of time" explained Pan.

"Ok, whatever. What time is it anyway?" Derek asked groggily.

"It is time to resume your instruction. You must regain your ability to operate without a body. I will help you. Come." said Pan in his characteristically firm, self-assured, commanding tone. At the same time Pan's pervading care always made Derek feel as though he was in the company of a life-long friend.

"Where are we going?"

"On a journey. A journey through the past, to help you recall your personal identity." Pan mused.

At that moment Derek looked down on the land as though he were a soaring bird, high above the earth. He knew this place, though he could not name it.

"As you may recall, these are the ancient cities of Akkad and Sumer. The fertile fields along the alluvial banks of the Euphrates River in southern Mesopotamia, which runs south into the Persian Gulf. To the east lay the foothills of Elam, rising to meet the wild forest of the Zargos Mountains" Pan said, directing Derek's attention.

Across the river to the west stretched a vast sea of sand, the Arabian Desert. On either side of the river stood cultivated date palm orchards and golden fields of waving grain. Herds of grazing cattle, sheep and scattered goats flourished.

"Along the original course of the ancient river lay the cities of Sippar, Kish, Nippur, Uruk and Ur. As time goes by, the river will jump its banks and change course at Sippar, giving birth to the cities of Agade will be the glorious Babylon" Pan continued.

Derek scanned the expanse of ancient civilization below him. Along the river were built several walled cities adjacent to towering mud-brick pyramids called ziggurats.

"These were once called 'The Staircase to Holy Heaven, said Pan.

"Step-pyramids, supposedly built to provide the gods with a means to descend to Earth from the heavens. A massive mound of earth covered with bricks and painted with iridescent blue facing stone. The temple at the top of each pyramid is built to honor a patron god." he indicated the immense, precision built structure to Derek by leading his attention westward from the river.

"It was here, a mere 5,000 years ago, I first arrived at the planet Earth. I ruled in these lands and was hailed by all as Enlil, God of Creation, God of Earth and Air. And God of the Underworld: the Unseen Spirits of the disembodied, the once-living, not as yet reborn. I taught my faithful to prepare the earth for planting, to tend and harvest grains and trees.

My people flourished and prospered in the land and traded with regions far away in Egypt and India. Faithful they were to me. They praised my name, keeping my temple staffed with slaves to clean and keep the fires lighted in my honor. The glory of victory in battle was celebrated in my name. I kept my people well and safe from famine and drought.

My people were aware of the spiritual essence of themselves and of the myriad creatures. They perceived and revered the life essence of all living things. Even in the killing of animals for food they gave thanks to the beast for giving up life so that others might live. Purity of thought and action were taught to the young, who respected those who taught them.

Innocent joy and selfless friendship were virtues then. To breath the pure air, to hear the serenade of songbirds, the fragrance of flora, the sunlit sparkle of dew-dampened dawn were passionate experiences. The hearth of heaven heated the invigorated soil to germination and gestation, followed by harvest.

Derek listened intently while scenes of life in the ancient land passed before him. He experienced life in antiquity as though it were present time. Everything that Pan showed him was vividly real and alive.

"My people needed no priests to know me", Pan continued. "They had no need of idols to symbolize my presence among them. No sacrifices of flesh were made to appease me. To my people I was known as I am: as the Wind is known. My voice was heard by my people as it is heard by you. The voice of one spirit to another. In this way I visited my people.

To those who sought my help I appeared through signs in nature: the wind, the clouds, in storms and gentle rains and through the rich harvest from the earth. They knew my presence through my softly colored aura or by the sweet aroma of pine. To those who called my name I appeared and commenced to aid them. Those were happy times. They were as children to me, and I their benevolent father."

Derek didn't quite understand how he was perceiving all of this. He had never studied the history of the Middle East. Yet he knew what Pan knew, he thought his thoughts, felt his feelings, lived the memory.

It occurred to Derek that in spite of how astonishing all of this seemed, at the same time, it was quite natural and routine, like actual, living reality. In fact it seemed much more real than any reality he had known before. And so familiar...as though he had been here before.

"Déjà vu ", he guessed.

"Yes, déjà vu ", said Pan.

"Oh, yes, I suppose. Quite a story. Impressive, really", Derek stammered, not knowing what to think or how to express himself.

"It is no storying my friend. It is as you have seen for yourself." Pan said.

"Uh, yes...I mean, I didn't mean to say I thought it was a story, like fiction. Just quite a story." Derek replied.

"Exactly" said Pan.

"It does seem very familiar to me, somehow", Derek paused in thought, trying to rummage through his own memories for some scrap of recognition, but found nothing certain, only vague emotions.

* * * * * * * *

"OK gentlemen, (sniff) let's take another run over the area. Officer Johnlaw, you come with me. Officer Peeler, you and Brickman will search from east to west. We will search from north to south." said Sheriff Gumshoe, pointing a plump finger across the meadow where Derek had been shot.

"Let me remind you once again gentlemen, that (sniff) persistence is the key to good criminal investigation (achoo!). Now remember, we're looking for anything that will provide evidence of a premeditated assault on the (sniff) victim. (A-a-a-chooo!)"

Bubba had already given the same speech three times already that morning and at least seven times the day before. The assisting officers in the investigation each swore under his breath as they spread out for yet another search across the trampled ground they'd been scrutinizing for the last 36 hours.

So far, they had accumulated a treasure trove of incriminating evidence. Plastic baggies containing, in order of discovery: 1) one spent rifle shell-casing 2) thirteen cigarette butts 3) 12 beer cans from the campsite. They had also acquired, with effort, the following items: plaster cast impressions of footprints, tire tracks and deer hoof prints. They recovered the weapons the Jaras brothers left behind in their haste to get Derek to the hospital. Derek's jacket, back-pack, camera, and several bloodied remnants of Derek's shredded shirt were new evidence.

"All we need (sniff) is that one little piece of evidence. A second shell casing. The boys at the lab will have a field day if they find that both rifles were fired! Those guys probably (sniff) ditched the extra empty shells. But we could find (sniff) one they missed. You know, Jerald, this case could mean a lot to the department and to my career too (aachoo!). Let's check those tree trunks over there again". Bubba waved his soaking-wet handkerchief in the direction of a row of small pine trees at the edge of the meadow. "See if you can find where those other bullets hit ... (sniff)".

   * * * * * * * *

"If you would like to hear a story, instead of the simple truth of reality, I will tell you a story. It is an ancient and simple story, but you will find it entertaining and instructional. It is the story of how the Evil Ones came to Earth to ruin our tranquility. It is told in the ancient Myth of Homosapus."

At that moment a 1930's style movie theatre marquee appeared before Derek, complete with a border of white blinking lights. The story title and cast of characters scrolled up across the marquee like the credits at the end of a movie. Derek thought he even smelled buttered popcorn. In the background music tinkled on an upright piano like they used to play in movie theaters to accompany silent movies. He recognized the tune: "When The Saints Come Marching In". A Greek Chorus of male voices chanted the words as they appeared on the theater marquee:

"The Pandemic Players

Present:

A Play portraying The Pangenesis of Planetary Perversion

Starring a Panoply of Players in:

THE MYTH OF HOMOSAPUS

Derek and Pan hovered together over rows of tiered stone steps cut into a mountainside which formed a circular outdoor amphitheater. The performance was given on a sunny spring day, attended by a capacity audience of men and ladies, gracefully dressed.

The robed members of the chorus stood below in the circular orchestra as they collectively narrated the story being acted behind and above them on the "logeion". This was the stage built on top of a shallow, colonnaded building called the "proskenion". Behind the stage stood the "skene" which housed three rooms from which the all male cast entered and exited the stage. The actors were too far away from the audience to be clearly seen, so they each wore a large mask to depict his respective character. The cheerful murmuring of the audience hushed in anticipation as the chorus filed into the orchestra from the doors of the logeion. The play was beginning. The chorus swayed in unison as they chanted the story:

[CHORUS] *"From the other side of the galaxy, a spaceship came when Earth was young. Plague One, was her name and Her unsavory crew was led by Shamanus, The Priest. The craft is halted at the Gate of the Heavens. Our Hero, Homosapus, stands against them alone: the sole Guardian of Man. With his Shield of Truth he challenges the ship, ready to defend us*: (entering from stage left Homosapus shouts:)

"Hail! Who goes there?!" (The audience whistles and applauds)

[CHORUS] *"See how brave Our Hero is! See how his muscles bulge! See his shiny shield of Truth! See his bold and noble chin. Surely we are safe from harm! Oh, joy! Oh, joy!"*

"Hail to you friend! I am Shamanus, High Priest of the Creators. I come with my faithful wife Psychles, my lovely virgin daughter, Donnabella. We seek only to serve our fellow beings."

(Hoots and jeers from the audience. Several vegetables are thrown onto the stage.)

"Greetings to you sire. Please state your business here" Homosapus replied resolutely.

Shamanus, responding in his most unctuous voice said, "Good sir, we are sent from The Creators to purvey their blessings to the beings of your world."

(More boos and some rotten vegetables hit the stage)

"Hold! I have been Guardian of the Gates of Earth since the Beginning of Time", Homosapus replied unimpressed, "yet I have not heard of these Creators of yours. Of what benefit could such an association be to anyone here on Earth?"

(Cheers, applause)

[CHORUS] *"See how Shamanus is abashed by our wary Hero. Homosapus reigns supreme!"*

"We have traveled long and far seeking you my child. We bring the gifts of the Creators. Come to my ship, that I might show the glories of the Creators to you. Shamanus paused gravely, saying, "You must lay down your Shield of Truth while you enter our ship. There is no room for it within".

[CHORUS] *"We know Our Hero will not submit! He cannot be so easily tricked. His Shield protects us still."*

However, Homosapus, having no other duties at the moment and overwrought with the monotony of his post of guarding a planet that was never visited by anyone, thought no harm could come of this apparently innocent diversion. After all, he'd been guarding the Gates of Heaven for all Eternity so far and he needed a break. So, laying down his Shield, which he had, heretofore, never been without, enters *Plague*. (Shouts from the audience of "No! Don't do it!" and "Stop, you fool!")

[CHORUS] *Oh, fie! What treachery is this? What abandonment of duty? Why are we forsaken thus? How can he leave his Shield of Truth without?"*

The doorway was so low that Homosapus had to prostrate himself in order to enter the inner sanctuary of the vessel.

"Please excuse me for a moment so that I might alert my wife to prepare a refreshment to honor our guest", Shamanus said.

(Exits stage right followed by boos and hoots from the audience)

[CHORUS] *"Oh see how he conspires to outwit Our Hero. But never fear. Homosapus will not be duped!"*

(Shamanus enters stage left)

"Donnabella, go into the outer sanctuary where you will find the Guardian of the Gate of Heaven, Homosapus. Entice him to accept this cup and drink from it. Tell him that the drink will renew his strength and vigor".

[CHORUS] *"See how the evil Psychles prepares a chalice of fragrant liqueur, carefully laced with drugs. Beware, Our Hero! Beware!"*

(The Chorus swoons to their knees with hands upon their brow.)

"Once our guest recovers from the unconsciousness caused by the drink" Shamanus continued, "entertain our guest so that he will desire your favors and become amenable to us".

[CHORUS] *"She how Donnabella prepares herself with cosmetic cover-ups. She her curvaceous form beneath the see-through gown. Our Hero greets her graciously and accepts the offered cup. What naiveté! What wicked ways! Pray that He will catch on to the trick and save us!"*

(Donnabella enters stage left)

"Homosapus, you seem so familiar to me. Your face is more pleasing than any I have seen before. Have we ever met?" (Someone in the audience shouts "Don't fall for that line you fool!")

[CHORUS] *"See how the whore is blushing. Her cup is raised to make a toast. She hopes to do Our Hero in!"*

"May we remain in close proximity, but mystery, forever", said Donnabella (Screams from the audience of "Stop!" and "No!" Several women in the audience faint and are carried out.)

[CHORUS] *"The Cup! The Cup! She how he drinks! He is oblivious! Who knows what tragedy he brings upon us all!"*

(The Chorus slumps prostrate, on the floor of the stage, weeping.)

"I drink to the enduring health of Shamanus and to the surpassing beauty of his daughter. (The crowd boos loudly. More debris is thrown on stage).

Homosapus reels and spins, slumping to the floor as the cup slips from his hand.

"Anyone whose daughter is so lovely must be worthy on our trust..."Homosapus said.

In that instant the potion cleansed his memory and with it, all knowledge of his true identity and all future hope for Man.

[CHORUS] (raising themselves to their elbows) *"Injury enough we've suffered not. Shamanus has won! Lo, he has overwhelmed our Guardian! Guile and treachery cast salt upon our open wounds and treads us under foot! Oh, spare us! Spare us from our doom!"*

Shamanus spoke with the polished elocution of his trade:

"We, having been sent forth to Man by The Creators, come to you humbly as their chosen servants and messengers. Though The Creators live far beyond the ken and view of Earth, they remain One with us always.

We were sent to Earth to teach the Will of The Creators, that Man might have concourse, through Us, with them. In as much as The Creators have been and will always be The Creators, who know all, see all and tell all, we, as Their humble servants, are instructed to deliver The True Word to the men of Earth.

[CHORUS] *"Shamanus now rules the world. Our Hero is no more. Oh, woe to Us! The Deed is done! Oh, woe! Our Doom is sealed!*

Shamanus enters center stage, draped in flowing robes. He wears a crown of gold and jewels, with matching sepulcher:

"Hear now the Word of The Creators:

"Man is an Animal, Flesh and Dust. Like the beasts of Earth is he. He has no say in his destiny.

It is not for Man to understand, but merely to obey the will of The Creators and their Servants.

You must yet evolve to a higher state. As everyone knows, you are evil, unless controlled. Yet, Man in his lowly state, may someday complete his own perfection through compliance with the Will of The Creators.

Only The Servants of The Creators know Their Will. Learn The Way to Truth through them."

[CHORUS] *"Oh my, we are impressed with his noble dress and rhetoric! See him gesture and genuflect with such drama effect! Our Hearts are one, Our trust is won. The Creators are the Ones!"*

(A storm of rotten vegetables, stones and pot shards are thrown on to the stage from the audience.)

All the actors file on to the stage center to take a bow and exit. The Chorus marches off the stage with heads bowed in cadence to a Dixieland band which plays a mournful arrangement of "Nearer My God To Thee".

The stage and amphitheater are left in shambles and clutter. The marquee lights dim and fade...

-- THE END --

"You may applaud now", said Pan, concluding his apocalyptic presentation.

"Great!" complimented Derek, clapping with imaginary hands. "That was the saddest story I've ever heard! But I didn't understand one thing: who are The Creators?"

"An excellent question" replied Pan, enjoying the fact that Derek had paid attention to his mythological skit.

"You realize, of course, that the characters in this story are all purely allegorical and are not intended to represent any actual persons or professions, unless of course, they actually do. Inadvertently, of course."

"Oh, sure, of course...right" replied Derek.

"However, I can well image that The Creators might not be unlike the sort of beings who operate covertly to control Man for their own interests: priests, politicians, the press, bankers and lawyers. Their game is the same regardless of the guise. Any being who seeks to control the minds of men for personal gain is without moral standing.

They move surreptitiously, hidden from view. Their actions are disguised. Their words are duplicitous. The rotting stench of their crimes is perfumed by pretended benevolence toward the very people they enslave.

Fortunately, the light of truth is as deadly to them as sunshine to a vampire. The only power they truly possess is the power granted by each of us who, through apathy, inaction and irresponsibility, give them a license to endure. In this way, every man places the shackles of servitude around his own neck."

"Oh..., well, of course..." said Derek.

CHAPTER V

MENS CUIUSQUE IS EST QUISQUE.

"THE SPIRIT IS THE TRUE SELF."

-- Cicero - *De Republica, Vi.26* (c. 106 – 43 BC)

Jenny finally slept after a 48-hour vigil at Derek's bedside. A small stack of cards, faxes and e-mails from well-wishers stood between several floral bouquets on the night stand. A daybed was arranged in the corner of his private room. He had been released from intensive care early that morning. Though Derek remained unconscious, his vital signs were stable. A team of doctors agreed that his condition was still critical.

Jenny was exhausted. The doctors and nurses, phone calls from friends, the attorney and the office were very stressful. The threat of loss of her precious Derek had numbed her, but the necessity of having to persist through the ordeal raised her courage far above what she ever imagined she could endure.

* * * * * * * *

Paula hung up the phone. She had been handling all of the media questions and employee confusions since the accident. Coffee cups littered her desk. She was already on a first name basis with the Mercy of Mother Mary front desk receptionists: all three shifts. Each of her hourly calls got pretty much the same reply, "I'm sorry Paula, there is no change in Mr. Adapas condition. But we'll let you know if anything changes".

She, in turn, had repeated the same story over the phone to dozens of executives from other companies in the PC industry, as well as to several company VPs who were acting as information relay points to employees.

"No, there's no change yet...Yes, his wife is there with him...We don't know yet. The police are still investigating at the scene...Yes; I'll call you if there is any change. Thank you for calling (Mr. or Mrs. or Ms, etc.) so and so.

A gut-wrenching nausea hit her again. She made it to the bathroom near her office just in time, as she had done several times during the past two days. The stress of Derek's accident, the strain of no sleep and all the coffee, were too much for her, she thought. She was sick with worry. She didn't really feel physically ill except when periodic moments of nausea occurred. At 11:30 PM there was nothing more for her to do at the office so she forwarded the phones to the answering service and left to go home. She needed rest.

The next morning, although she had slept soundly, the nausea returned. On the way into the office she stopped to see Dr. Stevens at the clinic. After a brief exam, a few questions and a urine test, his prognosis was short and certain:

"Yes, I'm completely sure Paula. There is no mistake. You're pregnant".

* * * * * * *

"That Sheriff Gumshoe is crazier than a coot, Virg", said Billy Joe squinting beneath the brim of his orange, weather-beaten, 'Scotty's Lumber' baseball hat which he'd worn constantly for the past three years, except in the shower and in bed.

"Buuurrrp!" burped Virgil, "know what ya' mean little brother. He's damned curious", as he popped open another can of beer.

"What the hell. Let him and his boys do their sorry-ass investigation. There ain't nothin' for him to find up there anyhow" Virgil said, throwing an empty can onto the growing pile near the front porch of Billy's trailer house.

"Just the same Virgil, I think we oughta get us a lawyer. Know what I mean? Throw me another beer, will ya'?" Billy said, sitting down on the porch next to his brother.

Virgil spit across the porch onto the gravel driveway in front of the trailer. "Take it easy Billy Joe; don't get yer shorts all bunched up in a knot. There ain't nothin' to worry about."

* * * * * * * *

"Behold! *Kmt*, the Black Land and *Dsrt*, the Red Land! Hail to you, oh Nile, sprung from Earth, come to nourish Egypt, wherein are built the Houses of Eternity", Pan intoned dramatically."

"Therein reside the Sons of Ra, together with all the Earthly possessions required to keep them through life everlasting, forever and ever, for millions and millions of years. Amen!" Pan chanted with lofty sarcasm, continuing his theatrical salutation.

"In this land I was known as Min, Lord of Fertility and Harvest. He whom Pharaoh offered the first-cut sheaf of grain in gratitude from my plentiful harvest. All travelers invoked my blessing before the journey. Min, he of the erect phallus. He who holds the flail to thresh the bountiful grains of the fertile delta. I am Min, companion and friend of Asar, Lord of Death and Rebirth. Min, favored by Asar, the Great Mother, binder of Spirit and Flesh; giver of Life. Min, playmate of the beautiful Bastet, Goddess of Cats, she who protects pregnant women from evil."

Pan and Derek hovered before a painted hieroglyphic inscription deep within the massive Old Kingdom tomb of a long-dead, god-king. Pan read the words of the Supreme God Ra, as they were carved shortly after the unification of Upper and Lower Egypt under the first Dynasty of Pharaoh. This is the Hymn to the Creation of the Universe from the Egyptian Book of The Dead. Listen carefully, said Pan.

"I am the Eternal Spirit; I am the sun that rises from the primal waters.

My soul is God; I am the Creator of the world. Evil is my abomination, I see it not.

I am the Creator of the Order wherein I live. I am the Word, which will never be annihilated in this, my name: Soul.

The Word came into Being. All things were mine when I was alone. I was RA in all his first manifestations.

I was the Great One who came into being of himself. I fulfilled all my desires when I was alone, before there had appeared a Second to be with me in this space.

I assumed form as the Great Soul wherein I started being creative while still in the Primeval Waters in a state of inertness, before I had found anywhere to stand.

I considered in my heart, I planned in my head how I should make every shape. This was while I was still alone.

I planned in my heart how I should create the Myriad Forms of Life and that there should come into being their children and theirs".

Pan concluded the reading and rose from the dark within the tomb, dragging a rather over-awed Derek with him. They soared high into a cloudless sky. Derek looked in amazement across a panorama of the Nile River and the valley delta: verdant plains of cultivated grain fields met the brilliantly azure horizon at the Mediterranean Sea to the north. The gargantuan, geometric stone mountains of Giza gleamed under the scorching desert sky.

The majestic Great Pyramid of Khufu ascended above the desert as testimony to the surpassing enterprise and prosperity of the Egypt. Nearly every Pharaohnic Dynasty pursued a career of architectural self-glorification designed to overshadow his predecessor, funded by tribute from conquered nations in addition to the immense wealth of his own land. The mammoth monument been built with one hundred thousand stone blocks, each weighing two and a half tons, each quarried and dressed by hand. Every stone had been transported across miles of desert sand and precisely set into place by 200,000 paid laborers: free men, not slaves. No physical evidence existed to demonstrate that the pyramids of Giza were constructed by any Pharaoh. The priests of Amun maintained that they had existed for 15,000 years.

The benevolent dictatorship of Pharaoh, the living man-god, in cooperation with the gods of the heavens, had served Egypt well. The kingdoms of the Upper and Lower land had flourished and prospered through more than three thousand years of systematically stable expansion. Organization, protection, expansion and progress were administered by Pharaoh.

Derek had seen black and white photos and Hollywood movies about Egypt, but the real thing was beyond his wildest reckoning. The brilliantly painted and inscribed hieroglyphic colonnades and temples surrounding the dazzling white facing-stones of the Great Pyramid soared 40 stories above the Earth. These were escorted by the lesser, but still magnificent pyramids of Khafre and Menkaure, each completed with smooth facing stones. The entire panorama was a vividly grandiose scene, especially when viewed from five thousand feet above the valley floor.

Pan pointed to the formation of the pyramids as they are laid out on the ground adjoining the River Nile to the left from their vantage point facing north.

Suddenly, bright sunshine turned to a brilliant black sky, glittering with stars in the chilly desert night.

"Notice that the formation of these pyramids at Giza are an exact duplication of the formation of the three brightest stars in the "belt" of the constellation of Orion, relative to the Milky Way to its left" said Pan, directing Derek's attention first to the ground and then rising above the atmosphere of Earth to view the 'night' sky.

"Oh yeah, I see what you mean" said Derek in his moment of realization after looking carefully at the stars and the ground, comparing them. "If the Milky Way represented the Nile

River, the pyramids are laid out just the way the stars are laid out in the sky. What a coincidence!" Derek commented.

"In the year 10,450 BC, " Pan continued, "during the Golden Age when Thoth, God of Wisdom, who directed the design of the pyramids at Giza, lived on Earth, the three stars in the Belt of Orion were formed in an identical pattern as viewed from Egypt, as these three pyramids on the ground. You will notice that the two Dashour pyramids to the north also correspond identically to the position of the two Hyades stars in the constellation of Taurus, which are called the Eyes of the Bull. The right eye is the star Aldebaran and the left eye is Epsilon. These are the stars from whence the Earth societies of Mesopotamia originated" Pan said plainly.

Returning to daylight, Pan and Derek now surveyed other royal tombs, causeways, monuments, temples, dwelling places and the smaller pyramids of the queens. They visited the expansive market places of Memphis to the east flowing with thousands of people and livestock. The view, to Derek, evoked an eerie, magnificent awe within him.

In a blink Pan, with Derek in tow, swooped into a large, precisely carved room in the center of the largest of the tombs.

"This is the burial chamber of the Pharaoh Cheops, the alleged builder of the pyramid of Khufu.

"It's something to see, isn't it?" said Pan.

"Wow," Derek replied in a breathless whisper, "so this is Egypt. I would never have imagined it was like this!"

"Yes, it was quite an impressive place to be." replied Pan. "Before this temple stands the great Sphinx, symbol of the god Heru, God of Light, who faces the rising Belt of Orion, from whence Osiris came to Earth. He bears the likeness of his Earthly son, Pharaoh, embodied with the strength and dignity of

Anubis, the Dog, protector of the Two Kingdoms of Upper and Lower Egypt," said Pan.

"After the founders of Egyptian culture returned to the stars, a Man-King was appointed to rule in place of the gods. However, through the centuries, the priests of Amun gradually manipulated Pharaoh and his court for their own purposes. They used false information and threats, saying that to betray their wishes would be to incur the displeasure of the gods!" he spat.

"Of course, these imposters, just as Shamanus in the *Myth of Homosapus*, had no communication with the actual gods of Egypt at all. They never had anything to do with any of us! Everything was stone with them: gods made of stone, temples made of stone, tombs of the dead made of stone and souls made of stone…" fumed Pan as his anger increased with the memory of the centuries he had spent in Egypt.

"The only desire of the priesthood was to maintain and accumulate power and wealth for themselves. Always hidden behind the power of their degraded imaginary gods, hidden behind the earthly symbols of celestial power: Pharaoh and his royal family."

"Sounds like you didn't really care for priests all that much. What did they ever do to you" Derek ventured timidly.

"You are very astute", replied Pan sarcastically. "To me they did nothing. I desired nothing from these parasites. They simply manufacture lies to mask the simple spiritual truths of existence. It serves their purposes to enslave the ignorant and feed from their subservient lives".

The acrid odor of ozone filled the air as the wrath of Pan burned the oxygen in the atmosphere around him.

* * * * * * * * *

Paula drove to the office. Although she was shocked to discover that she was pregnant, she was nevertheless pleased. Derek was the father of her child. There had never been anyone else. And now, there never would be. She felt wonderful, really. "Motherly" was the only word for it.

She flipped on the car radio absently. Some music would be nice. She felt good. No more nausea since her visit to the doctor.

"Hello America! Russ Loudmouth here! The radio show that champions the cause of imperialism and industrial might!" blared the radio.

"Today's topic: Global Warming or Global Hoax? According to scientists, our planet is four and a half billion years old and it'll take hundreds of years for our industrial waste emissions to raise the global temperature enough to be harmful. Meanwhile, our scientists can figure out ways to solve the problem. Don't worry about the rain forests. It's a scare campaign put out by the liberal press, short and simple. And it's designed to destroy American jobs. I for one will not stand for anything that will harm the U.S. economy! These liberal environmentalists can't prove anything..."

Paula pushed a button to change to a station playing music. "What a jerk...that guy misses the point of environmentalism totally", she thought.

"It's not about global warming or ozone holes or economic pressure or lost jobs. The real point of it has to do with our children. And with their children and the grandchildren who will inherit the planet as we leave it to them. Will Earth be inhabitable? Will they be able to vacation on clean shores, to walk through forests of trees? Will they have to breathe the air through a mask and drink water full of chemicals? Eat artificially manufactured food, devoid of nutrition? Will we leave them a defoliated landscape of asphalt and Astroturf?" Paula thought.

"It's really about survival for our children's, children's, children. After all, those future children will be *us*".

*   *   *   *   *   *   *

Jenny sighed and put the magazine down. She rose from her chair and smoothed the hair from Derek's forehead with her fingers, leaned over to kiss his face. She wished that she and Derek had children together. What if he didn't recover? He would have no one to inherit his name.

*   *   *   *   *   *   *   *

Pan was silent.

Derek reflected to himself about his experiences with Pan.

"That was an interesting myth...er, story or whatever, about Homosapus. But then I always thought that Pan was a myth too, that is until I met him in person. The characters in the story weren't real like him though, were they?"

"Don't be ridiculous. Of course not!" Pan scolded, abruptly cutting into Derek's thoughts.

"Get real. It's just a myth. It was told to me by the Cat Goddess, Bastet. I first met her long ago in Egypt. We were introduced by Ast, whom the Greeks called Isis. She was queen of the gods in Egypt. They came to Earth from a planet in the twin-star system called Sirius. However, the story is, allegorically speaking, true enough."

"Isis? You've met Isis? You mean she is a real god like you? From another planet?" Derek strained to grasp the idea that the gods of ancient mythology could have actually existed; notwithstanding his experience since meeting Pan.

"There were once many godly beings here on Earth" Pan replied matter-of-factly. They had different names, given them by the men of various countries, but they were all the same beings. In spite of the many names given me and the stories told about me, I am the same Being. It is the same with men: no matter how many different bodies you have inhabited and identities you have assumed in various lifetimes, you are still the same being: always have been, always will be."

"I'm beginning to understand that myself now unfortunately" thought Derek, reminded of his own disembodied situation.

"Historically, the kings of every nation, the tyrant of every city-state, the caliph of every desert tribe on Earth sought to claim divine origin for his rule. Each one sought to be ordained as the Son of God on Earth. However, since they were really only men and very ungodly men at that, they had only three devices with which to create the illusion of godliness.

The first method, which used to be very popular, was to hire poets and songwriters and sculptors to create aesthetic illusions about themselves.

The second method is to buy popularity among the people with feasts, sporting events, sacrifices, public monuments, paid for with taxes and plunder of foreign conquest, of course.

The third method, and the most popular with rulers, has been to hire armies and police. The people are then convinced of his divine right to rule by the point of a spear. This has always been a very convincing technique."

"Yes, I get the point" Derek chuckled.

"What about Isis and the planet she came from?" Derek asked, intrigued.

"Many of the gods came to Earth long ago from a planet near the star Sirius." said Pan. "This also explains why the Egyptians were obsessed with the star for thousands of years. It is the brightest star in the night sky as seen from Earth. It is the uppermost star in the constellation of Canis Major. It's called the 'dog star'. By an interesting coincidence the Egyptian word for 'dog' is 'au-au', and the English word 'god' is 'dog' in reverse.

"Sirius is a twin star. One star is visible from Earth and the other is an invisible dark dwarf star which is very dense and heavy compared to our sun and creates no visible light. The two are known by your modern astronomers as Sirius 'A' and 'B' which they did not 'discover' until the 20th century. However, the ancient peoples of Sumer, Egypt, China, Africa and Central America have known about both Sirius stars for thousands of years.

The two stars orbit elliptically around each other. One revolution requires 50 Earth years. Sirius A is only 2.5 times heavier than the sun, but is 28 times as bright. The light of Sirius A takes 8.6 years to travel 51 million miles to Earth. Sirius B is 61,000 times more dense than water and 2,000 times more dense than platinum. Anyway, this entire trivia is significant to me only because so many of my friends came from there."

"Did you come from there too?" asked Derek.

"No. Where I came from is unimportant. I am here now."

"Yes, well, I guess so...just curious." thought Derek.

"Of course", Pan continued, undistracted, "the priests of Isis were very interested in Sirius also. Egyptians have always based their calendar on the movements of Sirius, rather than by the movements of the sun or moon. The Egyptian star-clock is kept by tracking the nightly rising of Sirius above the horizon. Based on these movements, the civil calendar of Egypt was used to date financial transactions and all civil holidays. Their year was one of 360 days, equally divided into 12 months of 30 days each. The modern time keeping system of 24 hour days, was based on the movements of Sirius.

The first day of the Egyptian New Year is celebrated on the day Sirius first reappears above the horizon after having not been visible for the previous 70 days. The rising of Sirius corresponds to the beginning of the spring flooding of the Nile. The flood season is still called the 'dog days' inasmuch as Sirius has always been referred to as the 'Dog Star'.

The priests told the people that the star descended into "Duat", the Underworld during this period of 70 days in which Sirius remained below the horizon. They also decreed that all dead bodies must undergo a process of embalming and mummification which required exactly 70 days, in honor of Sirius.

Of course it doesn't take 70 days to embalm a body. But it gives the priests a lot of time in which to perform complex funerary rituals to ensure "safe conduct" of the dead through Duat. They charged a handsome fee from the family of the dead for these 'services'.

I tell you, if I live to be a trillion years old (which I will) I will never understand how men continue to be so easily tricked by the deceptions of priests." Pan pondered, and then continued.

"In the Egyptian language Sirius is called "Sept", which means literally "seventy". The major events of the Egyptian calendar year continue to be observed, even in modern times.

The Christians still observe the "Septugesma"; the period of 70 days preceding Easter which falls on the day of the 'resurrection' of Sirius from its 'death' in Duat.

The priests invented several sacrificial rituals in connection with Sirius. They knew that the orbit of Sirius is elliptical, egg shaped. So, they used eggs in the New Year feast on the day of Sirius rising to symbolize the reappearance or "rebirth" of the star. The eggs were always dyed a red color, as this is the color of Sirius when seen through the atmosphere of Earth on the horizon. The priests used to sacrifice a red dog on this day also.

Coincidentally, the rising of Sirius is preceded by the rising of the constellation of Orion, which the Greeks call 'The Hunter'. This is followed immediately by the constellation, Lepus, the hare or rabbit. In other words, The Hunter (Orion) chases the Hare (Lepus) with The Dog (Sirius). Thus the origin of the ridiculous 'Easter Bunny' and the ' Easter egg'.

There remain to this day primitive tribes of black people in western Africa near Timbuktu whose ancestors were priests, driven out of Egypt. Their tribal name is the Dogon. They say that their ancestors came to Earth from a planet whose sun is Sirius A. They know all about the binary star system, including the details of the invisible, heavy metal dwarf star, the exact time and pattern of orbit and about the planets of the system, which are invisible even through the most powerful telescopes.

The Dogon say that the gods came to Earth in flying ships and were amphibious men. They say the gods came to Earth to teach men the skills of civilization in Egypt, but, like the priests of Egypt the Dogon have kept all of this knowledge hidden in layers of symbolic ritual practices. These rites and their true meaning were shared with only a select few who were initiated into the cult of elders each generation."

Pan paused in his instructional diatribe.

Silence...

"Derek!" shouted Pan noiselessly, but with considerable intention.

"Oh! What the...! Jeez...oh, sorry. I must have drifted off for a minute there" fumbled Derek, waking abruptly from his bored stupor.

"Uh, what were you saying? Gosh, I guess you lost me there somewhere…" he said, trying to save face.

"Oh, that's OK" laughed Pan. "I got off on a tangent I suppose. Anyway, let's get going."

"Going? Where to now?" asked Derek, still feeling a bit foggy.

"To the temple of Amun-Ra in Thebes. There is something there which will be of much greater interest to you."

In less than a blink they were gone.

CHAPTER VI

"How often have I said to you, when you have eliminated the impossible, whatever remains, *however improbable*, must be the truth?"

-- Sir Arthur Conan Doyle, *A Study in Scarlet* (c.1859 – 1930)

      Derek's private room at Mercy of Mother Mary hospital to which the hospital staff referred to simply as "MOMM", was a maze of tubes, tanks, wires, cords and tiers of electronic gadgetry designed to monitor and sustain the life of Derek's deserted but still breathing body. Each device was attended periodically by a doctor specializing in a field of medical science characterized by highly technical and expensive paraphernalia, the operation of which and interpretation of the resulting data derived there from, required no less than four years of post-graduate study, financed primarily by federal government student loans, and four additional years of specialist internships at a prestigious institution of medicine.

      Several of the nations leading medical specialists had flown in from various parts of the country and were temporarily encamped at the most expensive resort hotel in the area, only 20 minutes away from MOMM by chauffeured limo.

The body's condition remained stable but unchanging. Heartbeat, blood and urine, brain waves, endocrine system, respiration rate and muscle reflex responses all remained constant. Aside from the chest wound, Derek's body seemed to be relatively healthy.

Jenny had taken a suite at a nearby hotel, the *High-Up Regency*, which served as her base of operations for the moment. She had reviewed proposals from each of the medical experts, each retained at considerable expense, recommending that Derek be moved to their respective "most-qualified-to-care-for-him" medical facility located in various cities around the U.S.. She chose to keep him at MOMM for the moment. Jenny couldn't see any advantage to moving, even though most of the costs were covered by his insurance company, *Strong Arm Insurance Group*.

Besides, she did not want to face the additional strain of moving, or returning home to face family, friends and business affairs. Paula seemed to be doing a fine job of handling things at home anyway. But most of all she had an intuitive feeling that Derek should stay at MOMM, near the forest where he had been shot.

*   *   *   *   *   *   *   *

The next morning Paula called her attorney, Barry Barrister, to discuss the ramifications of her pregnancy. After considerable discussion, they agreed that a public announcement should be made. Should Derek die, as seemed possible, the legitimacy of the child's parentage would become more difficult to establish. While he lived, a DNA sample could be more easily obtained as proof. After all, Barry insisted, the financial security of the child must be considered… (not to mention his own).

* * * * * * * *

Jenny was told, rather unceremoniously, about Paula's pregnancy by Derek's attorney, P.R. Proctor. After the initial shock of incredulity subsided, she was horrified by the news. She spent several days in bed, saying she had the flu, to sequester herself from the world and to hide the renewed anguish of her already terrible grief.

* * * * * * * *

In light of the now exposed affair, Sheriff Gumshoe became more enthusiastic than ever in his investigation of the "alleged" hunting accident. Billy and Virgil, together with their newly hired lawyer, Pete Pleader, from the firm of Pleader, Kryor and Saub Inc., had been subjected to several hours of intense questioning and coercion to reveal their relationship with the friends, family, associates or person of Paula Cadmus, prior to the shooting.

It was all-too-obvious to Bubba that he was dealing with a conspiracy to murder Derek Adapa. He was thrilled! Bubba's investigation of the shooting had top priority now – made all the more important due to the national press exposure of the illicit romance. Bubba celebrated by giving himself carte blanche access to the "Special Investigations Fund" to finance his newly intensified inquiry. Bubba was, in Virgil's words, "happy as a pig in shit". He had already gained a good deal of personal celebrity after being interviewed about the shooting by no fewer that 13 magazines, 28 newspapers and 7 TV stations.

* * * * * * * *

News of the scandal was all-to-soon on the front cover of every sleazy tabloid in the country, thanks to the quick thinking and opportunistic "reporting" of the ever-zealous, free-lance reporter, Lenny Liescribe. The *National Inquisition* was able to hit the grocery store news racks with the "exclusive story" on Derek and Paula 24 hours ahead of the competition.

Lenny, with his usual facility for "creative reporting" had coincidentally "discovered" no less than seven other illegitimate children fathered by Derek, complete with photos ranging from bare-bottomed babies, to toothless first-graders and one high school freshman. According to Lenny's unnamed "reliable sources" Derek had slept with approximately 4.7 percent of the entire population of San Jose, California during the past 20 years and that the incorrigible rouge, in spite of his currently unconscious state, was having an affair with an as-yet-to-be-named nurse at MOMM also!

* * * * * * * *

Aching slashes of grief and anger ripped through Jenny in irrepressible floods. Her jealous imaginings of Derek and Paula together in forbidden lust were a living nightmare. His pretended innocence while continuing to live his routine daily life with her, apparently unchanged, tormented her. What must he have said to Paula? How did he touch her? What had she been doing when they were together making love? Why had she not noticed anything different about him? How long had this been going on? With each new question came a new attack of anguish. The pain permeated the center of her being during every waking moment. Her only brief respite from exhausted weeping was in a fitful, sleeping-pill-induced slumber, too soon renewed on awakening.

Jenny was momentarily compelled to unplug all of Derek's life support systems in revenge. But the impulse passed. She still loved the god damned, two-timing shit head too much to harm him further. She had loved him since the first day they met.

After of few days of introspective review of their life together, Jenny began to realize that she herself must assume some responsibility for the affair. She had obviously not been paying enough attention to him to notice what was going on. How could she have been so blind?

* * * * * * * *

Paula grew increasingly involved in handling the operation of Nimbus Software. Jenny had no legal control over the company and no power to fire Paula. Besides, regardless of her personal feeling toward her, Paula was too valuable to the business to be let go: baby or no baby.

Ironically, since the news of the scandal had been ejaculated all over the media, business at Nimbus Software was booming. Sales of ThunderCalc were always expected to be at least 8 to 10 percent higher each year, following the normal annual growth in personal computer sales.

Vern, the VP marketing confided privately to Paula, *"The National Inquisition articles are great for business. As disgusting as these tabloids are, we never got this kind of response from our paid advertising!"*

* * * * * * *

Billy Joe and Virgil, now under a court order not to leave the county, stayed home and stayed drunk.

* * * * * * *

Paula's attorney, Barry Barrister, managed to keep Bubba's sleuthing inquiries away from her so far. As there was absolutely no evidence whatsoever of her involvement in a plot to kill Derek he was able to get a court injunction against police interrogation. But all of that work meant nothing to him. There was a lot of money to be made through the paternity suit he was preparing to file on Paula's behalf.

Paula decided to have the baby and there was no question of terminating the pregnancy. Despite that fact local TV news reporters contrived a story speculating that she would abort the child. The resulting "pro-life" and "pro-choice" controversy inflamed confrontations in front of Nimbus Software headquarters resulted in battle which left 7 persons injured and 35 people arrested.

* * * * * * * *

"The pennants attached to the flagstaffs outside the temple are supposed to indicate the presence of the god Amun-Ra in the temple when blown by the wind", scoffed Pan.

Pan and Derek glided through the twenty-four foot thickness of precisely crafted stone blocks to emerge on the interior of the sanctuary of the Temple of Amun-Ra at Karnak near the ancient Egyptian capital of Thebes. The massive complex had been progressively expanded and elaborately enhanced by the priests of Amun over a 200 year period during which an Egypt continually conquered foreign lands. The riches of conquest held in the state treasury were under the control of the priests at this temple. Towering columns and thickly plastered brick walls were boldly incised and artfully painted by the finest artists in the ancient world to praise of the omnipotence of Amun-Ra.

"People actually believe these camel dung stories made up by the priests! They will say anything to convince the people that the priesthood is supreme and inviolate", indicating to Derek the wall paintings, hieroglyphics and statuary in the dimly lighted sanctuary. The musty odor of myrrh hung like a burlap cloak in the stale air.

"Look at this junk! Who dreamed up this stuff? I'll tell you: a bunch of temple scribes and artists, that's who!" Pan ranted, sweeping his attention to the gilded stone statues of Amun-Ra.

The granite god was a man with the head of a hawk, crowned by a disk encircled by an asp. Beside him the lion-headed image of his wife, Amunet.

"These are symbols of the Sirius star", Pan indicated, "the snake, symbol of supreme power; the disk, symbol of the star itself; the hawk represents the transcendent soul. Usually the statues of Amun show him as a frog-headed man: the Nommos or amphibians, described by the Dogon tribes of West Africa.

In fact, the planet near Sirius is a watery planet inhabited by amphibious men. They were sent here to teach civilization to Men long ago. Of course the priests, saving literacy and writing for themselves, keep this knowledge a secret from the people. What the people do not know can be used to control them." he said.

Pan directed Derek's attention to the hieroglyphic murals covering the temple interior. Derek looked about curiously for a moment and began to read the symbols painted on the walls:

> "Hail O Amun-Ra! Sun disk of Heaven.
>
> Thou art the Source of all Life in Heaven and Earth.
>
> And of the Spirit Underworld.
>
> Praised be Thy name.
>
> Thy Invisible Creative Power is above all gods.
>
> There is no other god like unto Thee.
>
> Thou art the one One. There is no second One.
>
> Blessed be Pharaoh, Amun-Ra incarnate on Earth.
>
> Lord of Man. The Divine consort, They Queen

doth lay with Thee in the temple to beget the

Children of Amun-Ra.

The Sons of Pharaoh are the Sons of Amun-Ra, God of Gods."

Derek concluded. "I see what you mean".

"This is propaganda to make it look like Pharaoh is the son of god on Earth", Derek commented.

"Exactly!" agreed Pan.

"What angers me is that *I am* a real god, who actually exists and I receive no recognition at all!

I worked here for centuries making sure the Nile didn't flood too much. I protected the crops against locust and defended the cattle, kept them free from disease. I protected the camel caravans along the trade routes from bandits and storms. I kept the females fertile with seed. But people, who used to thank me for my troubles at the annual festival of the New Year, do not pay attention to me anymore. It is by the hand of the greedy, lying priests that I am now ignored. D*amn* them!" raged Pan.

A jagged shaft of lightening scorched the desert air. The walls and floor of the temple swayed and trembled. A huge, shattering crack streaked down the north wall and struck the floor. Dust and pebbles sprinkled from the ceiling. A crackling roar of thunder echoed across a cloudless sky and through the hills surrounding the Valley of the Kings.

"Whoa, take it easy!" shouted Derek ducking the debris instinctively, but unnecessarily. He caught himself short, stopped in dumbfounded astonishment and said, "Wait a minute! How did I know that stuff? Jesus! I read those hieroglyphs just like they were the Sunday newspaper. What the hell?!"

"Well, it appears you are starting to remember a few things", glowed Pan. "That's what we are here for. To sweep the dust and cobwebs from your memory."

"Memory? You mean I've really lived *here* before?!" Asked Derek, alarmed with the realization of his own knowledge.

"I didn't say that you *lived* here before. However, how else might you explain your reading of the walls?" Pan kidded him with half-suppressed mirth.

"I don't know...I guess...I mean, this place...Egypt seems very familiar to me. I can read these walls - no problem. God, this is really amazing! Derek glowed with delight and excitement. "Incredible!"
"Not so incredible my friend", Pan soothed. "You will remember more as we go along. You and I have seen and done many things together during our Earthly time trek".

"Really? Me? Jesus!" Derek spouted, still astonished.

"No. Not Jesus..." prompted Pan.

"Oh, well I didn't mean that I thought I was Jesus..." Derek started to interject.

"Yes, I know. However, as part of our quest to recover your memory you must know this:" said Pan more soberly. "Man, to the degree that he considers himself not to be a god, is not at cause over his own life. Man thinks he is not a god. That he is the body only. Priests teach such lies. Man is a god to the degree that he can operate as a spiritual being – that is, to communicate and cause things to happen as a spirit, whether inside the body or outside. The greatest lesson I can teach you is this: In order to operate as a spirit, you must first become aware of spirits – not the false spirits of priests – but with truly living beings like me. Your ability to communicate with other beings will increase your own awareness and power."

The entire body of "religious art", as the walls within this temple demonstrate, is nothing more than an elaborate enticement: a beautifully orchestrated carnival side-show of priestly lies and mysteries. Beauty is the carrot, dangled alluringly in front of the donkey's nose to keep him pacing the treadmill of endless subservience. The donkey forgets that he is able to find his own carrots."

Chapter VII

"And when the tomb was finished the sun had already set, but the afterglow was rosy on the huge bulk of Pan. And presently all the enlightened people came and saw the tomb and remembered Pan who was dead and all deplored him and his wicked age. But a few wept apart because of the death of Pan. But at evening as he stole out of the forest, and slipped like a shadow softly along the hills, Pan saw the tomb and laughed."

-- Lord Dunsany, The Tomb of Pan (c. 1878 - 1957)

Jenny was beginning to despair of Derek's chance for recovery. The surgery had gone well, but the doctors could find nothing to explain his continuing unconsciousness.

The team of medical authorities in attendance were led by Dr. Benny Troche, credited by the American Medical Monopoly as the leading expert in nuerotraumatic pharmacology Dr. Lance Butcher was the foremost practitioner of neurophysiologic surgery procedures. They sat in a conference room at MOMM while they explained Derek's medical situation to Jenny:

"What we have here Mrs. Adapa is a probable disruption of the reticular formation found throughout the midbrain, pons, medulla and cerebral cortex. As the reticular formation serves to control the overall electrical activity of the central nervous system, it plays a major role in maintaining a state of sleep or wakefulness by allowing the passage or filtering out of various sensory impulses to the cortex" he explained, pushing his coke-bottle thick, gold-rimmed glasses higher up on his ski jump nose.

"However, prolonged electroencephalogram analysis of the alpha, beta and delta waves produced by Derek's brain give no clue to the condition, even when enhanced by automatic frequency analyzers and average response computers. Further, chemical analysis of amino acid content in the brain showed normal levels of glutamic acid, tryptophan and nicotinic acid, but a peculiarly elevated level of serotonin. I will defer to Dr. Troche at this point to further elaborate based on his extensive pharmaceutical expertise", he said, nodding to his associate to pick up the diatribe at this point.

"Yes, well, an attempt can be made, with your permission of course, to inhibit the action of monoamine oxidase, using antidepressant drugs such as PROZAC. However these have proven to have a few minor side-effects, such as addiction, nausea, liver damage, sexual dysfunction, memory loss and death.

"The general theory here", he explained to Jenny with veiled condescension, "is that man is basically a machine, as every school child knows, composed of a complex concatenation of chemical compounds. One need only guess the right combination of drugs to combine with the natural chemical components of the body in order to affect a remedy for any ailment".

"However, in this unusual case, I propose that exploratory surgery is needed to discover the source of the traumatized neuralsynapses of the midbrain, the regions of the brain thought to be responsible for conscious analytical thought and motor stimulus-response generation of the body."

Dr. Troche looked to Dr. Butcher for acknowledgement. They both turned to Jenny, fully expecting her complicity with their expert recommendation.

"I will take your proposal under advisement, pending other opinions. I'll call you if I need you." Jenny responded coldly to their suggested use of drugs and surgery.

Nonplused, the doctors began to stammer a protest as Jenny got up and left the room. She had heard enough. She quickly left MOMM and drove back to her hotel.

*   *   *   *   *   *   *   *

Paula didn't want to file a paternity suit against Derek, or his estate, in the event of his death. She was sure that once Derek recovered he would want the baby too and that he would take good care of both of them financially. Meanwhile, she was making good money working as the temporary President of Nimbus Software, appointed by the Board of Directors to handle the company during Derek's absence.

However, Barry was quite insistent. His argument in favor of a lawsuit seemed coldly logical. He seemed to be so genuinely concerned for her well-being and for the baby. Barry carefully explained to her the various legal contingencies, liabilities and fiduciary encumbrances of her primogenital maternal-familial situation, the successful resolution of which would not cost her a dime, inasmuch as his fee, a mere 50% of the awarded or negotiated reciprocal concession, would come from the aforementioned party or estate of the patriarchal defendant. He reassured Paula, most sincerely, that he was thinking only of her best interests, of course.

* * * * * * * *

Bubba was having a great time. He hired a new personal secretary and a staff of three full-time inspectors to assist him in his conspiracy investigation of the alleged hunting "accident". Bubba's secretary drove him to the airport this afternoon to catch a flight to Washington D.C.. He hoped to gather the vital information he was missing to prove a premeditated assault on Mr. Adapa. He would get an indictment against Paula Cadmus and the Jaras brothers if it was the last thing he ever did as Sheriff of Sasquatch County!

It was obvious to Bubba that Paula, knowing she was pregnant had hired these two hit men, disguised as hunters, to bump off Derek Adapa. With him out of the way, she could sue his estate for everything, being the mother of his sole heir, and pay off the Jaras brother and no one would be the wiser.

But she hadn't bargained for a run-in with Bubba Gumshoe! He hadn't fallen off the garbage truck yesterday. Yes, he was too smart for her. He ordered 24 hour security placed on Derek's room at MOMM just in case they tried to finish the job before Bubba could get them legally. He also ordered 24-hour surveillance of both Paula and the Jaras boys, including wire taps. Just let them make one wrong move....

The central computer database at the national headquarters of INTERPOL in D.C. would give him access to every file kept on anyone who had ever been assigned a social security number. Files were kept by every government regulated financial institution and every agency in the country including the FBI, CIA, DEA, IRS, each branch of military intelligence, Social Security Administration, as well as local, state, regional and federal police, sheriffs, marshals, troopers, and highway patrol. A truly awesome accumulation of information pulsed through the INTERPOL data files and it was all at his disposal.

Bubba sniffed with satisfaction as his pudgy, sweating fingers clasped the handle of his briefcase. He sneezed and started down the stairs to the parking garage.

*   *   *   *   *   *   *

"Damn! Ain't this a buncha' shit? said Virgil, shaking the itemized bill he had just received from the Law Offices of Pleader, Kryor and Saub.

"Git me another beer will ya'?" he shouted into the kitchen as he plopped down on the couch in front of the TV.

"Shit" hollered Billy "Git yer own friggin' beer! I gotta take a piss and get ready to go to my night job so I can pay the goddamn attorney bills".

*   *   *   *   *   *   *

Pan stirred the air above a crumbling stone temple, leaving in his wake a few swirling dust-devils on the dirt streets below. Derek was amid the barren, mid-day ruins of present time Egypt. A flock of flying ducks passing over head was swept up abruptly in a draft of heat rising above Pan as he continued to curse the priests of Amun-Ra. The birds fluttered momentarily and continued on their southerly flight.

"The five of Us: Isis, Osiris, Heru, Bastet and I, decided to take action against the priests. Not so much in revenge, but in an attempt to awaken the people to their evil-intentioned power game. We chose a vehicle through which to affect our plan just as the cult of Amun-Ra reached the pinnacle of power".

"What did you do to them?" asked Derek. "What it gruesome?"

"I'll show you," said Pan, "in the year 1370 BC, that is, Before the Calendar changed…".

Chapter VIII

"When I investigate and when I discover that the forces of the heavens and the planets are within us, then truly I seem to be living among the gods."

-- Leon Battista Alberti (c. 1404 - 1472) Italian architect, philosopher, poet

"Thy rising is beautiful in the horizon of heaven thou Aten,

Who hast thine existence in primeval time.

When Thou rises in the eastern horizon, fills every land with beauties.

Thou art beautiful to see, and art great and art like crystal, and art high above the Earth.

Thy beams of light embrace the land, even every land which Thou has made.

Thou are as Ra, and brings Thyself unto each of them.

And binds them with Thy love.

Thou art remote, but Thy beams are upon the Earth," intoned Akhenaton in his slightly lisping, effeminate voice.

"I wrote this hymn to our beloved Aten myself. How do you like it?" asked the young Pharaoh, turning to his enchanting and splendid wife, Queen Nefertiti, mother of his 6 daughters.

"It is truly wondrous" she replied politely, placing the fruit and flowers she held on the mud-brick alter of the Holy of Holies. The pair stood in an outdoor temple which had been built virtually overnight, according to the exact specifications given by her husband to his army of architects and artisans.

"It will be engraved in the sanctuary I am building at the new Royal Temple near my Pleasure Garden", said Akhenaton with the anticipation of a small child about to receive a new toy.

They bowed to a huge symbol of the Aten, The Sun Disk, deeply chiseled into the stone and brightly painted wall above the altar. Together with his retinue of bodyguards, servants, musicians, dancers and selected nobility, the pharaoh turned and slowly began to return the 870 yard length of the brick-walled temple grounds. They passed along the central causeway through a series of smaller chapels and a rectangular maze of baked brick tables built to receive ritual offering from royalty and citizens alike.

Pharaoh and his entourage shuffled reverently between the gargantuan crimson pillars of the Gem-Aten, (The Finding of Aten) altar. They marched ceremoniously through the massive, towering walls of Per-Hai, The House of Rejoicing and exited the temple compound to the west from the sole entrance to the sprawling, cumbersome, Temple of Aten.

The small herd of companions to Pharaoh during this daily outing turned north along the King's Way, a broad dirt road serving as the main thoroughfare of Aketaten, the newly constructed capital city of Egypt, whose name means "The Resting Place of Aten'. The road stretched along the course of the nearby Nile, through an expansive central city of temples, palaces, government buildings and the national treasury. Within half an hour the procession reached the bridge which joined Pharaoh's living quarters to the awkwardly spacious buildings, the open square of the Great Palace and the main assembly hall of the city.

Pharaoh paused briefly at the windows in the center of the bridge to wave limply, but with affection, to a scattered throng of curious but unenthusiastic citizens in the dusty street below. Everyone wanted to glimpse the graceless figure of Pharaoh whose bizarre features were not repulsive, but uniquely deformed. Above his elongated face and chin, thickly protruding lips and large, oriental eyes Akhenaton wore the stately crown of Upper and Lower Egypt: the supreme symbol of his dominion over a multitude of tributary nations. Spindly legs supported a protruding belly and broad feminine hips.

In spite of his bizarre countenance, this grotesque man-god held the crook and flail, keys to the power of Egypt, in his thin, elongated fingers.

"Isn't this just too absolutely perfect?!" squealed Bastet in delight. "He is the greatest laughing stock in the entire world! Can you believe how deliciously silly that hymn was that he made up?"

Through Pan's memory Derek stood by as Bastet surveyed the growing urban sprawl of Aketaten from several thousand feet above the city along the western desert bank of the Nile. Aketaten was situated on a plain six miles long and three miles wide, at the exact geodetic center of Egypt: equidistant between the pre-dynastic capital city of Behdet in the north and the southernmost limit of Egypt at 24^0 00' north latitude (as reckoned by a rigorous adherence to the mathematical laws of cosmic order which the dimensions of Egypt are thought to embody).

Derek gaped at the scene below. An entire city, consuming most of the awesome creative talents and physical resources of the most highly civilized and powerful nation on Earth, had been erected in a desert at the instruction of a deformed religious fanatic in just two years.

"Yes, we've all done our parts well", agreed Heru. "The power of the priests of Amun has been completely destroyed. All of the wealth of the Amun-Ra has been taken from them and restored to the state. The temples are closed and barren. The priests are stripped of power. Taxes have been lowered and the granaries are once again open to the people. The hatred of the priesthood, which I have given the new pharaoh, has served our purposes well."

"Indeed", laughed Isis, " and likewise, his religious has produced this absurd aberration of the 'one and only god'. It's perfect! No more will the people be forced to pay tribute to stone idols. The sun-god, Aten, so childishly conceived by Pharaoh will discredit Amun-Ra forever. Now, we can restore the awareness of Men of the true gods – us! No one can possible take this notion of 'one and only god' seriously. It is too ridiculous, even for children to believe. Wonderful, is it not?" giggled Isis.

"You are right. As long as we are congratulating ourselves, do not forget that I gave him his perverted obsession with sex. The whole world is disgusted that a Pharaoh could be so sexually promiscuous. He keeps his wife and grown daughters all pregnant, producing congenitally deformed idiots, while fornicating with every serving boy and concubine he can get his hands on. Pharaoh thinks of nothing other than his love of sex and his sun-god Aten" said Pan, promoting his own contribution to the demise of the priesthood.

"This will be our lesson to the priests. The world will never forget Akhenaton" said Pan, gloating with self-satisfaction.

"And don't forget Bastet, by withdrawing her maternal protection from his mother, Queen Tiy, while she was pregnant, allowed the deforming disease to enter her womb".

"Oh, it was really nothing", Bastet purred modestly.

Derek was smitten by the sensation of Bastet's being. Her presence was overwhelmingly sensuous. Feline and feminine, he thought lustfully.

"Yes, she is indeed a beauty", Pan commented, sensing Derek's desire.

Derek still wasn't used to the idea of telepathy – that Pan could *feel* this thoughts and emotions. He'd have to be more careful to edit his thoughts in the future…. "Oh, er…well, yes…uh…" Derek stammered, as the scene faded from view and Pan returned their attention to present time.

"So, this must have been a great victory for all of you. Eliminating the power of the priesthood like that. Very clever." Derek complimented.

"And so it seemed for an all-too-brief moment in history", replied Pan soberly.

"In spite of our apparent success against the priests, our joy was short-lived. Almost immediately after their demise at the hands of Akhenaton, the disenfranchised priests of Amun-Ra and the corrupt political establishment at Thebes mounted a massive whispering campaign designed to slander and discredit Pharaoh. Such attacks were extremely dangerous in Egypt where Pharaoh had absolute authority over all life and property. Never-the-less, the priests, having lost everything, had only their lives left to lose by attacking Pharaoh. It was a gamble they thought worth taking.

Their goal was to create an uprising among the people and foreign enemies of Egypt sufficient to overthrow Akhenaton.

They did not succeed. So deeply entrenched was the conviction of the divine right of Pharaoh to rule, that the people would not rise against him. And adjoining rulers had too much to lose by openly breaking diplomatic relations with Egypt, much less risking the wrath of Pharaoh's army.

"However, the priests, masters of treachery, finally managed to alienate some key military leaders from Pharaoh and even his faithful wife and co-regent, Queen Nefertiti.

Derek once again watched through Pan's memory as a group of cloaked soldiers under the command of General Ay, kidnapped Akhenaton from the safety of his palace bedroom under the cover of night. Pharaoh's muffled cries for help faded beneath the clatter of horse's hoofs and grinding chariot wheels, as they sped off into the cold desert night.

The sun god Aten searched the dawning dust with golden hands to warm Akhenaton, man of god and god of man. But his namesake was slain by slashing swords seen only by the silent moon. The dismembered king lay hidden beneath an unmarked tomb of desert sand.

Ay, the former Keeper of the Royal Horses for Akhenaton's father had by treachery, extortion, and murder become the Vizier of Pharaoh. In his jealousy of Pharaoh he conspired with the priests to slay Akhenaton and was eventually rewarded with the Crook and Flail of Egypt. He fulfilled his end of the bargain by restoring the decadent, criminal power structure of the priests in Thebes.

Within 20 years Horemheb, former commander of Pharaohs army had assumed the throne. Under his jealous rule, the capital city was returned to Thebes. At the direction of the priests, every monument, statue, building and inscription erected by Akhenaton was defaced and destroyed." Pan concluded his story with noticeable, and uncharacteristic, melancholy.

"I'm very sorry" said Derek sympathetically. "It must have been upsetting for all of you."

"Indeed. However, that was not the worst of it. In our despair at the failure of our plan to defeat the priesthood, Isis forgot to remove her curse of religious zeal, which fostered Akhenaton's idea of the 'one and only god'. This "one god" notion was adopted by the Jewish slaves, who hated Egypt, and subsequently by their leader. As you know, his idea survives to this day. The philosophy has flourished as a scourge in the hands of the priests, who have used it to debase and pervert the spiritual awareness of the people on nearly every civilization on Earth since that time. This disastrous accident taught me one of the most valuable lessons I have ever learned." said Pan, pausing to reflect.

"What's that?" asked Derek.

"Do not be the effect of your own cause", Pan tutored. "When you set fire to the city of an enemy, be sure that your own village is not consumed by the flames".

*   *   *   *   *   *   *

News of the paternity suit filed by Paula's attorney came as no surprise to Bubba. He had her figured out from the start. It was just like he learned in his class in Criminal Psychology 1-A: the first correspondence course Bubba took in law enforcement. Just another money-hungry, psychopathic, nymphomaniac killer-type. She was a routine, psychology textbook case.

Bubba stepped out of his taxicab in front of a nondescript brownstone building in Washington D.C.. which served as the US. Headquarters for INTERPOL. He was sure he could turn up the incriminating evidence he needed to indict Paula and the Jaras brothers here.

Questioning the Jaras brothers regarding their relationship to Paula Cadmus had been a complete waste of time. Criminals never tell the truth. Paula's slick, big-city lawyer had blocked every attempt he made to gain access to interviews with her. Not that interrogating her would do any good.

As Bubba mounted the brick staircase to the entrance landing, he sneezed furiously. He was sure that the smog and inner-city filth of D.C. was going to kill him, that is, if some local drug gang didn't get to him first. This building was in a pretty seedy part of town. Actually, all of D.C. was pretty seedy except where the Federal Government buildings were, which everyone knew were even seedier, in spite of their outward appearances.

Bubba was met by a frumpy, gruff, middle-aged lady who, after examining his California drivers license and police ID very carefully, showed him down the hall to the data processing managers office.

"Pretty good (sniff) security here", Bubba said.

"Welcome to V.I.P.E.R., Mr. Gumstick. This is INTERPOL's state of the art computer database, the Voluntary Information Processing Exchange Registry", said the computer room control clerk, indicating a chair in front of a row of computer terminals.

(sniff) "Catchy name", said Bubba. "My name is Gumshoe, by the way…"

"Uh, yes. Indeed...Well, let's see, once you have read this simple 150 page instruction manual on V.I.P.E.R. access codes and procedures, you will be able to address, merge, sort, search and cross-reference every file we keep on private citizens, corporations and churches in the entire U.S.. Just use the appropriate key code to get the data you want: birth, employment history, personal finances, medical records, purchasing history, tax return, sexual habits, names of associates and family members. If you have any questions, just press the red button on the desk in front of you. You may ask for me personally if you like. My name is Werner. Oh, and there are tissues in the restroom down the hall, first door on the left."

"Uh, thanks. (sniff) No problem." said Bubba.

Verner bowed stiffly, clicked his well-polished heels together, just as he had been trained to do in the S.S. during WW II, turned crisply and left Bubba to thumb through the computer manual on his own.

       *   *   *   *   *   *   *

Seth Mountebank, Doctor of Psychiatric Sciences, graduated from the Chicago Institute of Psychiatric Studies (CHIPS), class of '69, Magnum Cum Laude in a doctorate class of two.

Dr. Mountebank, or "Mountey" as he was nicknamed facetiously by his classmates, had invented a new "science" which he called *psycho neurophysiology*. His research was given to exploring the psycho synthesis between psychosexual and psychotropic therapies: Drugs and sex, basically.

The psychology textbooks Mountey read didn't mention the fact, as any school child knows that the word "psyche", meaning "spirit or soul", is the root word of psychiatry. The concept of a spirit or soul was purely inconsequential in the actual practice of psychiatry. Mountey thought that Man was no more than a complex, tool-making, flesh and blood animal evolved from a primordial sea of ammonia. His post-graduate internship on Santa Monica Boulevard in LA, as well as his brief tenure in private practice on 8th Avenue in NYC, had been living application of his theories: he proved, as least to himself, that any man or woman could be persuaded to have sex with him, if given enough drugs.

As with any self-respecting psychiatric theoretician, Mountey had taken an early retirement from private practice, right after he went broke. Besides not getting laid enough, the few weirdo patients who actually paid for his "therapy", expected to be cured of their problems! Naturally, any psychiatrist worth his diploma knows this is an absurd impossibility. Once a weirdo, always a weirdo.

So, he had happily accepted a research grant from the Federal Government for "continuing studies". This was known in the trade as the "mouse and maze game". All one had to do was set up a simple experimental laboratory using mice in a maze or mutilated monkeys in cages: whatever works. When the federal inspectors came around at the end of the fiscal year to check the progress of his research, he simply typed up a multi-page report full of "psychobabble", a lot of very technical sounding nonsense language, and turned it in with a copy of his new budget proposal. Of course his request for continued and increased funding always concluded with the standard psychiatric catch-phrase, 'Of course no one can really understand the human mind, but with continued funding we hope to learn how to control it."

Since the philosophy of the federal government has always been that "the only good mind, is a mind under OUR control", Congress, in their infinite foresight, had continued to fund psychiatric research. Budget subcommittees doled out billions dollars every year.

"Yes", he thought, "a very lucrative business indeed. And I don't have to talk to any weirdoes anymore either".

Mountey had been referred to the Adapa coma case through the very best authority in the field of psychiatry, the Chairman of "A.S.P.", the <u>A</u>merican <u>S</u>ymposium of

Psychoneurophysiologists, who happened to be an old drinking and whoring buddy from American Psychiatric Association conventions which were held one week each quarter in either Las Vegas or Atlantic City.

Dr. Mountebank flew out to California from his private research laboratory housed in the second level subterranean basement of the Center for Human Psychosexual Studies (CHumPS), near Bethesda, M.D..

Upon arrival, his initial interview with the patient's wife clearly indicated an advanced condition of traumatic psychosexual behavioral impairment of physiological stimulus-response hormonal secretions resulting in manic-hysterical psychosis. This became evident when Jenny screamed at him and slapped his face when he suggested that she go to bed with him as a "therapy" to calm her upset about her husband's continued coma.

Anyone who read Newsweek Magazine knew that at least 65% of all psychiatric patients were sexually involved with their therapist. So, what was the big deal? She was obviously incapable of making sane decisions.

*   *   *   *   *   *   *

"I'm afraid there really isn't anything more I can do at the moment gentlemen" said Pete Pleader, using his most sympathetic attorney telephone etiquette.

"We'll just have to wait and see. Your case is still under investigation in Sasquatch Country. They might still charge you with involuntary manslaughter (or maybe poor marksmanship)", he thought to himself, suppressing a chuckle.

"Damn!" said Billy over the kitchen wall phone. "Shit!" said Virgil over the extension phone in the back bedroom of Billy's trailer. "However, gentlemen, there is the small matter of your bill with our firm..."

"Click!" went Billy's phone.

"Click!" went Virgil's phone.

Chapter IX

"I ask, as a fool who knows not His Own Spirit:

Where are the hidden traces left by the Gods?"

-- Rig Veda, Book I, Stanza 164, Lines 5 A & B, (c. 8,212 BC)

"We will visit another land where I once served as the God of Fertility, together with my friend and lover, the precious Parvati. This is one of the love songs I wrote for her", said Pan.

"I Am that I Am: Lord Shiva, Destroyer and Creator of Life anew. Parvati, The Light of Love is my eternal companion. Hear Our Hymn of Love and rejoice with us:

Jewel within the Lotus

Phallus and the Womb, The Source of Life Anew.

We are really No-Things

Beings joined with Form:

Animating Matter

The Cause of all that grows.

All creation springs from Love,

Heaven joins the Earth:

We are Souls united with the Flesh.

Death is joined with Life.

I am like Air. You are like Fire.

A hearth is made in Our embrace.

Our loins the fuel, our kiss the spark,

We fan the Flame with Our desire.

Rising smoke from each caress,

Our Love the heat, Our Joy the pyre

Wherein Our Seed and Soul are met.

Every Cause has an Effect.

One reaches, One withdraws.

Positive flows to negative,

In and out and ebb and flow

are rhythms of the Universe.

One is born as One grows old

Life and Death, a single thread;

Endless circles joined by endings.

We are Spirits causing Life."

In one timeless instant Pan and Derek transported across a thousand miles of space and thousands of years of time from Egypt to India.

Derek emerged among moist white clouds, far above a verdant river valley. He soared through sparkling sunlit mists of amorphous moisture. Each crisp, clean droplet drifted, serenely in space. A flock of fleecy white gulls flapped and floated through him. Three thousand feet below him sprawled a pristine, verdant panorama of pastoral serenity.

"Wow! This is really *flying!*" enthused Derek, like a child on his first roller-coaster ride. "If I'd known that not having a body could be like this, I would have given it up a long time ago!"

Flowing foothills of the hallowed Himalayas towered jaggedly on the northern horizon. Tributary streams snaked into the shimmering surface of a broad river flowing away to the south. Directly below lay an ancient, deserted city.

"Harappa" Pan pointed with intention.

"Along the course of the Indus River there were once 1,000 cities. The towns and temples are abandoned now. Their people long since gone, consumed by the advance of the nomad warriors descending from the Iranian plateau below the Caspian Sea.

The people of Harappa once lived in sophisticated cities complete with sewage systems. A shift in the crust of earth in this area caused the river to leave its course. Towns along the river were submerged in marshy lakes. Crops and grazing lands were spoiled, and so the people died or moved elsewhere.

The Harrapan were the first on Earth to farm rice and cotton. None of their written language is understood by modern man. The Harrapan were also seafaring traders who kept written records of their commercial transactions with Mesopotamian cities along the coast.

They developed Sanskrit as a written language to record the wisdom of the Seven Sages, passed down to Man in the year 8212 BC. For thousands of years their teachers memorized and passed this wisdom from one generation to the next verbally. After the Aryan nomads settled in India they began to write these teachings. These were called the Hymns of the Veda and remained unchanged since then. They are still recited by the faithful in modern times.

Many secrets of this universe are contained in these writings. Mysteries of the spirit and of the laws of this universe are contained in four books of more than 20,000 stanzas" said Pan.

"Really? I've never heard of it." Derek said.

"Typical of a western man. The Christian priests have worked hard to ensure that men do not know about the Hymns of the Veda. However, for your benefit I will recite some verses from the Rig-Veda. I will start from the beginning – the Genesis – you might call it", Pan proceeded without a hesitation:

"Stanza one:

In the beginning even Nothingness was not, nor existence.

There was no air then, nor the heavens beyond it.

What covered it? Where was it?

In who's keeping?

Was there then cosmic water, in depths unfathomed?

Stanza two:

Then there were neither death nor immortality,

Nor was there then the torch of night and day.

The One, who breathes without air, breathed windlessly

The energy of self-generation, The Self-sustaining Power.

There was the One then, and there was no other.

Stanza three:

At first there was only darkness wrapped in darkness.

All this was only as fluid water,

Unillumined and indistinguishable.

The One which came to be, enclosed in

Nothing, arose at last, born of the Self-generating Power.

Stanza four:

In the beginning desire to experience caused creation.

That was the primal seed, born of the Mind.

The Sages who have searched their hearts

With wisdom know that which is,

Is bonded to that which is not.

Stanza five:

And they have stretched their cord across

The Void, and know what was above and what below.

Seminal powers made fertile forces.

Below was the male energy.

Above this was the female intention to Survive..

Stanza six:

But, after all, who knows, and who

Can say whence it all came, and

How creation happened?

The gods themselves are later than

Creation. So who knows truly whence it has arisen?

Stanza seven:

Whence all creation had its origin,

He, whether He fashioned it or whether

He did not, He who surveys it all

From the highest heaven, He knows-

Or maybe even He does not know."

Pan finished his recitation, paused, and then added, "This is a theory of the Creation of the Universe. What do you think of it?"

"It sounds sort of like the Bible" Derek mused.

"Indeed" replied Pan.

"This is the original, unaltered version, before the Jewish priests wrote their own testaments while captive in Babylon in the 600's BC.

"No kidding? How do you know all these things anyway? In fact, it seems like you know everything?"

"It was easy. I was there. However, there are some things which I choose not to know". Pan said without hubris.

"Did you memorize all 20,000 stanzas of the Vedic Hymns?" asked Derek.

"No, but there are many through the millennia who have done so without changing a single word: a truly remarkable feat", Pan declared with admiration.

"Unbelievable!" thought Derek. But so was just about everything he had experienced with Pan. It all seemed so real and it was getting more real all the time.

"Our beautiful India was a place where priests and kings flourished. And, like all of their kind, perverted the truth of the Vedas. Once again we took up the fight against these evil beings. However, we soon learned that not all men wish to be free. There are multitudes of men who seek slavery as a willing release from responsibility.

They claw at survival by dragging each other down into the boiling waters of Life, like lobsters in a charred cooking pot, waiting to become a meal for their masters."

*   *   *   *   *   *   *   *   *   *

Jenny spent the morning in Derek's room. To pass the time, she watched a weekly summary of U.S. Congressional proceedings on PNN, the Political News Network. It was a lot more entertaining than she imagined it would be. Congress had a lot more bedroom farce, scandal, crime, tragedy, dramatic acting and sexual situations than any soap opera she'd ever seen, and with fewer commercials!

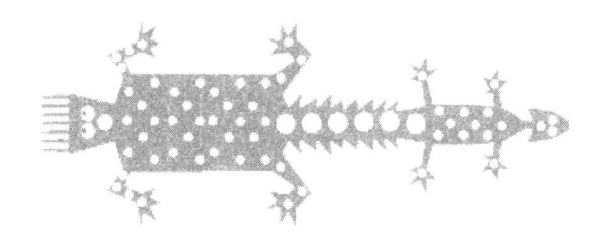

Chapter X

"...the dead are not powerless. Dead, did I say? There is no death, only a change of worlds."

-- Attributed to a speech given by Chief Seattle in January 1854 as it appeared in the Seattle Sunday Star on Oct. 29, 1887, in a column by Dr. Henry A. Smith.

Mitosis and meiosis: an intelligent pattern of predetermined cellular division resulting in growth of a newly conceived life-form. RNA, DNA, genes, x and y chromosomes; the natural genetic components of cellular construction.

Paula didn't know or care about any of the technology behind pregnancy. All she new was that she felt wonderfully robust and healthy. She was pink with vitality. Her morning sickness had passed. Her appetite was tremendous. Although her breasts were slightly sore she felt no adverse effects of being pregnant. On the contrary, in spite of the turmoil surrounding the circumstances of her pregnancy - Derek's unchanging condition, the police investigation, her money-crazy attorney and the occasional hate letters from abortion rights activists, Paula felt serenely purposeful and positive about her life. Motherhood pleased her!

    * * * * * * *

Jenny sat next to Derek's bed absently flipping through a magazine. The blipping, beeping sounds of life-support machinery blended softly with the rhythmic inhale-exhale of his breathing. Jenny looked across at the supine, expressionless face next to her chair. She slowly lifted his hand and caressed it to her cheek.

"Oh Derek, my dearest darling. I love you so much. Please live! Please, please come back to me. I need you", Jenny wept. Tears wet her cheeks and fell on to Derek's limp, unresponsive hand as she kissed the open palm and hugged it to her mouth. Worn down by the weight of her loss, she no longer tried to dam the flood of aching grief which swept her into as sea of sobbing hysteria.

"Jenny! I'm here! Jenny! Jennnnyyyy...! I'm right here honey! Oh, Jenny. Don't cry baby. I'm here. I'm O.K.!" Derek shouted soundlessly, hovering above Jenny and his own body.

Jenny didn't respond. She couldn't hear him or perceive his presence. Derek recoiled in agony as he reached out to pervade his body in a desperate attempt to communicate to her through it. He tried again and gasped in anguish at his inability to let Jenny know he was with her.

"Oh my precious darling. How I love you. I've hurt you in so many ways. I've never really told you how much I love you, how dear you are to me. Oh God, Jenny". He was overwhelmed by remorse, more intense than bodily agony could ever be.

His perception of the Jenny, the hospital room and of existence as himself, faded into an abyss of despair, failure and regret. Baleful oblivion submerged him in unawareness of everything except the overwhelming torment of his sorrow.

       *   *   *   *   *   *   *   *

The next morning Jenny sat up in her chair, awake, alert, and refreshed. She patted Derek's hand and placed it back on the bed. Cedar scent suffused the air in the soft morning light of the room. She stood and stretched without stiffness. Jenny felt secure, certain and strong. She kissed Derek gently and slipped silently from the room.

Derek too, felt cleansed and composed. The orange-pink glow of dawn spread slowly across the pointed boughs atop the pine forest below him. Crisp, cool, pine-scented woodland air breathed life across the earth and its creatures. His grief was gone.

He perceived Jenny again, sitting in front of her hotel room mirror brushing her hair, humming happily. He shuddered a bit at a fleeting recollection of the emotional abyss he'd fallen into last night, astonished that he'd come out of it so quickly. Yet, everything seemed fine and bright to him now.

"God. That was horrible...I thought I was going to die of grief." he thought.

"Many beings do at such times. However, I was here to raise you from that Realm of Wretchedness." said Pan with resolute compassion. His emotion was free from the gooey sympathy one usually gets from friends during such moments of loss.

"God, thanks man" Derek said gratefully.

"I think it's the other way around actually" Pan said, joking.

"Huh?" thought Derek, not getting the pun. "Uh, well anyway, what happened? I was really upset last night. It was horrible!"

"This is why I am Lord of the Underworld. I do not fear death. I know the Black Abyss and do not flinch. Men of all lands and ages have various names for it – Hell is one. Many have been there but have no memory of it. Many beings who descend there do not return. Spirits, overwhelmed by life, lose themselves there.

The road out of that oblivion is recognizing one's own responsibility for the past and for creating the future. Death of the body alone can not condemn one to the Underworld: it is his own decision *not to be* that prevents one from living, whether with a body or without", Pan finished consolingly.

Both you and Jenny have an important mission to fulfill, too important to be postponed by dismal emotions."

"Well, last night was as much Hell as I'd ever care to be in!"

Derek thought about it some more, looking back on the ideas he'd always had about death: mostly learned from Sunday school.

"I never believed all that stuff about heaven and eternal damnation. There is a bit of truth to it though, I suppose".

"A teaspoon of truth makes swallowing lies more palatable", replied Pan.

Derek returned to MOMM and looked again at his body lying in the hospital bed.

"You know" thought Derek, looking down at the body, circumfused with life-support contraptions, "I feel funny seeing my body like this now. I don't think of it as being ' me' any more". He pondered, musing philosophically, "It seems more like…the label on a record. It tells people the name of the song and maybe the composer and the name of the orchestra. But the sound of the music when it's played, that's me. All the subtle intonations of melody, rhythm, volume and harmony. The passion and the joy of performing and hearing. That instant of creation when sound becomes aesthetic: the infinite variation of my own composition. That's who I really am. You know what I mean? The best the body can be is an instrument through which to play my song…so it can be heard by men who can only hear with ears".

"As you say, my friend" agreed Pan.

* * * * * * * *

Bubba hung up the phone excitedly.

"I have some good news (sniff) for you boys", Bubba said to his two minions in the most authoritarian voice he could muster. Officers Johnlaw and Peeler were seated in front of Bubba's desk. They looked at each other, rolled their eyes to the ceiling and said in sarcastic, sing-song unison, "Oh boy!"

Bubba returned just this morning from his trip to INTERPOL headquarters. He had been very lucky in D.C. last night too. He got drunk and picked up a hooker at a bar around the corner from his hotel. Even thought she had stolen $375.00 in cash from his wallet after he'd passed out in his hotel room he didn't care. What the hell, it was all department money anyway. He put it on his expenses voucher as an "entertainment expense". Besides, he was pretty sure he had gotten laid, although he didn't really remember much after he left the bars, especially about how he came by the bump on the back of his head.

"OK, you guys. Cut the crap. This is (sniff) important. I just talked to the Federal prosecutor. He says he can get a conviction on those two Georgia clowns (sniff) with the data I got from INTERPOL files and with some testimony from you two. All I need you to do is sign an affidavit (sniff) saying that you found their campfire still burning the morning we went up there to look around. There'll be a little (sniff) something extra in it for you guys. Know what I mean?" The two deputies left the office shaking their heads.

*   *   *   *   *   *   *   *

"Like all men, you have a very limited memory of the past, not much beyond what they ate for breakfast, relatively speaking. Until recently, you have been ignorant of spiritual matters -- much like a mole that spends his entire life beneath the ground, yet thinks he knows all about the world above. Have you ever asked a mole for his opinion about men?"

"Well, no...." Derek began to reply.

In an instant, Derek faced a fuzzy, brown mole on the floor of the forest just emerging from his burrow. It sprayed dust and hairs everywhere as it shook the dirt from itself. The squinty-eyed rodent twitched his enormously long whiskers and bared his huge, sharp teeth. He sniffed, sensing the presence of something, but not knowing what.

Derek was alarmed by the relative size of the mole with whom he now 'stood' face to face.

Pan introduced himself to the mole by mocking up a very convincing illusion of being a mole himself. After a bickering exchange of squeaks and twitches, Pan was able to convince the mole that he was only passing through and not trying to invade his territory.

"Have you seen any of the great monsters near here?" Pan asked, loosely translating his thought into "mole speak".

"Well, of course I've seen them! I am an authority on those monsters, you know." said the mole dully. "Know all about them, I do. They're all the same, as every mole knows. Big, stupid creatures. They don't even live under the ground. Imagine that! They just stomp around up here above the ground. I've been close enough to smell one several times. Heard them passing by once, don't you know. Terrible, thundering sounds they make. Yes, you've come to the right place all right. I know all about them. Oh, yes indeed!" squeaked the mole, scratching intensely at a flea.

Pan thanked the mole for the information and turned to Derek.

"Well, do you see what I mean?"

"Oh...well, yes...I guess I do", said Derek, a little astonished.

*　　*　　*　　*　　*　　*　　*　　*

"Your scientists know little of the history of Earth before a few million years ago and nearly nothing of human existence before 3500 BC. They rely too much on the false teachings of priests as the basis for their 'scientific' theories.

Life in this universe has existed for a nearly infinite time. Trillions of trillions of years. As spiritual beings we are indeed immortal. We have all lived a lot of life. Just because it is not socially acceptable to remember having lived before does not make it false".

Derek was rather nonplused by what Pan was saying, yet his growing awareness that there may be other realities beyond those of mortals made him more attentive now.

"If I were to tell you", Pan continued, "the unaltered truth about the origins of Life on Earth, you would not believe me. Yet you believe the lies of the priests out of ignorance. However, in order to help you regain your own memory, I will share with you some of what really happened."

"You mean, like about evolution and all that?" Derek quizzed.

"No, not myths or fairy tales like evolution. About history – what actually occurred, long before I ever arrived on Earth myself", corrected Pan.

"I used to work for a very large biological laboratory in a galaxy not far from this one. It was called the Arcadian Regeneration Company: A.R.C., for short.

We created and supplied new life forms to uninhabited planets. There were millions of star systems with millions of inhabitable planets in the region at that time. I was an engineer in the company and directed the work of a large staff of technicians.

There were many such biological laboratory companies. They produced every conceivable species throughout the galaxy. My company specialized in mammals for forested areas and birds for tropical regions.

We contracted with various planetary governments and independent buyers to provide life forms for a variety of planetary habitats. We created animals that were compatible with the variations in climate, atmospheric and terrestrial density and chemical content, etc. We had to integrate our specimens with other biological organisms already living on a planet.

In order to do this our staff were in communication with other companies who created life forms. There were trade shows, industry publications and a variety of other information supplied to us by companies who were working on related projects. There was more than enough work for everyone during that period.

Our researches did a great deal of interstellar travel to conduct planetary surveys. The data gathered was accumulated in huge computer databases and evaluated by biological engineers.

Based on the data gathered, designs and artistic renderings were made for new creatures. Some designs were sold to the highest bidder. Other animals were created to meet the customized requests of our clients.

The design and technical specifications were passed along a sort of engineering assembly line through a series of biological, chemical, and mechanical engineers to solve the various problems of integrating all the component factors into a workable, functional and aesthetic finished product.

Prototypes of these creatures were then produced and tested in artificially created environments. Imperfections were worked out, modifications made and eventually the new animal was introduced into the actual planetary environment for final testing.

We monitored the interaction of the new animals with the planetary environment and with other indigenous life-forms. Conflicts resulting from the interaction between incompatible animals were resolved through negotiation between us and other companies. The negotiations usually resulted in compromises requiring further modification to our creatures or to theirs or both. In some cases changes were made in the planetary environment.

One of the contracts we got from the government of this sector of the galaxy was to build a planetary zoo and fill it full of animals. The contract required that we deliver animals from all over the galaxy to Earth.

It was a joint project between A.R.C. and a company called N.O.A.H., which stands for Natural Oceans and Artificial Habitats, Inc.. They were a planetary landscaping firm we sub-contracted to create the living environments which would be suitable for the huge variety of life forms we were supposed to supply to the zoo-planet.

The dinosaurs that dominated this planet at one time had to be removed. They proved to be a bad experiment -- very impractical and unpopular with buyers and incompatible with other life forms too. The company that developed them lost a great deal of money on the idea.

When we started the zoo project here most of this planet was a desert, very few oceans and forests. So, N.O.A.H. used their engineering skills to alter the chemical content of the atmosphere, create water, fill up the desert areas with oceans and plant a wide variety of trees, shrubs, flowers and grasses. It was their job to create a planetary zoological garden and aquarium for us to fill with animals and fish and insects.

The skill required to modify the planet into an ecologically interactive environment that would support billions of diverse species was an immense undertaking. Specialized consultants from nearly every bio-tech company in the galaxy were brought in to help with the project.

Once it was done, tourists came from all over the sector on vacation. The government collected tourism fees and the whole planet was maintained as a kind of nature preserve for a very long time.

What you see now on Earth is the huge variety of life-forms left behind. Your scientists believe in the fallacious "theory of evolution" as an explanation for all the life forms here. These anomalies are very baffling to them. The truth is that all life forms on this and any other planet in this universe were created by companies like ours. How else can you explain the millions of completely divergent species on the land and in the oceans of this planet?" Pan asked Derek.

"Wow! You mean to tell me this whole place was put together like a kind of gigantic, intergalactic Disneyland?" Derek asked incredulously.

"More or less" said Pan. "Evolution by 'natural selection' is science fiction".

There was a long, silent pause while Derek muddled through all this in his mind. He'd seen science fiction movies. He'd read a few science fiction books and fantasy stories. But this was different. How could something so incredibly far-fetched seem so reasonable? It sounded practical enough in some ways, after all, doctors were practicing a kind of biological engineering right here and now on Earth. Heart bypasses, cloning, test tube babies, organ transplants, plastic surgery - but still...

Derek looked around at the panorama of woodland mountains, glittering lakes and softly drifting clouds around him. He sighed a breathless sigh.

"This all seems very strange to me Pan. But, I'll take your word for it", he thought with exasperation.

"Truth is what is true for you. Not because I say it is so", said Pan. "Observe and recall for yourself."

"Well, one thing is sure; I'll never look at a bug or a flower the same way again…" Derek offered.

Chapter XI

I have gone through many rounds of birth and death, looking in vain for the builder of this body. Heavy indeed is birth and death again and again! But now I have seen you, house builder, you shall not build this house again. Be vigilant and go beyond death. If you lack vigilance, you cannot escape death. Those who strive earnestly will go beyond death.

-- *The Dhammapada*, the teachings of Buddha – (6th Century BC)

Bubba was pleased. He knew the Feds could get an indictment on any case they decided to prosecute. They were masters at it. If there were no laws already written that they could use to indict someone, they'd get new ones drawn up. If that didn't work, they could always use the Ricco Act. You could convict anybody of anything using conspiracy laws. All they had to do was to pay some government witness to say that the defendant had knowledge of the crime and he'd be guilty of conspiracy, which carried the same penalty as actually committing the crime. And the catch-all, the Anti-Drug Abuse Act of 1988, H.R. 5210, P.L. 100-690 took care of just about any other loophole.

Bubba hadn't even been able to figure out how to get the menu to come up on the INTERPOL computer. However, he had been able to pay Werner enough cash to help him come up with some useful information.

It seems that the Jaras brothers grew up in Georgia and moved to California a few years back. There was a record of them having bought hunting licensees and rifles while they were in high school in Geogia. But there was no record of a hunting license or guns purchased in California. It was a lead...a miracle of modern law enforcement technology.

Sure enough, a phone call to the Federal prosecutor paid off. The Jaras brothers could be convicted on charges of interstate transportation of arms and hunting on Federal lands without a license: both Federal offenses. Also, charges of building an illegal campfire could be thrown in as an extra bonus. Perfect.

So far, Bubba's investigation had cost the taxpayers only $132,796.27 (including travel, personnel, salaries, cars, special surveillance equipment, wire taps, bonuses, overtime pay and entertainment costs). Still, as yet he hadn't been able to find a single piece of incriminating evidence on Paula Cadmus.

However, the Jaras brothers would soon be convicted felons. All he needed now was to piece together a connection between Paula and the Jaras brothers. The threat of a five year prison sentence would be a very persuasive tool in forcing a "confession" from the brothers to implicate Paula in a 'conspiracy to murder' her lover.

"One step (sniff) at a time", thought Bubba. "So (sniff) far, so good (sniff)."

*   *   *   *   *   *   *

"I want you to meet another dear friend of mine, Derek. I first met the Old Master lingering above a forest in China about 2,500 years ago" said Pan, introducing the other being to him. Derek had never read the writings of Lao Tzu, though he had heard of Taoism. This being, Derek observed, was quite extraordinary; gentle, yet powerful and certain. The space he occupied glowed with an undulating aura of soft, golden light. Derek thought this is what a halo must look like.

Pan emanated a similar radiance, along with the scent of cedar, which filled the space, especially when he was happy about something.

"I had grown to be an old man and had enough of living", said Loa-Tzu, telling his story to Derek, by way of introduction.

"I prepared to depart from my village to find a quiet place in the distant forest from which to depart my body, away from the needless lamentations of my grieving students. As I approached the city gate the gatekeeper asked to know the reason for my departure. When I expressed my intention to him, he barred the way saying, 'Old Master, I cannot allow you to depart the city until you have left behind a written record of your wisdom for those of us who wish to follow your way'.

So, I returned to my lodgings briefly to commit such thoughts to writing which I felt were most essential to living a life of integrity. I distilled these thoughts from my life-long study of the ancient wisdom of India which I was able to obtain from traveling merchant caravans and my own observations about life.

I also included such truths as might serve the needs of the gatekeeper, inasmuch as he was a man of little formal learning. This I presented to him as I departed the city. I am amused that my small, simple book has affected the lives of so many since that time".

"Well, what did the book say? I mean what was so impressive about it?" asked Derek curiously.

"The book has been altered by priests over the years in an attempt to obscure the original wisdom, but as I recall, the original was something like this", said Pan.

He recited from memory the original version of the *Tao-Te Ching*, 'The Way', as told to him personally by the author long ago:

"Without seeking, one may know all under heaven;

Without finding, one may know the way of heaven.

The wise man knows without searching,

Understands without thinking, accomplishes without acting.

To know when one does not understand is a virtue;

Failing to know that one does not understand is an error.

A wise man treats errors as errors.

He becomes more perfect each time an error is corrected.

Be honest with those who are honest. Also be honest

With those who are dishonest; thus is honesty attained.

All beings are basically good. However, prevent those who

do evil from harming others, for even they are basically good.

What separates goodness and badness?

What difference is there between yes and no?

What distinguishes beauty and ugliness?

Front and rear join in the center.

Being and non-being is a circle of decision.

The way of heaven conquers without war,

Speaks little but answers well, is always present

Without being summoned, is not rushed but is well planned.

The wise man is skilled in all of his undertakings.

He who is skilled at counting needs no counting devices.

He who is fluid in speech needs no script to guide him.

A man of skill practices skill and conquers reality.

A man who fails to practice is conquered by failure to practice.

Walls form and support a room, yet the space between them is most important.

A pot is formed of clay, yet the space formed thereby is most useful.

Action is caused by the force of nothing on something, just as the nothing of spirit is the source of all forms..

One suffers great afflictions because one has a body.

Without a body what afflictions could one suffer?

When one cares more for the body than for his own spirit,

One becomes the body and loses The Way of The Spirit.

He who looks will not see it; he who listens will not hear it;

He who gropes will not grasp it.

The formless nonentity, the motionless source of motion.

The infinite essence of the spirit is the source of life; spirit is self.

The Self, the Spirit, creates illusion.

The delusion of Man is that reality is not an illusion.

One who creates illusions and makes them more real

than reality, follows the path of The Spirit

and finds The Way of Heaven".

* * * * * * *

"Hey y'all. Thanks for hauling all that shit away for me!" Billy Joe hollered, waving a half-drank can of beer at the scout master's truck as it backed out of his driveway.

"Hey Billy! All you got in here is frigging *light* beer! shouted Virgil rummaging through the refrigerator in the kitchen.

Local Boy Scout troop 342, "The Panthers" collected $11.35 from the cashier at the county aluminum recycling center for 45 pounds of beer cans they collected from behind Billy Joe's trailer house. It was the biggest single contribution to the troop recycling fund drive all year.

* * * * * * *

"There is yet another being from whom you can learn", said Pan, imparting his thoughts to Derek telepathically, as always.

Derek entered into Pan's mind, his memory, his experience, as though it was a living reality. Derek saw the image of a man in a plain robe seated calmly beneath a fig tree, in meditation.

"Feel the experience of this man. Assume his viewpoint as fully as you can", instructed Pan. "Permeate and pervade the space and observe without adding any thought of your own. Let his thought be your thought, his mind your mind, his being your being. Empty yourself and be him".

Derek reached out, cautiously at first. He'd never tried to do anything like this before but felt safe doing as Pan directed. Gradually he became aware of all that surrounded the man, as though the body were his own. The eyes were closed, yet there was sight and awareness all around him. The patter of passing children, intent on their play. The distant chatter of women weaving mechanically, concerned more with gossip than work. Chirping birds squawked and fluttered in the branches above as loosened leaves fell to earth on a warm breeze.

Time progressed. One day turned to the next. Heating sun and glinting glare. Cool and cold rain and rushing wind. Dark of night, dew of dawn. Day and day and day again. All perceived within the sphere of awareness surrounding the body with no thought or response to any motion, sound or sensation. Just a persistent, unwavering interest.

Throughout the meditation, which seemed to have no time or location, he experienced a parade of emotions – imposed on him from some external source. Some were familiar, though he could not tell if they were from his personal experience or from the other being or from other people passing by. Perhaps disembodied spirits pervaded his space and thought, it deemed as though he perceived the common experience of many beings.

Longing loneliness for love and loving; aesthetic ache of lust for lovely ladies: observed only. Gnawing, gnashing, craving hunger for savory scents, taste and texture. The body beseeching to be fed: acknowledged only. Painful pressures prodding with unendingly urgent, reasonable requests to care for the body, to move, depart, succumb, submit: no reaction. Deathly despondent despair. Angry outrage and grief. Hostility, hatred. Apathy, shame, regret and blame at failed fulfillment, fallow futures: each emotion was felt without flinching.

Myriad mental manifestations of terror and trials; tumultuous turmoil of timeless tribulation: of lives past. Born and buried ten thousand times. Every game gone; every love lost; every friend forsaken. Every gain, a loss; a passing parade of pain; disease, distrust, death, desire, deserted destruction; wanton war and wailing; never winning, never ending; hope and help betrayed at every hand: these were confronted without emotion.

Icy, infinite hostile heavens of molten masses. Stars and planets far from Earth's eternal turning. Every guise and form wherein spirit merged with matter was seen and felt and heard and recognized with understanding.

"Aware of being aware...just 'be'...all motion passes…illusion…. The 'I' that 'I Am' persists: I am indivisible, imperishable, immortal. I move, yet am unmoved. I am life and senior to life: source of all I perceive. Reality's reality".

With a soaring surge of exhilaration Derek returned to present time, awesomely awake and shouting, "Yes, I see!"

Derek laughed and laughed and laughed and laughed: the laughter of him released.

Pan smiled. A serene cedar-scented smile.

*   *   *   *   *   *   *

Virgil and Billy Joe left the courtroom after an overnight stay in the custody of the Federal Marshall, having been arraigned by the Honorable Judge Woody Hatchet to hear the indictment brought against them by a Grand Jury Indictment. After they each posted a $10,000 bond with the bailiff, they were released into the custody of their overpaid and under-appreciated attorney, Peter Pleader.

Pete was just one of the 756,000 attorneys practicing law in a country that imprisoned more people per capita than any other nation in the world. By coincidence, the number of practicing attorneys had tripled during the last 30 years; by further coincidence, so had the number of Federal lawsuits.

Peter opened his briefcase and gave each of his clients a copy of the indictment which had been supplied to him by the Federal prosecutor, who by even further coincidence, happened to be one of Pete's old law school buddies. It was a formidable looking, legal-sized document which began:

THE UNITED STATES OF AMERICA

VS

VIRGIL & BILLY JOE JARAS

Damn!" said Billy Joe, "I don't like the looks of our odds here. We gotta fight the whole goddamn government!"

The indictment continued in officially obscure, obtuse and esoteric legal nomenclature which meant simply that Billy Joe and his brother were about to go to prison for a least 5 years and pay a sizable fine, as prescribed by U.S. Criminal Code, Chapter 44, Section 922 (a)(1) and (a)(3) as well as Chapter 91, Section 1856, et. al, etc., ad nausea.

"OK, Pete. So what'a we do now? You're gonna get us out'a this shit, right?" asked Virgil, assuming, naively, that anything could actually be done about the situation.

In reality, the only thing they could do was pay an attorney to plea bargain with the federal prosecutor to get them off with the minimum allowable mandatory prison sentence required by the Federal Sentencing Guidelines.

"Well, the first thing you boys will need to do is come up with $10,000.00 each in order for us to get started on your defense" said Pete apologetically.

"What?! We already gave you all the cash we had! What about all the money we already paid you? What was that for? How the hell do you think we're gonna pay you another ten grand?!" Billy was pissed.

"Well, I don't think you really have a choice, unless you want to plead poverty to the judge and let the court appoint a public defender for you. But you would really be taking your chances. Most of those guys are rookie lawyers, just learning the ropes and so overloaded with work they don't have time to take a shit, much less work on your case", rebutted Peter in his most innocently diplomatic voice.

"You slime-suckin' pig..." thought Virgil to himself.

"OK, I guess we ain't got no choice, but you better make damn sure you get us out of this mess!" Virgil threatened out loud.

"We'll give it our best effort to prepare a convincing defense. But, as you know, the final decision is up to the judge and jury", shrugged Peter.

"OK, so if we're gonna pay you all that money, you better make sure the judge decides right. I'm gonna have to sell my truck and mortgage my trailer to pay you. And I want you to know that where I come from a man's truck is more important than his dog and maybe even his wife." Billy fumed. "You get my drift?"

As Peter stepped into his luxurious leather upholstered, high-performance sports car he reflected that the few years he had spent at law school had paid off very handsomely. He had learned to play the game well. Criminal law had been very, very good to Peter.

The court system required that defendants hire an attorney who could speak the legalese which had evolved through centuries of British and American jurisprudence and which had become literally indecipherable to the layman. The hoops and jumps of trial procedure were a legal dog and pony show. Litigants were required to hire or have appointed for them an attorney to serve as a safety-net between the high-wire acts of esoteric courtroom procedures and the unyielding ground of incarceration, should one happen to take a fall. As a defendant, the best you could do was to pay the price of admission and sit through every incomprehensibly suspenseful act in which only highly trained showmen could perform.

Peter had performed well enough to buy a new custom-built 5 bedroom lakefront home and maintain a very healthy investment portfolio. Although he knew that he could expect to lose more than 97% of every Federal case he tried, the national average, he managed to manipulate a very healthy income from his clients. Many of his clients, now serving time in prison, felt that what Peter did for a living was equivalent to legalized extortion. However an equal number were somewhat grateful to him for saving them from having to serve a much longer prison term.

Peter's courtroom theatrics and legal acumen had much less to do with his prosperity and reputation as a "good attorney", than the fact that he ate lunch and played golf regularly with every judge and prosecutor in his district.

When he felt that his clients had paid him all the cash they could borrow or raise from asset liquidation (that is, what the government hadn't already confiscated under the comprehensive criminal and civil forfeiture laws) he could set up a speedy out-of-court settlement with his buddies and move on to his next victim. Pete planned to retire at age 45. Maybe sooner.

*   *   *   *   *   *   *   *

"Here is a lecture I heard 2,500 years ago" said Pan to Derek. His recollection of the event was as though it were happening in this moment.

The same man with whom Derek experienced meditation spoke to a small gathering of men and women of all castes. Even to the Brahmans who came to scorn him. The crowd of curious seekers assembled in a deer park near the small village of Benares to hear the words of a prince of the Shakyas clan: Guatama Siddhartha Shakyamuni, the Silent One. Buddha.

Derek tracked with Pan through his memory of the Buddha's lecture. They hovered amid a crowd on the cool grass beneath the bohdi trees as though it were now. Experiencing the 'now' of Pan's re-experience of 'then' was more 'now' than any 'now' Derek had ever experienced before.

"Some of you are like the lotus flower, deeply submerged below the water. Others float freely upon it. It is to those who are yet below but yearn to touch the sunlight that I come to teach. Yet only those who seek freedom from desire for water and sun shall find it".

"To be free from the sufferings of life in the physical universe you must release your desire for it. You must be willing to experience anything, to be anything, and to be nothing. You can be free from *samsara*, the cycle of birth, death and rebirth. You can be free from *karma*, the unknowing cause/effect of your own misdeeds. You may attain *nirvana*, which is, Being without desire; Joy without suffering; Ownership without attachment. Cause without unwanted effect; Love without longing;

You must learn to distinguish the real from the unreal, illusion from appearance, the pleasant from unpleasant and permanent from the impermanent. You must conquer your own desire in order to discover the simple, eternal truth of you".

Chapter XII

We have to keep our God placated with prayers, and even then we are never sure of him. How much higher and finer is the Indian's God. Our illogical God is all-powerful in name, but impotent in fact; the Great Spirit is not all-powerful, but does the very best he can for his (Indian) and does it free of charge.

-- Mark Twain (c. 1835- 1910 AD)

Bubba was thrilled. Life was good. More criminals brought to justice; another feather in his cap. As soon as these crooks were behind bars he could go the next step in his plan to prove his conspiracy theory in the Adapa "assassination" attempt.

He knew Paula Cadmus and the soon-to-be-infamous Jaras brothers were in this together. He'd soon have the leverage he needed to get a confession out of the Jaras boys, "proving" they acted as hit men for Paula while posing as deer hunters. All he needed was the 'cooperation' from these good-ole-boys.

If Bubba could make this case pay off he might even try to go for the big time: a job with the CIA. That was *real* police work, with no lawyers or judges in the way to slow down the wheels of justice!

"Aaaachooo! Shit!" Bubba's reverie was broken by a violent sneeze, which caused him to piss all over the front of his best suit pants instead of into the restroom urinal in front of him.

*   *   *   *   *   *   *

"There are children, as yet unborn, of whom you are the father" said Pan solemnly.

Pan and Derek appeared in the bedroom of a second story apartment. An ornate Persian carpet was spread beneath a queen-size bed covered by a heavily quilted comforter. The over-all motif was more or less middle-eastern, although the dominant colors were pink and mauve, accented by fluffy silk-satin cream colored throw-pillows encased in fine, hand-crocheted lace. Three very fluffy Persian cats lounged sleepily on the bed. Paula sat before a large ornate oval mirror, calmly brushing her raven hair in long, even strokes. Her dressing gown was open in front revealing her slightly swollen belly beneath her round, bare breasts.

"Paula?...she's...she's...pregnant?" Derek stammered in shocked embarrassment.

"As you can see for yourself" said Pan.

Derek knew it was true. Though he certainly had no right to expect her to be faithful to him, he knew the child was his.

"Oh my God! Jenny! What about Jenny?! She must know!"

"Indeed." Pan replied dryly.

"She knows about the baby? She knows I was unfaithful to her? She knows about Paula?"

Pan remained silent in assent.

"And she still loves me?" thought Derek in astonishment. "Oh my Jenny! What have I done to you?

Pan remained silent as Derek struggled for a long time with remorse for his actions and tried to come to terms with the shock of this new revelation.

"The body known as Derek Adapa will soon die, but the children will be well cared for by their mother.

"Children?! What do you mean *children*?"

"Twins." said Pan proudly, as though he were a new grandparent. "Paula will bear twins".

Derek considered the situation in stunned silence.

Pan continued, "At the moment these babies are born, you will assume the body of one. There are many things you must do in your next life and you have much to learn to prepare for your new responsibilities", Pan directed solemnly.

"What? You mean you want me to be Paula's baby? My...*my own baby*?!" Derek stopped.

This was too much. He'd just gone from being shot, to being dragged all over the world, all over the time track by a Greek god, becoming the father of his own bastard twins and now he was supposed to become the son (or maybe even *daughter!*) of his own secretary, while he was still married to someone else.

Derek's mind was spinning. He had to think. Very slowly. Very carefully. He tried to do this for quite some time. Calmly. Slowly, step by step. He strained his wits to find at least one thing of which he could be certain and hang onto that.

"You want me to be the father...of myself? Jesus!"

"No. Not Jesus. You have another destiny. Your future is with the child's mother. There is important work for you to do together."

Derek continued to stumble mentally, reeling under the overwhelmingly complex and imperative news.

"Our work together...our work together on Earth...?" he queried desperately.

There was no answer, so he gave up trying to think. It wasn't doing him any good.

"Shit! I don't know what.... My body is just laying there in the hospital rotting anyway. It's keeping Jenny from getting on with her own life. Jenny is well cared for by my life insurance policy and my stock in the company. I guess I should let her get on with it. Jeez, how can I face her now, anyway?"

"Never mind" said Pan, "bodies have a way of resolving themselves in time."

"Meanwhile, there are still many lessons for you to learn during the next few months", beckoned Pan. "If we are going to restore your ability to act as a god, we must work quickly. Let us get on with it."

They were gone.

Chapter XIII

Live life.

Thou shall not die.

Thou shall exist for millions and millions of years, a period of millions of years.

I am Shu [the god] of unformed matter.

My soul is God, my soul is eternity.

Soul to heaven, body to earth.

Thy essence is in heaven, thy body to earth.

-- *Egyptian Book of The Dead* - VIth Dynasty (c. 2345 BC)

      Derek died. That is, his body was dead. After a few moments of sober reflection, he took his attention off the body. He disconnected from it, let it go. Without his connection to it, the body did not continue to function. Except for a few lingering cell colonies, it was just 175 pounds of meat and bones. He had another future now, a new purpose, a new game to play.

* * * * * * *

Jenny discovered the body at 2:14 A.M. She awoke suddenly on her bed in Derek's room where she slept several nights each week. A whistling alarm made by the electronic monitoring device roused her. She sat up, peering in panic across the darkened room at the solid horizontal blue line on the heart monitor. The screen told her instantly what had happened. Without looking at the machinery she knew he was gone.

Yet, she knew he was still with her. A sense of him she had never felt before.

Jenny walked to the bed. She bent over the body, kissed the forehead, then rested her head on the now unmoving chest and hugged him goodbye. She could not be sad. His pain was over and so too her vigil. Oddly, she felt they were together now, more than ever before.

Moments later the doctor rushed into the room to examine the body. The futile attempts of the staff to revive him verified what she already knew. After every emergency procedure failed, the life support systems were disconnected, the body removed to the morgue. For the doctor, all this meant a lot of paperwork. The death certificate recorded the cause of death: "gun shot wound".

* * * * * * *

"Where are we?" asked Derek. He was surrounded by what seemed to be an endless expanse of glittering blackness.

"This is the Milky Way." Replied Pan casually. "We are located on the outer edge, more or less, only several light-years from Earth. How do you like it?"

Derek gasped breathlessly and gaped at the immense expanse of emptiness shimmering with stars. "I've never seen so many stars! Not even when I was camping at night in the mountains. There are billions and billions of them, above, below, on all sides…everywhere! I never imagined there were so many stars. There's *a bazillion* of them!" he marveled.

"Yes, there are a great many, but I assure you that the number of stars is quite finite. Perhaps not as measured in earthly terms, but finite nonetheless. All things in the physical universe are limited." Pan observed.

They remained silent for quite some time without moving, thinking or talking. After a while Derek began to feel overwhelmed by the immensity of the universe. The most disturbing sensation was a lack of any known point of reference – he just seemed to be floating, motionless, in an unending vacuum of black, empty vastness. He couldn't stand it any longer.

"Well, what are we *doing* here?" he demanded anxiously.

"Nothing." said Pan.

"Nothing? You mean we're just going to sit here? How come? What for? How long do we have to do this?" Derek blurted, no longer able to disguise his discomfort.

"We don't have to be here at all. I thought you might enjoy the relative peace and calm of the wide open space after all you've been through recently. You know, what with dying and all. I realize this can be very upsetting. I've found that a change of scenery can sometimes have a calming effect. I often come here myself to gain some perspective.

"Well, it was nice for a few minutes, but I'm starting to get the willies out here! I feel so incredibly... *tiny,* compared to all this space" Derek said, feeling queasy and skittish.

"I see" said Pan. "I know what the problem is. You just need to re-orientate to your actual size. You have been encumbered by a body for so long that you have forgotten how big you *really* are. Having a body always makes one feel very small compared to the rest of the universe. Although it may not seem so to you now, I assure you, you are as big as you think you are. Your size is limited only by your own point of view and the volume of space you conceive yourself to occupy".

With some instruction and coaching from Pan, Derek began to practice changing his "size" and "location". Without any movement or sense of motion, Derek was suddenly looking at the Earth from about 1,000 miles away.

In another instant he was hovering several hundred feet above a busy metropolitan freeway. The cars moving below him looked like toys as they slowly threaded their way along a maze of tiny highways.

Then he was inside a late model sedan being driven by an old lady with blue-white hair. She could just see the road between the steering wheel and the dashboard with the driver's seat moved all the way forward.

Now Derek was hanging in the stratosphere over an island continent surrounded by blue-green Ocean and partially covered by a thin layer of clouds.

Then he was looking at the bright blue ball of Earth from the barren, rock-cold-gray of the lunar landscape beneath him.

And now the rings of Saturn loomed magnificently before him. He felt as though he could walk across the boulder-strewn halo.

He was an ant, clambering clumsily over blades of grass on his way back home from foraging...

A bumble bee swooping over patterns of color in search of pollen...

A pig rooting the dirt sniffing for juicy roots...

Back in space, he confronted the horrendous hydrogen holocaust of the solar landscape. Without skin there was no heat. Without eyes, no blinding glares.

A porpoise racing to catch a fish beneath clear tropical water...

A hawk drifting on hot wafting waves of desert air in search of unwary rodents.

Derek saw planets and moons in orbital alignment to their suns, like marbles strewn in a three dimensional ring against a never ending void of blackness. He felt like he could reach out and spin each one on its axis like a series of toy tops.

With Pan as his guide he drifted through clouds of nebulous gas sprinkled with twinkling points of light: each one, an entire galaxy of billions of stars, moons, planets, and asteroids.

Finally, once again they were above the familiar trees of Pan's pine forest.

"Wow! What a trip!" Derek enthused, once they had stopped the exercise.

He was not quite sure he'd actually *been* to all those places. It wasn't anything like what he'd ever seen in the movies. But, it wasn't the same as looking at things through Pan's memory either. Actually, there was a *big* difference. It had all been so...so, *real*! Just like being here in the forest right now.

"I'm pleased that you enjoyed it" said Pan. "However, the purpose of this demonstration was to point out to you that 'size' is purely relative. The concept of size, your own size specifically, depends entirely on your point of view. You as yourself are as big or small as you *think* you are. If you think small, you are small: think big and you are big. It is a simple lesson: size of viewpoint and viewpoint of size." Pan explained.

"I see..." said Derek, expanding his concept of himself.

It was a very airy, spacious experience. The more he practiced, the easier it got and the more he enjoyed the feeling. The size. The space. His confidence soared. Derek was beginning to feel...well.... almost, ...like a *god*!

"This is really great!" he said with rising exhilaration.

"Indeed. You must continue to practice this until you feel quite comfortable with it. Practice until you can change your size and viewpoint at your own discretion, without help from me." Pan said.

"That's going to take a lot of work", thought Derek, deflating a little.

"All states of being require a lot of work, large or small. Practice will make it effortless. Discipline will enable you to choose and control the size and quality of the state of being you stipulate", Pan encouraged firmly. "But now come with me. There are more of my friends I want you to meet."

*   *   *   *   *   *   *

The next few days were a blur for Jenny. Derek was gone. Even though he'd been hanging on the edge for such a long time, now the reality of his death numbed her. At the same time she felt him close to her.

The funeral arrangements were handled very efficiently and expensively by *Eternal Days Funeral Home and Cremation Services*, including transportation of the body back to San Jose. She didn't know why she had the body cremated. It was merely a feeling that Derek would have wanted it that way. Derek hadn't left a will. There was no other family. Neither of their parents were alive and they were both only children.

The memorial ceremony was elaborate and well attended by several hundred social and business friends. The press were forbidden. As an additional precaution, Jenny hired a team of bouncers to keep the paparazzi out of the church.

Pan hovered near the parish priest, Father Pryor Flamen who had been very happily assigned for the past five years to the affluent suburban parish of the Church of The Virgin Madonna. The priest stood solemnly, hands folded across his floor-length, embroidered silk-satin robes before the assembled throng. A massive pipe organ groaned the chords of a traditional funeral dirge, reverberating through the towering vaulted beams of the elaborately stained glass cathedral. He waited for several late arrivers to be seated by the ushers in the crowded pews before beginning to read the traditional burial liturgy laid out on the pulpit podium.

Derek stayed near Jenny, doing his best to comfort her with his presence. He was unsure if he was able to make her aware of his manifestation beside her. Although Jenny felt his presence, she had no idea that he was *really there*. But, in spite of her sobbing, he knew that she would be OK. She would carry on with her life without him. The living forgets the dead.

Derek pervaded others in the audience to feel their thoughts and emotions. Some of the women cried softly, mostly because it was a funeral and it was supposed to be sad.

Paula sat with dignity, though her tears streamed down the front of her black maternity smock from beneath a black laced veil. Paula felt Derek near her and he too, became aware for the first time that she knew he was there. He was quite startled, but happily surprised. Was this some sort of spiritual bond between mother and child?

His friends from Nimbus Software were solemn. Derek could make none of them aware of his presence. All of their attention was on the priest and the urn containing ashes of his cremated body. The only awareness of him in the rest of the crowd was in their personal memory of him as a man.

"How utterly absurd" he fumed in exasperation. "*I'm right here!* "He thought with all the intention he could muster.

Nothing. No one batted an eyelash. Not Vern, or any of his friends. Each of them viewed death through a dim, false concept: "He's gone to Heaven now to meet his Maker' or 'Death is the inevitably final end of everything". No one except Pan and Paula had the vaguest idea that he was present among them at this very moment. Of course, if he had not run into Pan, he would have been thinking these same dim thoughts too or none at all!

Derek realized that Pan was right. The priests really had done their work well. No one was aware of spirits anymore. At best, he was a ghost now, and ghosts were supposed to be scary, weird, and taboo: forbidden subject matter for "reasonable", "god-fearing" men. Indeed, the gods were feared - and ignored. The situation made Derek realize that he still had a lot to learn about operating as a spirit.

With a nod from Father Flamen the organist stopped playing the dirge which had now been repeated 43 times. He stepped forward into the pulpit, straightened the liturgy before him and opened his mouth to read. But the words he heard coming from his own mouth were not those written on the page in front of him.

Pan manipulated the body of the hapless priest as though it were a marionette puppet. To all outward appearances Father Flamen was heard to deliver the following brief, but passionate memorial service:

"Hear Me, all you gathered here to grieve the death of your beloved Derek. Know this and mourn no more: He is not lost to you, though the flesh he once inhabited is now turned to ash and vapor and is no longer among you."

"Cast off the false teachings of the priests. Free yourselves from slavery to the body. Free yourself from the false notion that animating a flesh body is the only life and experience you have", Father Flamen intoned with apparently practiced emphasis. He leaned over the pulpit with a sweep of his flowing ecclesiastical sleeve across the assembly and continued.

"Know that your Derek is immortal, as you are yourself!" The priest paused, looked heavenward and continued with deliberate drama.

"He is now free from the chains and walls of living as men live. He is free to see and feel, to know and act, to create and play, unencumbered by the finite considerations of survival. He is free to be himself, not just to become someone, as it is among the living. He is free from the cumbersome demands of caring for the body: working to make money to buy food and shelter and clothing and companionship. He is free from the pain of disease and cravings of the body. Were each of you not falsely indoctrinated by the priests, he would be free to communicate with you now, so that you might truly know him."

Father Flamen turned the page before him, as though he were reading from it, shrugged his robes about his shoulders and looked back to the audience with an air of resolute conviction.

"The legacy of Derek Adapa in death, if not in life" he said softly so as to draw the attention of the audience toward him, *"is to seek the truth of this universe and of his own spiritual universe".*

With increasing volume Pan preached emphatically through the unwitting priest:

"To unlearn the false appearances propagated and promoted by religion; to expose the treachery of suppressive overlords, and to help of those who choose to be free of the illusions of mortal reality."

In a final flourish of uplifted eyes and arms Father Flamen concluded the eulogy.

"His Shield is Truth, his Sword is responsibility, and his Armor is having no need of armor."

He paused and leveled a stern gaze from face to face across the audience, pointedly. *"He offers you a challenge and opportunity: Join him now my friends! Take up the Crusade for Freedom in Life and be forever free from death!"*

The priest concluded by bowing his head toward the organist, who, after a moment of befuddled hesitation, began to play the dirge once again. But now the fingers on the keys of the massive pipe organ were directed by Pan to play a stirring, military marching anthem, to which Father Flamen marched, swinging his arms in time to the music, striding up the center isle to the front entrance of the cathedral. There he stood calmly outside the opened doors, having now returned to "normal", not realizing that anything unusual had occurred, and waited to greet the funeral guests as they exited the sanctuary.

Inside, the funeral guests sat for a moment in shocked and curious amazement. A few looked around at each other tentatively, then to the rear of the church. The music continued to play as the guests stood up and filed out of the cathedral.

Father Flamen nodded solemnly to each of the guests, shaking hands with some. He paused to listen to one mans' comment on the service.

"That was certainly an...uh...well... unusual service Father. I don't think I've ever heard that particular eulogy before. Was that a recent translation from Latin?"

The priest, not really understanding the comment, thanked him blankly, shook his hand and turned to the next group of people emerging from the church.

*   *   *   *   *   *   *

Virgil and Billy were both arrested at their respective places of employment by Federal Marshals. They were held without bail at the Sasquatch County jail. About five hours later, Pete Pleader finally checked in with his secretary from his cell phone and got the message from Virgil and Billy. Pete sighed and made a call to the federal prosecutor's office. He was out of his office. Pete left a voicemail on his machine saying he wanted a meeting to discuss a plea bargain agreement for the Jaras brothers and left his home number.

Pete really didn't think the chances of beating second degree murder and conspiracy charges were very good, even though he knew his clients were innocent. He'd stop by to see them in the morning before the arraignment.

"What a hassle", he thought.

Pete pulled into his driveway and trotted up the stone stairway to his house. He had to shave and get dressed for an 8:00 dinner engagement at *Chez Lilliane*. He and his partners were meeting to discuss a joint venture with a big real estate contractor to develop a luxury condominium/golf course project. It could mean big bucks for him.

Billy gave his baloney sandwich and grits to Virgil. He didn't feel like eating his first dinner in jail.

* * * * * * *

Bubba met with the federal prosecutor for breakfast at 9:30 A.M. the morning after Derek's death was announced at MOMM.

"I need those two scumbags to put the finger on Paula Cadmus. I need a conspiracy indictment against her. You can put together a nice plea bargain agreement for those two in exchange for a confession, right?"

The prosecutor picked up the plain brown envelope full of cash which Bubba shoved across the table and nodded as he put it into his coat pocket.

* * * * * * * *

"Yes, we've been enjoying our company together here for some time now. How long has it been? I can't say really. Does it matter?"

Pythagoras gestured with his attention toward the other beings he had known since his days in Greece. Below them the azure Aegean and Mediterranean Seas glistened, bordering the islands off the coasts of what had once been ancient Thessaly, Aachea, Peloponnese and Boeotia wherein the classical cities of Thebes and Athens lay. The islands of Lesbos, Chios, Samos and Rhodes lay to the southeast. The ancient shores of Asia Minor once flourished with prosperous city-states of the Delian League. Through the clouds beneath them rose the majestic, though diminutive peak of the once sacred Mt. Olympus.

As the Aegean Sea faded into the shadows of sunset the group lingered long enough to enjoy the glow of twilight as seen from 50,000 feet above the water.

"I love to watch the sunset from here" said Pythagoras with his usual cheerful serenity. "No matter how often I see it, I never tire of the Mediterranean. It is like no other area on the planet, don't you think?"

"Indeed my friend", Penelope sighed silently above the shimmering sunset sea. "Derek, is it small wonder that Zeus and his court once dwelled here above the clouds of Olympus? Such beauty as this befits the gods. Although it is now no longer as it once was. The gods are gone and the horizon is now too often gray with the smog of Athens."

"Uh…yes", Derek agreed.

Penelope turned her attention to Pan affectionately.

"Pan, my dear, it is so lovely to be with you again. I miss you're not being here with us as often as you once were. How have you fared?" she said, plainly showing her affection for him.

"I have been well, as always, My Fairest One" replied Pan, emanating a glowing affinity toward her.

Derek thrilled in the intense purity of their emotion. Pan's clean caring caress surrounded Penelope and filled the space for all to share without shame or shyness. The sensation was unlike any he had felt from Pan previously.

"This is a very special being indeed" thought Derek to himself. "Pan has such intense feelings for her."

"She is most certainly Derek" said Pan, picking up Derek's thought. "This is Penelope, my 'mother' " he said in jest.

"Oh?" said Derek, not getting the joke. He paused, thinking, "Mother? How could a god have a mother?"

"It's an honorary title only I assure you. A private joke, Derek." Penelope said with delight.

"Pan and I have known each other for a very long time. He teases me about my being his 'Mother' because of the poetic license taken by Homer and other human poets who have allegorically related Pan to me as the product of my affair with his 'Father' Zeus, or some say Hermes. It's a rather charming story actually. I take it that Pan has never told you about it?"

"No. He hasn't." Derek smirked at the thought of hearing about Pan's 'birth'. "I'd really like to hear it though, if you don't mind telling me."

Derek was already enchanted by Penelope's charisma. She emanated an aura of unpretentious, feminine grace. Derek delighted in being near her – not due to any sexual sensation aroused by her, but rather a delightfully pure essence of feminine beingness that embodied the best of all that is feminine – a combination of mother, sister, lover, friend.

Pan turned his attention to Pythagoras and Democritus who chatted among themselves as Derek listened raptly to Penelope's memoir:

"Eons ago, it happened that Zeus, foremost of all the gods of the Greek pantheon, became infatuated with me. I was embodied as a young girl in Greece at the time. He visited me repeatedly cloaked in the form of a surpassingly handsome and charming young prince. At first I was overwhelmed by his endearing charm and then by his profoundly impassioned lovemaking.

　　　I later learned, he was infatuated with a great many other young maidens also. Well, my jealousy got the better of me, thinking that I should be the only one. When next Zeus came to me in mortal form, I coyly asked him to grant me one favor. I was careful to make my request at a most impassioned moment for him. He promised, swearing an irrevocable oath on the unholy river Styx that he would fulfill any wish I made. Before he had quite recovered his strength I said, 'I request that you make love to me as you do with your wife. I wish to have you as she does, unfettered by restraints of the flesh. Love me once with all your heavenly splendor, so that I will know that you truly love me.' My words were out before he could stop me, thus binding him to his promise.

　　　When next he came to me, Zeus returned in his natural form: as the Great Zeus – Lord of the Gods. He was the embodiment of raw electric force, without physical form, the timeless creator of space and the forms therein. With sadness for his foolish but irrevocable promise, he reached out to me without restraint, knowing full well the effect his touch would create upon my frail human form. In one gloriously sensational instant my body was charred to vapor and ash. In that same awesome moment I knew the ecstatic exhilaration of his embrace and discovered my eternally ethereal self." Penelope sighed, recalling her moment of pleasure.

　　　"Wow!" Derek marveled.

　　　"Exactly! What an orgasm", said Penelope giggling girlishly but without embarrassment. Derek laughed hysterically himself, caught up by her contagious, unselfconscious amusement.

After they had recovered from laughter Derek asked, "What happened after that? How did Pan get 'born'?"

"You know he didn't get born at all, silly. That's just a story a poet made up, saying that I got pregnant and gave birth to Pan. It's been a joke between us ever since. Many of the poetic stories of mythology are quite true, but obviously, gods are not 'born', any more than a smile is born.

Anyway, Zeus allowed me to stay with him and the rest of the gods. After an experience like that, I rediscovered who I really am and what sensation can feel like between beings. There was no way I could go back to being human again.

"Actually I've known Pan for a very long time now. I suppose you might say that I gave birth to him in a way. My escape from the cycle of birth and death was very encouraging to Pan. It gave him hope that other beings might be able to make it out of that infernal trap as well. Since then he has been able to help others make it out also, like you".

Derek knew that Pan had been trying to help him deal with his death and to rehabilitate his memory, but he'd never thought of himself as being in the same league as the gods of Olympus! He suddenly became more acutely aware of the reality of where he was at the moment and with whom he was keeping company. The order of magnitude of the beings to whom Penelope referred so casually, included the legendary Greek philosophers Pythagoras, and were having a conversation with the Greek god Pan within the range of his perception.

"Don't devaluate your own worth or ability with such thoughts Derek" Penelope prodded him compassionately. Be aware of your own potential and use your abilities fully. We will all help you. It is our purpose to help rehabilitate beings we feel may, in turn, be able to help others."

"Yes, well, thank you very much. I'm flattered, but..." Derek started to say with the automatic self-abasement which is customary in human social conversation.

He caught himself in mid-sentence, remembering what Penelope had just told him, before continuing.

"Pan has been a very great help to me. I will not betray his trust" Derek said confidently. Penelope acknowledged him with a Cheshire catlike grin and continued her story.

"After awhile Zeus got over his infatuation with me and took to chasing after other mortal maidens. And I too grew tired of his unfortunate addiction to mortal sexual sensation. It proved to be his ultimate ruin, as it has been for so many beings" Penelope observed sadly.

"I'm sorry to hear that" Derek sympathized, not quite understanding.

"What ever became of Zeus? Isn't he still here?"

"Oh no, he and most of the others gods have long since departed the realm of Olympus. In truth, only Pan is left."

"Well, where'd they go?"

"Zeus inhabits a body in Boulder, Colorado now. His name is Buddy Ballard. He owns a 'titty bar' called "The Olympus Bar & Grill". He always liked mountains, big ones and small ones.

Anyway, you know, he was never the same after the Trojan War. He sulked endlessly that his chosen side lost the conflict. It was the beginning of the end for many of the gods who debased themselves by too much meddling in the affairs of men. Because of their sexual dabbling with mortal bodies and interference in the petty activities of men, they sunk into the mortal state themselves."

"Really? I don't understand. I don't know a lot about it, but I thought the gods have always interfered in the lives of men."

"No, not at all!" said Penelope earnestly. "Long ago the gods stayed to themselves and attended to their own creations. They were far too busy with much bigger and more interesting games than could ever be played by mortals.

A man inhabits a chunk of fragile flesh for only 50 or 60 years, suffers, dies and remembers nothing of his former life. He operates within a tiny, fragile realm of solar time, atmospheric pressure and temperature, confined by Earthly distances and the need for food and sleep. Meanwhile, the gods fly in thought between galaxies and universes where no time exists. They create their own space, energy and objects.

However, immortal omnipotence does have one burdensome liability: Boredom.

The gods grew tired of eternal responsibility. The gods who gathered at Olympus decided it would be amusing and restful to observe the men of Earth for awhile, much as one might spend an hour on a lazy summer day watching a colony of ants toil at building a nest. But as the gods became more familiar with men, they grew attached to certain favorites among them.

"It got especially bad when they started fooling around with sexual sensation. That was the unseen trap door right down the dark twisting tunnel to temporality.

"Well, one thing led to another, as you know, and the gods descended into the anthill, so to speak", Penelope thought wistfully.

"Hmmm...who would have thought?" thought Derek.

He remained silent in intense thought for some time. After awhile, Penelope rousted Derek from his reverie with a 'flitter beam'. It felt to Derek like an explosion of tingling orgasmic exhilaration. It was like free-falling into a sensuously sparkling sea of children's laughter.

"Don't take things so seriously Derek" Penelope chided playfully. "Nothing is worth getting serious about. It's all just a game anyway. Pan will be the first to tell you that, I'm sure" she laughed. "Let's go see what the others are up to, shall we?"

"Oh, my god!" said Derek, still swooning as he floating after her. "Can you do that again?"

CHAPTER XIV

THE GODS ARE COME DOWN TO US IN THE LIKENESS OF MEN.

-- Christian Apostle, Luke, *Acts 14:11* (ca. 62 AD)

Virgil and Billy shared a sink, a toilet and a bunk in an otherwise barren cell at the Sasquatch County jail. They played checkers. They smoked cigarettes. They waited to hear from Pete Pleader.

"This really sucks man" Billy Joe kept saying.

"Tell me about it" said Virgil shaking his head.

*   *   *   *   *   *   *   *

Pete had a meeting with his old law school buddy Anthony Lucretia, the federal prosecutor. They ordered lasagna and garlic bread at *Luigi's*, a local eatery.

"Let me give it to you straight Pete. What we are willing to do is this. In exchange for testimony from your clients that they conspired with Paula Cadmus to murder the late Derek Adapa, we will be willing to reduce the charges against them from 2nd degree murder to involuntary manslaughter. This means a substantial reduction in sentence for your clients. Our investigation so far has not been able to come up with much on Paula Cadmus yet. She has covered her tracks very carefully. Without testimony from your clients we don't have a case against her.

On the other hand my office will be able to cooperate with you in the future on other cases which may prove to be much more financially rewarding to your firm than this one. You know, one hand washes the other", said Tony, wiping tomato sauce from his mouth.

"Listen, I gotta run. Call me after you've discussed our offer with your clients" he said as he slid out of the booth. Tony got his coat off the rack by the front door and left, leaving Pete to pay the tab.

  * * * * * * *

"The Brotherhood has much in common with the Orphic communities which sought, through the use of ethical codes and abstinence's to purify the spirit and enable it to escape the 'wheel of birth'."

Pythagoras stood before a group of men and women seated at his feet among the colonnades surrounding the *agora*, the sunny, open-air marketplace near the center of the Dorian colony of Croton in southern Italy. Most of his audience wore only a tunic in the noonday heat of early summer and sat on their blanket-like himations which they folded beneath themselves as a pillow. Some of the men sat with shopping baskets full of fruits, produce, fish and cheese from the morning shopping. A few women who had stopped on the way to the fountain house for water, sat with their painted pottery vases to listen.

One did not usually see women in the agora and never as part of such stoic conversation. But all were welcomed here. Several times each week citizens and freed men, even slaves who could beg permission to be away from their chores, came to hear the master speak about a new way a living which had grown increasingly popular and controversial during recent years.

"We forbid the eating of flesh and encourage men and women to refrain from sexual activity except for the purpose of producing children. I have shared the eating habits of many divergent peoples during my travels. I have journeyed from the Aegean through Persia to visit the Chaldean Magi on the River Euphrates, and the mysterious Brahmins of India and the priests in ancient Egypt. Nowhere in my travels did I observe that men attain an age greater than 120 years, yet most live no more than two or three score years. Few people of other lands eat meat, except on the occasion of sacrificial offering of animals to their gods, as do the Greeks.

The people of many lands cannot afford the expense of eating livestock. Oxen are rightfully kept as beasts of burden. Wool is gathered from sheep for clothing. Cows and goats give milk. Few can afford to raise domestic animals for food as grazing land is shared by many to raise grain to make bread and beer to feed themselves.

Throughout my travels I have observed the life-cycles of the myriad creatures, all of whom live to an age approximately six times the length of time required for their young to reach maturity. If a man grows to maturity in 15 years, he should then live a healthy existence of not less than 120 years.

The eating habits of the myriad creatures follow naturally the design of their bodies: the fierce predators tear the flesh of beasts with sharp teeth and sleep during the greater part of the day, conserving energy in order to digest this food. Their bodies have great power, but for short periods only. Conversely, grazing animals tear and grind grasses and leaves with teeth suited to this purpose. They are fleet of foot and have great endurance.

Though men are able, apparently, to eat all of the foods of nature, I have observed that an ideal diet exists for the bodies of man also. My conclusion is based on my observation of men who are the longest lived, most energetic and free from diseases of any on the Earth that I have met."

Pythagoras paused to allow a few new arrivals to be seated before continuing his lesson.

"These men consumed no flesh foods, neither the meat of any beast, fowl or fish. Indeed when I traveled to the East I met a race of people called the *Hunzukuts* in the northern provinces of India who live uniformly to an age greater than 100 years. These men and women maintained great strength and vigor, toiling daily in their rocky soil to raise vegetables throughout their long lives. The men continue to sire children at an advanced age. They drink the milk of goats, and eat exclusively the freshly grown fruits, vegetables, and grains of the earth. In so doing these men maintain a harmony with the composition of their own bodies, which is made principally of water.

Just as the soul is the harmonizing principle of the natural universe, so are the apple, melon, dates, rice and wheat harmonious with the body of man."

Pan, Penelope and Derek shared the experience of the growing crowd of regular students and curiosity seekers seated on the ground as Pythagoras spoke in the shade of a tile-roofed colonnade. They "tracked" with Pythagoras through his life in the Greek city-state of Croton of southern Italy. It seemed as alive in his recollection as if they were in present time. They re-experienced the incident as through the human eyes of the statuesque, darkly bearded body Pythagoras occupied during that life. He continued the lesson in a resolutely animated voice.

"However, these matters are of relatively little importance. Do not think that I am concerned overly much with the care and feeding of bodies however. Whether a man lives fifty years or five hundred, it is more important for the soul to be full of vigor; free from pain and disease. Ultimately, it is for each man to contemplate the injustice of inhabiting a body in this universe: that for one life form to live, another must die.

All life forms are animated by the spirit. The spirit departs the body at death and returns again, repeatedly, until purified through self-discipline. The slaughter of the bodies of other life forms for food, is usually unnecessary, and inflicts pain on beings who may have been your own brother and sister in another incarnation.

It is written in the sacred books of the East that what one does to others, so shall it be done to him. It is therefore a simple, but highly workable maxim that one should treat others as one would choose to be treated by others."

"*Ipse dixit*!" applauded several members of the Brotherhood who, seated randomly among the gathering, nodded and smiled at each other knowingly.

* * * * * * *

Penelope summoned Derek's attention again by surrounding him in a shower of softly shimmering sentience. He shuddered with delight. The sensation was so…well, just so…*sensational*! He had never been so completely aroused and relieved, simultaneously and instantaneously, with so many subtle and complex emotions. It was like experiencing all of the emotions one might feel from your wife, mistress, mother, daughter and high priestess, blended together. The feelings transcended physical sensation. It wasn't erotic, but the magnitude was definitely orgasmic! Penelope's communication was all at once lascivious, kind, empathetic, pervasively understanding, and innocent. Sex couldn't compete with a simple 'hello' from Penelope.

*　　*　　*　　*　　*　　*　　*　　*

After their excursion, Derek once again returned his attention back to the present, along with Penelope to the story Pythagoras was sharing with them. Several young men, returning from athletic practice at the gymnasium, bodies still glistening with olive oil used for cleansing the skin after exercise, stood at the rear of the crowd, smirking cockily to each other. Pythagoras recognized the oldest of the three as the son of Epimenides, the herdsman. Pythagoras had often sat near the edge of the *palaestra*, the open square at the center of the gymnasium watching the naked athletes practice at wrestling, boxing, javelin throwing and other martial sports, just as he himself had done for many years as a younger man. He regularly discussed his way of life with the athletes in the anointing rooms or at the baths.

For the most part, athletic training was done merely to enhance the muscular beauty of the body, so greatly admired as a virtue among the Greeks. Citizens often trained for hand to hand battle at the gymnasium in order to voluntarily serve as a *hoplite* in the infantry or navy of the city-state. But there was time afterward for philosophic discussion to strengthen the mind as well.

"As you know, I too have trained extensively in the gymnasium to serve with my fellow countrymen in the bearing of arms. I recently visited the Temple of Hera at Argos. I recognized my own shield hanging there amid the trophies of the Trojan War of which Homer has written" said Pythagoras, addressing the youths.

"But Master, how can this be? Agamemnon captured Troy more than 600 years ago?" questioned the youngest of them, in an attempt to mock Pythagoras.

"You are quite right, my young friend" replied Pythagoras.

"At that time I inhabited the body of Euphorbus, son of Panthus. I fell in battle against the Greeks by the spear of Menelaus himself. But not before wounding Patroclus, the friend of Achilles, so severely that he could then be slain by the lance of Hector" he said, smiling, though remaining earnest about his former life experience.

Some of the audience laughed nervously and others murmured their incredulity as the boy turned away to hide his embarrassment at having been singled out by Pythagoras.

"Most of you have the sight with which to recall your past lives, as I do, but do not use it. Others of you care not to remember your personal past. But to any of you who care to seek the truth of whom you really are, it is always within you. By simply looking, you may know it. The way of life of the Brotherhood seeks to remove the distractions and habits of living which prevent one from looking."

The scene faded from Derek's view as Pythagoras shared his thoughts with them in present time.
"Plato learned, through my student, Archytas, the concept of *anamnesis*: the "recollection" of knowledge. Memory. Simply knowing that one knows: that one has always known as an eternal being" said Pan to Pythagoras as an aside.

Derek and Penelope listened as they continued their conversation, gradually drifted off when the muses diverged into a too-technical discussion of mathematics and music. These were subjects that Pythagoras pioneered and evolved to a highly sophisticated level.

Derek ventured to leave Pan for the first time since he'd been out of the body to follow the playfully sensational enticement of Penelope. Pan didn't object or even seem to pay any attention to his departure.

"Let's go watch the sun rise over New Zealand, Derek" said Penelope, tugging him along toward the dimly lighted crescent of the southern horizon.

She envisioned the location for him so he could locate himself in the space above the northern island, rather than having to be guided by her. After a few hit and miss attempts, he got it right, and with a great deal of satisfaction Derek joined Penelope in the high altitude above New Zealand just as dawn gleamed across the snowy mountain peaks below.

"Magnificent" Derek thought.

"Uhhmmmmmmmmmm, yes!" sighed Penelope. "This is one of my favorite-est spots in the whole world."

The sunrise spent its' splendor in half an hour or so. As Penelope and Derek returned, the sages were conjuring the performance of a piece of music composed by Pythagoras. Derek was astonished to "hear" the telepathic rendering of a complete symphony orchestra".

He understood now how Bach must have experienced his own final triumph as a composer when he lifted his baton to the premier performance of his final and most famous composition, even though he could not hear with human ears the awesome symphonic strain of the musicians or the roaring ovation of the audience. The creation was complete in his mind and perfectly performed before a chord was struck by the orchestra.

The performance Derek and Penelope heard was a magnificent masterpiece of imaginings.

"Dance with me Derek" said Penelope.

So saying, she soared and swirled through space, mimicking music with motion. He followed, and with encouragement, contributed to her movements. Derek bobbed and bounced behind her. Penelope donned a tutu and a danced a ballet.

Through the night the maestro jammed and conjured metaphysical tunes. The delighted dancers swayed in symbiotic symmetry.

Infernos of energy twinkled distantly against the infinite ebony firmament that served as stage, studio, and ballroom of the gods.

Chapter XV

All the world's a stage, and all the men and women merely players: they have their exits and their entrances; And one man in his time plays many parts...

-- William Shakespeare, *As You Like It* (c. 1564 – 1616)

"You're wonderful Paula. You know how much I appreciate everything you did while I was at MOMM with Derek. I know it hasn't been easy on you either" Jenny sobbed.

Paula wiped her own eyes with a table napkin, half laughing and half crying. She sat across the table from Jenny at Le Petite Manifique Bistro, the latest fashionably discrete restaurant for wealthy valley socialites.

They met for brunch the day after the funeral. Jenny had no longer had any hard feelings toward Paula, aside from her natural jealousy over the affair with her husband. But she reasoned that this was not something that she should hold against Paula. Derek had been an attractive, wealthy man. Many women had flirted with him over the years certainly, though none successfully, as far as she knew. It wasn't as though Paula had tried to steal Derek away from her either.

Father Flamen's sermon had given Jenny's a new perspective and instilled a spirit of forgiveness in her. When she saw Paula from across the sanctuary on their way out of the funeral service she experienced an inexplicable emotional kinship with Paula. After all, she thought, they had both been abandoned by Derek.

She remembered Paula's kindness to her after the shooting and her steadfastness in handling the affairs of the company during her bedside ordeal with Derek. When Paula appeared with unabashed grief to mourn Derek's death publicly, Jenny felt compelled to meet with her in person.

Early dinner guests were beginning to arrive now. She and Paula had finished three bottles of Chateau Lafitte Rothschild champagne together, so far. The pink, bubbly beverage had reduced both of them to a state of blissfully blubbering catharsis. By now Jenny knew all about the sexual encounter in Derek's office. She also knew the names of all of Paula's cats and about the twin babies Paula would bear just five months from now.

Paula knew the life stories of Derek and Jennifer, as told to her by Derek, including the color of the first car they bought after they got married and about Derek's early morning bathroom rituals and about all the other intimate domestic habits one learns during years of cohabitation.

Paula listened compassionately as Jenny described the painful vigil with Derek, the blow-by-blow account of all the medical bullshit she'd been through with doctors and about the trial and trauma of her life at MOMM in general. Paula was a very good listener. She didn't interrupt or comment while Jenny talked. She just listened and acknowledged what Jenny told her. She duplicated her grief and shared her pain. She too, loved Derek.

As she talked, Jenny felt increasingly released from the painful self-pity and the desolate despair of her loss. The vacuous hole of emotion left by her outpouring to Paula was filled with relief and realization. Jenny felt safe with Paula. Ironically, she had gained a new friend in the mother of the children she never had with Derek. They were his only heirs now. Paula knew there would be no need of a paternity lawsuit now. Jenny would make sure they were all very well cared for.

* * * * * * *

"Uh, hello? Yes, yes, (sniff) this is Sheriff Gumshoe. Yes, Mr. Espion? Oh, yes, thanks for calling me back...yes; of course this is a secure line. Yes, Friday. That will be fine. Two o'clock. Yes. (sniff) OK. I'll look forward to seeing you at your office then (sniff).

Bubba hung up the phone. He was very excited about having made an appointment to fly to Arlington, VA. to meet with special agent Juan Carlos Espion, Assistant to the Departmental Chief in charge of Inter-Agency Operative Cooperation at C.I.A. headquarters. Juan Carlos always handled the minor jobs that his boss didn't want to bother himself with, like entertaining small-time big-shots.

Besides, he wanted to fly back to D.C. to get another chance at that hooker who ripped him off. This time he'd be sure to be awake when he got laid.

* * * * * * * *

Derek followed Pan and the procession of Athenian citizens from a vantage point three feet above and behind the dull gloss of Miltaides' helmeted head.

The senior citizens of Athens had ascended the steep stone mountain overlooking the city. The group reached the walled Acropolis as the rising sun repealed the night and swept the shadows from their path. The solemn parade of citizens, led by the generals was followed closely by members of the Council and the much smaller group of the *prytany* who saw to the execution of the council orders each day.

"We exhort you, goddess Athena Zosteria! Armor us for battle with your celestial might! We beseech you Athena Nike, to prepare the way to victory in the defense of our homeland! Our hour is near. The demon legions of the evil Persian King Darius march upon us. The oars of his black trireme fleet beat the water to our shore. Let your wisdom be our shield, your courage, our sword. Present our noble cause to the benevolent intervention of your Father Zeus, that we may again bring honor to his name!"

The elder statesman lowered his arms as he completed his invocation and backed away from the altar solemnly.

Miltaides, one of ten *strategoi,* generals of the Athenian army took his turn to toss a bloodied chunk of sacrificial cow into the charcoal fire of the Great Altar of Athena as part of this ritual offering to the patron goddess of Athens. He was flanked by other military leaders, who though without weapons, wore the tufted bronze helmet, metal grieves and bronze and leather cuirass which served as chest armor of the hoplite soldier. Scarlet capes draped from their shoulders dragged the ground as they knelt before the altar to fulfill the ancient pre-battle rites.

The much more numerous Assembly taciturnly trudged up the sculpted stone stairway and through the great columns of the *Propylaeum*, the immense marbled gateway, entrance to the *temenos*, and the grounds of the temple.

The pageant passed the spot at which the 30 foot bronze statue of Athena, the warrior would someday be built using metal smelted from Persian weapons captured in a future battle.

The Athenian suppliants continued with practiced pomp to enter the inner sanctuary of the Erectheion, wherein sat the oldest known statue of Athena. Across the Acropolis compound a track of stone had already been cleared and leveled to overlook the sea whereon the Parthenon would be raised during the next generation by the sculptor Phidias, the preeminent artist of the Golden Age of Athens.

Their routine ritual observances having been uttered amid the echo of the classic temple, the group exited through the temple entrance, turning left to mount the broad stairs of the smoking altar in front of which they were now assembled for the sacrificial finale.

"They actually hope that Athena will be appeased with burning flesh. It is no wonder their civilization was so short-lived" said Pan to Derek, whispering as though he were narrating the potentially winning putt on the 18th green of the final round of a golf tournament.

As the last man placed his offering into the smoking pit the sturdy Athenians dispersed into smaller groups to begin their descent from the Acropolis. Derek discerned from their mumbled debates that no tactical agreement existed between them as to how they would fight their battles against the mercenary Persian army and navy.

The only consensus reached among the warriors so far was that each of the 10 *strategoi* would take his turn to serve as commander of the Athenian warriors for one full day of battle before yielding to the next. This compromise had been made to resolve the disputatious proposals of each general and his individuated supporters, none of whom could agree on when, where or how they should deal with the imminent Persian invasion.

"Such organizational chaos would have ended the history of Athens within the week, had I not intervened to bring order and leadership to this mob of heroes", Pan commented quietly to Derek, as the scene continued to re-enact in Pan's memory.

"The Greeks were first to experiment broadly with 'government by committee': leaders selected at random through the choosing of lots. This *democracy,* as it came to be called, was an apparent solution to the brutal tyranny of self-appointed rulers", said Pan, filling Derek in on the technical details of the situation, as was his usual pedantic habit.

"However, they succumbed to the psychotic professional politicians, as all governments do eventually. Sane men do not usually want the job of governing others. Most wise men know that they do not know all of the answers and that they are not free from fault. Unfortunately, government by consensus of the *demos,* the common people, can only be as sane as the individual members of the group.

As Plato observed, the benevolent dictatorship of a sane man is always superior to decisions made by a group. The only thing any group shares are the lowest common denominators of human instinct, which when acted upon are invariably disastrous. Unfortunately, these degraded instincts are the baser qualities to which politicians appeal in order to gain a consensus and support" concluded Pan.

By mid-morning the Council, Assembly and citizens all of whom comprised the hoplite army of Athens had gathered at the *bouleuterion,* the council hall. Now they took up the debate to resolve the issues of leadership and tactics. Every man present was destined to fight to save their city against the formidable Persians whose force outnumbered them by more than two to one. The invaders included mounted cavalry against their own infantry. The Persians were practiced archers, weapons which the Athenians had abandoned for military purposes since the time of Homer. Only their spears, shield and short sword were used in hand-to-hand combat.

However, as the orb of Helios passed it's zenith at midday there was still no consensus forthcoming from the assembled soldiers.

Argument and internal conflict was the only product of democratic process, though their imminent confrontation with the Persian Empire demanded precision cooperation in order to save their city from certain destruction.

So far Callimachus, one of the civil leaders seated among the Assembly, had not contributed to the debate, but had grown increasingly impatient with the pointless proceedings. He stood and stretched his arms above his head, thinking dully that he should excuse himself and go home, have his slaves prepare a meal for him and take a nap.

Pan, witnessing impending disaster, contingent on continued irresolution, could restrain himself from intervening no longer. In a twinkling of time Derek witnessed the impassioned Pan seize the standing body of Callimachus and turn his yawning stretch into an outraged, fist-shaking tirade. Through the body of Callimachus, Pan shouted above the droning din of the debate. The voice filled the hall with resounding authority. As Pan delivered his invective against indecision, every eye and ear turned to the voice of the unwitting Callimachus.

"Athenians! The hour of our undoing is at hand. We can no longer afford this interminable interlude of disputation. King Darius and 20,000 armed invaders are encamped at the Bay of Marathon as we speak. The Empire of the East has already swallowed our Thracian and Macedonian neighbors to the north. Our messengers report that the Persian general Datis has besieged and captured the nearby city of Eretria. He is accompanied in his revengeful conquest by none other than the exiled Athenian dictator Hippias who in this evil alliance hopes to regain his power through Persian victory.

Are you all so blinded by your lust for personal prowess and glory in combat that none can yield command to the other *so that together we can be triumphant? Or are you merely women disguised as men, who loiter, enjoined in inconsequential gossip while the home fires grow cold and families go undefended?"* Pan bellowed his scathing diatribe.

A general murmur of shocked resentment rose in the assembly mixed with a few shouts of complicity with Callimachus. Urged by these few shouts of approval, Pan, directing the body of Callimachus descended the tiered seats of the *bouleuterion* to take the podium at the center of the room to continue his speech.

"Of all our able strategoi, Miltiades is, if each of us places self-importance aside, the obvious choice to provide the tactics and command for battle. He has proven himself against the Persians in battles already won and already leads our city in anti-Persian initiatives. Though our strength and excellence as individual athletes and soldiers is unmatched, we cannot hope to win against overwhelming Persian armaments as a horde of loosely affiliated heroes.

An organized force of a few well-trained, dedicated hoplites is a more lethal weapon than any convictionless rabble of foreign mercenaries, no matter how well paid". He paused to let cheers and applause subside.

"Citizens! Unite! Fold our fingers into an iron fist to fight our foe! Act as one to strike the blow! Let the warring wrath of Athena be our soul. Let the mind of Miltiades be our mind, directing the body of our army to swing our sharpened swords as one. The Persian dogs will fall and flee from our sacred shores!"

Callimachus raged and roared the words, shaking his clenched fists above his head, face reddened and voice nearly cracking with verbal bravado. The assembled citizen-soldiers leaped to their feet united in cheering affirmation of Pan's proposal. Four of the other generals relinquished their claim to command forthwith in favor of Miltiades. The others defaulted soon after. The gathering adjourned in unified enthusiasm to prepare for war under the sole command of Miltiades.

"Why didn't Athena respond to the Athenian prayers and sacrifice? This was her city wasn't it? Why did you have to step in to handle the situation?" burbled Derek after pondering the preceding scene.

"I was interested in the game of war at that time. Athena was not. Just because the citizens of Athens had chosen Athena to be their goddess, does not mean that she was interested or willing to play the part. Besides, she was probably off chasing butterflies in a quite meadow or something else she enjoyed. She was like that, you know. She was really not much of a warrior at all."

"Oh", said Derek.

"In any case, interest and willingness to play a game are more important than the ability to play. The men of Athens were pleased to have my help, whether they were aware of it or not. Observe", said Pan, as he flicked his attention back to the Athenians once again.

   * * * * * * * *

"You can tell that prosecutor to eat shit and die" said Billy.

Virgil took a long drag on his cigarette and shook his head in disbelief. An armed guard was watching through the glass of the tiny visiting room as they met with Pete Pleader across a small, gray, metal table.

"Man, to begin with he *knows* it was a hunting accident. And second, we ain't never even heard of this Paula chick. So how're we supposed to be in a conspiracy with somebody we don't even know? How can we plead guilty to something we didn't even do, for Christ sake? So, why not make them prove it was a conspiracy in court. We'll take our chances with a friggin' jury."

"I entirely sympathize with your feelings Virgil. However, that is the best offer I could negotiate with the federal prosecutor's office" Pete said, shrugging his shoulders.

He closed his briefcase, preparing to end his visit.

"I suppose our only alternative then is to take the case to trial. I must inform you, however, that it will be very expensive and that your case may not come to trail for many months. I'll do the best I can to get the judge to set a reasonable bail and to prepare a position for your defense. I'll let you know as soon as I can when the arraignment will be held" said Pete with a motion to the guard that the visit was over.

"Just how expensive is it gonna be?" asked Billy wearily.

"Well, it's hard to say for sure, but you can be sure that you'll need to post bond" Pete said as he reached the open door. "I'll need another $10,000.00 to get started with the pretrial preparations", he added as he turned to leave.

"Son of a bitch!" yelled Virgil, throwing his cigarette butt at the closing door.

    *   *   *   *   *   *   *   *

Darius I, sovereign king of a multitude of nations consolidated by force under his command, knelt on the deck of the anchored Persian flagship, bowed his head and recited an ancient incantation:

"Though one be armed with valor and the strength of wisdom, yet it is not possible to strive against fate."

His prayer was offered to Ahura Mazda, god of Zarathustra and taught to him by the Magi, priests of the Twin Spirits of good and evil, to ensure humility in his hour of self-assured triumph.

Miltiades surveyed the Persian position from atop the sloping plain a mile distant from the fleet of Persian triremes which lay at anchor in the Bay of Marathon. He raised his sword arm above his head in the autumn dawn as a signal to the assembled *hoplites* at his back. The Greeks poised themselves as one for the downhill charge on foot to engage the waiting heavily-armed enemy infantry.

They had marched double-time with 10,000 *hoplites*, recruiting another 600 volunteers along the route. The combined force, resolved in unity now, advanced against the horde of 20,000 Persian infantry, cavalry and archers to attack them on open ground.

For every soldier assembled here there were five supporting artisans, farmers, wives and slaves at home to supply their needs in defense of their homeland. Now the work of preparation was done and all came down to this single, well-planned charge.

Yesterday Phillipides returned after having run 150 miles on foot from Athens to Sparta in only two days. His heraldic mission had been a vain attempt to summon Sparta to their aid against the allied threat of Darius and Hippias.

"I trust that the news you bear from Sparta is as felicitous as your timely journey. How is it that you were able to reach Sparta and return so quickly? I cannot imagine such speed in a man. Did you travel by horse?" Miltiades asked amiably of his exhausted messenger.

"Master" panted Phillipides, "as I ran the road to Sparta on foot I was overtaken and accompanied by the great god Pan near Mt. Parthenion, above Tegea." replied his servant with breathless exhilaration.

Though physically exhausted, the thrill of his recent seraphic encounter suffused him with strength.

"He asked me why his help was not solicited at the temple, inasmuch as he is and has always been the friend of Athenians. Thinking that he meant to punish our ingratitude, my terror was such that I fell to the ground and begged that he not punish us or transform me into a goat or afflict me with some madness. However, the god did not punish me. Instead he raised me up with compassion and filled me with joyous confidence. The Great Pan insisted that he wished only to help us, but that in return for his benevolent intervention he wishes Athens to build a shrine in his name under the brow of the Acropolis and that a cult to him be established there."

"Did the mighty Pan indicate how his assistance might be rendered to us?" asked the general with hopeful anticipation.

"He said nothing further to me, but helped to speed me on my way to Sparta with your message. I ran with a lightness of foot and soul; as though I were carried on the wings of eagles." Phillipides said happily.

"And what of the Spartan army? Does the god Pan send them to conspire in our cause and aid our army then?" demanded Miltiades.

"Master, the Spartan general replied that he can not dispatch their troops to share in the attack for several days." said Phillipides, cringing a little as he offered the parchment scroll, bearing the written reply from Sparta.

Having read the message, Miltiades dashed the scroll to the ground cursing the Spartans and crushed it under his foot.

"They pretend to excuse themselves, because a religious festival is in progress from which they can not depart for fear of offending their gods!" he minced and swished mimicking feminine mockery, then spat on the document angrily.

"Damn their festival and damn their Persian-loving, fornicating fathers! They had best pray that the promise of omnipotent Pan proves potent enough to save their pretty posteriors from the Persian fleet!"

Miltiades' crimson cape swirled behind him as he turned on heel, stamping past his still kneeling messenger to attend to the formidable business at hand.

Late that night he rested fitfully having fallen asleep on one of several couches in the *andron*, the main room of his home next to the kitchen. His wife and servants had provided the evening meal of fish and vegetables followed by wine, fruit and honey cakes for himself and his generals. Though the others had departed to prepare themselves for the march the strategic planning meeting had lasted late into the early morning with little certainty that their agreed upon plan would succeed against a superior force of cavalry backed by archers, neither of which his own army of infantrymen possessed.

They were determined to rely on the tried and tested hand-to-hand fighting strength and skill of a charging phalanx: rank and file formed close and deep, shields joined and long spears overlapping in close array. Though they would march to meet the invaders at the Bay of Marathon the risk of Persian naval circumvention and invasion of an abandoned Athens by sea were balanced precariously on the strategic scales of chance and discretion.

The early morning half-sleep of Miltiades was faintly suffused by an aromatic aura. An ambient aurora emerged among the painted walls and mosaic floor. A vision drew him forth from his body. He was looking at the Persian army encampment, dimly illuminated by the late night moon above the foothills of Marathon.

He gazed down on the vaguely lustrous black triremes moored along the bay behind the fading glow of campfires which spotted the lengthy curve of beach. His drowsily surreal perception of the moonlit scene was pierced with a startled cognition: there were no horses! Suddenly he was filled with inexplicable certainty that the Persian cavalry were absent from their camp, foraging in the forests for fresh meat.
He became urgently aware that he must march his army double-time to Marathon to engage the enemy during this apparent lapse in their defense. Miltiades' mind filled with an image of the formation he would use. His bold and brilliant battle plan was to surround and collapse the Persian ranks, driving them into the sea and away from the shore.

Pan's nocturnal epiphany faded as Miltiades roused and awakened. The general sat up in the pre-dawn darkness, knowing that *Nike,* the God of Victory, would inspire the offensive assault of his hoplite heroes this historic day. The subtle scent of cedar filled his sinuses.

"Emeritus!" he shouted, to summon his personal slave. "Prepare yourself to bear my shield and sword on the march to Marathon at dawn!"

On the evening of that fated day, the shades of sundown crept across the field at Marathon, sculpting a solemn sepulcher of shadows across sixty-four hundred fallen bodies of dead Persian soldiers. Only 192 Greeks were slain in the perfectly planned and precisely executed attack on the unwary army.

* * * * * * * *

"I have often tried to envision the state of prosperity that could have or may still exist for man and the myriad life forms on Earth had all of the energies which have been applied to war been invested in the creation of survival mechanisms instead." said Pythagoras, as Pan and Derek returned their attention to the present time.

Penelope smiled and snuggled to them with her usual bright sensuality. They chuckled at Derek's thrilled embarrassment over her unabashed affection, and then returned their concentration to the sophistic musing of Pythagoras.

"Envision what might have been created with the resources consumed by any one of the major wars. Not just to reverse the destruction of uncountable lives and resources, but to not have expended the time, energy and inventive thought on such destruction in the first place. Not to mention the natural resources of land, buildings, trees, minerals and food stuffs.

To have used those same creative skills to the solution of survival problems: food supply, weather control, water management and purification, environmental maintenance, construction of living quarters, energy production, cures of disease, animal and plant husbandry, transportation, communications systems, education and the arts. You could name many more.

The construction projects which could be accomplished in one year alone with the personnel and funds consumed by the armies of earth currently under conscription could provide comfortable housing for all of the peoples of Earth.

The technical progress advanced by western civilizations in the 20th century, without the consumptive waste of armies and navies could have been redoubled one hundred times over. The potential for such constructive action compounded through history is beyond the mathematical calculation of any geometric progression.

War is an admission of the inability of leaders to communicate with ideas. Swords, spears, bullets and bombs are sadistic substitute for ideas.

Most men, having lost their memory of the past, are careless of the present and oblivious to the future. If each man realized that he had to live with the result of his present time actions throughout the rest of eternity, he might consider his current actions more cautiously."

Pythagoras paused and turned his gaze toward the distant Earth.

"These are things I taught during my incarnations on Earth with some success. Most men are well-intentioned and work for prosperity. But the majority is too often overwhelmed by the few, who in their fanatical efforts to destroy themselves, drag every other being down with them. The pity is that the majority continue to allow a few madmen to lead all of them to destruction."

*　*　*　*　*　*　*

Derek and Penelope let their attention drift away from the sages, who continued their seemingly endless philosophical discussion. Derek thought to himself for awhile about all that he had seen and experienced recently. He was still puzzled over something Penelope mentioned earlier.

"What ever happened to the other gods of Olympus? Did they all end up becoming human beings like Zeus?"

Penelope remained silent for some time. Derek sensed that she was looking for something or someone…

CHAPTER XVI

A man should feel confident concerning his soul, who has renounced those pleasures and fineries that go with the body, as being alien to him, and considering them to result more in harm than in good, but has pursued the pleasures that go with learning and made the soul fine with no alien but rather its own proper refinements, moderation and justice and courage and freedom and truth; thus it is ready for the journey to the world below.

-- Socrates, *Plato, Phaedo,* 114d (c. 469 – 399 BC)

"Well, thanks for coming anyway, Sheriff Gumball." said Juan Carlos, patting Bubba on the back as he held the office door open for him.

"That's Gumshoe" said Bubba meekly.

"Oh, yes... er, whatever.. uh, take care." said agent Espion, closing the door behind himself. He adjusted the too-tight shoulder-holster under his sport coat and muttered, "What a bozo! Where do they dig these guys up?"

Bubba waddled down the stairs leading to the guest parking lot near one of the nondescript structures he'd been guided to earlier that morning by the gate security guards. He found his American-made rental car and squeezed his stomach under the steering wheel and into the driver's seat.

Well, the trip hadn't been a total loss, he thought. Even though the CIA couldn't help him prove his conspiracy theory, he still had the FBI to try.

Bubba spent all morning listening to a rather indignant, though somewhat informative lecture on the purpose and activities of the CIA, which unfortunately for him, did most definitely NOT include investigating the Chairman of the Board of a major American corporation.

Juan Carlos had been quite incensed that Bubba could be naive enough to think that the CIA could ever participate in the kind of investigation Bubba proposed, especially since he hadn't even offered a bribe!

The interview started out well enough. Bubba explained his purpose, seeking the assistance of the nearly unlimited resources and investigatory acumen of the CIA in his attempt to expose Paula as the secret perpetrator in the conspiracy to murder Derek Adapa. Juan Carlos had read about the software magnate's death in the *National Inquisition*. He was even interested in the investigation until he checked on his computer link to V.I.P.E.R. only to find that Paula Cadmus was now listed as the Chief Operating Office and Chairman of the Board of Directors of Nimbus Software, Inc., a California Corporation with assets worth hundreds of millions of dollars.

According to recent IRS entries in the file, Paula had very recently assumed the senior executive post, having been granted proxy for the position by the majority stockholder and with the written endorsement of the widow of the now deceased owner, Jennifer Adapa.

At this point, J.C. proceeded to explain to Bubba in very emphatic terms that the CIA worked *for* American Corporations. Who did Bubba think paid for their congressional political protection? The $35,000,000,000.00 annual "no-questions-asked" intelligence-agency budget? The media cover-ups concerning CIA covert operations? "Have you never heard of the "military-industrial complex"? asked J.C. with near horror of disbelief in his voice.

Bubba fumbled an apology, but was silenced by a 45 minute lecture about the sacred relationship he had presumed to violate. Bubba listened as J.C. explained the honorable CIA tradition of defending American corporate interests internationally.

With a series of flip-charts, which seemed to have been prepared for just such situations, J.C. showed that the CIA itself employed more than 25,000 American workers and had tens of thousands more "unofficial" workers on its payroll world-wide, all of whom served the interests of the Fortune 500.

Fixing foreign elections, infiltrating foreign governments, carefully continuing the "cold war" with Communism are all part of the game plan. Arms trading with drug lords and even known enemies, like Iraq, are all in a days work in the service of American Corporate interests.

With an eloquent tear of patriotic zeal in his eye, J.C. revered the "War on Drugs": the massive infrastructure maintained by the CIA that allows America open access into foreign affairs and therefore guarantees an open door for American Corporate Enterprise to exploit the resources and markets of the world.

And finally, J.C. reminded Bubba that the kind of revolutionary forces that overthrew British imperial taxation of the Colonies in 1776 and eventually brought an end to the slave trade, would never be allowed to get off the ground in the modern U.S. of A.! If British intelligence agents had been on the ball back in 1775, the American Revolution would never have happened!

J.C. wiped his forehead and dried his eyes with the handkerchief Bubba offered and slumped into his chair, exhausted.

Bubba couldn't take any more either. He retrieved his handkerchief and blew his tearfully runny nose. He was overwhelmed with appreciation for the magnitude of this most noble organization. But even more, he was ashamed of himself for presuming to compare the relative insignificance of his own petty ambitions to that of securing safety and sanctity for the very Foundations of The American Way of Life!

For a minute, as he stood and prepared to leave, he even considered giving up his investigation of Paula, given her corporate connections and all...but, quickly decided that would be stupid. After all, he had to look out for himself first.

* * * * * * *

The Carthaginians were devastated in 396 BC by an epidemic of smallpox. The importance of this plague on the civilizing process of the western world was that it prevented Carthage from controlling Sicily and thereafter from conquering Rome.

Without the pox, the relatively brutal and barbaric culture of Rome may have been supplanted, under the brilliant military maneuverings of Hannibal, by the vastly superior civilization of Carthaginian traders, which would have resulted in the predominance of a commercially based society thousands of years before that of the modern era.

(This message has been brought to you as a public service by the Historical Retrospective Society of The Long Since Vanquished and Now Extinct Phoenician Merchants of North Africa)

*   *   *   *   *   *   *

Barry Barrister was not amused. Derek's death was bad news. It meant losing the possibility of collecting 50% of Paula's awarded settlement in legal fees from her paternity suite. When Derek died and could no longer be sued, well, it ruined his whole day.

What made matters worse was that he hadn't charged Paula anything up front either. Even though he'd done many thousands of dollars worth of work for her. The hours he'd spent fending off investigative reporters from the press were worth a small fortune in legal fees alone. The legal injunctions he'd been able to secure, through his personal connections with judges, to keep the Sasquatch County Sheriff from poking around her personal life could have easily paid for a new Porsche.

Well, it didn't matter now. Just this morning Paula called him on the phone. He would not need to sue Derek's estate to recover his fees after all. As though anticipating his concerns she had appointed him to represent her personal and corporate interests as Chairman of the Board of Nimbus Software, Inc.. And, inexplicably, she requested that an itemized bill for all of his services to date be sent to her office for payment. He couldn't understand the integrity of such a move on her part, but what the hell...money is money.

*   *   *   *   *   *   *   *

Jenny was feeling chronically weak. She had just come from a check-up with her long-time physician and friend, Dr. Doris Mederi. Doris couldn't find anything wrong with her, but ran a number of tests to see what she could find out. Doris said that her symptoms were probably due to the stress of what she'd been through with Derek. Stress was known to be a primary cause of an immune system disorder called "Chronic Fatigue Syndrome".

Jenny felt great spiritually. Derek's death released her from a living nightmare, although it was still difficult for her to be at home alone sometimes, surrounded with all the reminders of their life together. So, most of the time she stayed in the newly furnished tenth floor condo she had leased at the beach. The view of the Pacific Ocean soothed her. It filled her with space and calm.

Paula was a godsend for her. She arranged everything through her attorney: the condo, moving, the sale of the house and all of the legal details of Derek's estate.

In addition to all of that, Paula officially took over the corporation. Paula was the one person that everyone came to for information and advice in his absence. She was the only person who knew everyone that Derek had known. She knew everything there was to know about the company, how he did business, when, with whom and why. She was the only choice to take over the corporation when Derek was no longer there. All Jenny had done was make it official with her signature. Paula was an extremely effective executive secretary. Now she was just as effective as the CEO and Chairman of the Board.

The babies were doing great too.

*   *   *   *   *   *   *   *

The sun sparkled from Aristotle's ostentatiously bejeweled rings as he twisted the curls of his balding head. What remained of his carefully cropped and curled red hair was as eccentric as his coxcomb clothing.

"I will grant that there is a certain incipient insobriety inspired by the seductive scents of the spring solstice which sway the soul to sensuality," observed Aristotle emphatically with a carefully effected, effeminate lisp, "but, what say you young gentlemen? Does Aphrodite win your attention away from my instructional annotations with the amorous arousal of her fragrant flowers? Or is their enough concentration left in you to learn the lessons you will need to fulfill the grandiose designs prescribed by your regal parents to carry on their self-ordained destiny to rule over nations?" he shouted above the din of laughter from his students, stamping his heel for emphasis.

Aristotle rebuked his ribald entourage with a sweeping arm, indicating the blossoming, shaded avenue of fruit trees which lined either side of the stone walkway along which they sauntered slowly. However, while supposedly absorbed in the instruction and indoctrination imparted by their Peripatetic mentor the adolescent attentions of his academic apostles were attenuated by the urging of Athena. What started as a sophomoric series of playfully platonic pubescent pranks gradually degenerated into a giggling, jostling joust of grab-ass.

Together with his brilliantly bigoted tutor, Alexander shared these strolling instructions through the Gardens of Midas, the verdant wine country of the Macedonian Precinct of the Nymphs, with other future kings: Cassander, Son of Antipater and Ptolemy, son of Lagus. Alexander, said to have been born of divine origin by his mortal mother Olympia, was the mortal son and heir of King Philip of Macedonia. Alex walked hand in hand with his beloved friend, and future second in command, Hephaestion.

*　　*　　*　　*　　*　　*　　*

Derek was becoming somewhat alarmed at the prolonged silence of his companion, the usually cheerful, open and talkative Penelope.

"Don't be concerned Derek" she said finally. "You know, I hadn't really thought about my old friends for a long time. When you asked me about the gods – what's become of them – I realized that I had really lost track of most of them. So, I went looking to see if I can still perceive any of them. You may recall I told you that Zeus is running a strip joint in Colorado. He was always a womanizer, you know.

But, the others…I don't know…except for Pan, I can't really find any of them. The aura of their being has faded so much that I just can't seem to distinguish them clearly from any others. It's quite of depressing actually. It makes me feel rather lonely."

"Oh, I'm sorry" said Derek sympathetically. "I really didn't mean to upset you, honestly! I had no idea…"

"It's OK. One must be ones own company and create ones own universe in order to be truly happy. I am happy to be with you though, here and now", Penelope said, returning her attention to him and to the present.

"If you are interested, I will tell you the real life, true story of how Zeus fell from power as the Father of Olympus" she told Derek.

"Oh, yes. Of course. That would be great!" Derek said with enthusiasm generated more by his relief that Penelope had recovered from her melancholy, than from an interest in hearing the life story of Zeus, her former lover.

"Derek. There is no reason for jealousy!" she teased, sensing his true emotion.

"Oh, well, it's just that…well; you know I really like you very much. I've never met anyone quite like you before…" Derek stammered with embarrassment.

"I know. However, I'd like to tell you the story of Zeus anyway, if you don't mind", at which she continued, without waiting for his approval.

*   *   *   *   *   *

The first true departure that Zeus made from Olympus was to take a body – that of Alexander, the Macedonian prince. As soon as he took over the body, he lost his memory of himself. Amnesia is the condition common to all humans. (As you know, the demands and sensations of the flesh can be quite overwhelming to the being and consume all of one's attention). Thereafter, Zeus spent all of his time trying to regain his memory of his true self. For example, in his travels across the world, Alexander paused at the Temple of Claros near the western shores of Ionia along his route to Persian conquest from Greece. With a few of his retinue he camped for several days to consult the oracle staff, searching for the answer to his lost omnipotence, yet not knowing what questions to ask them.

At the outset of his crusade for personal power he crossed the Dardenelles from Thrace with 100,000 soldiers and camp followers. Alexander stopped at Ilium to see the hallowed walls of Troy, though without his memory, not really knowing why. By that time he had already severed the famed Gordian Knot with his sword. This was the deed he used to legitimize his divine destiny of conquest to the plunder hungry hordes of his ever-growing army.

The Oracle of the ancient and prestigious Temple of Apollo at Delphi had already reaffirmed his godly origins. Or so he cared to think. He arrived at Delphi to seek the prediction of the oracle priestess concerning his future as conqueror of the world, at a time she thought to be unpropitious for the god Apollo to entertain his request. She refused to see him and told him to wait for a time more convenient for the god.

Alexander was outraged at her impudence and demanded an audience with her. Again she refused him. Not to be put off by so lowly a one as the prophetess of Apollo, though highly revered by the rest of the Greek world, he ordered her brought to him by force. Spitting, swearing and struggling into his presence, held by his soldiers at spear point, she screamed at him, "You are incorrigible!"

At this admonition from the priestess, Alexander waved her away. Thinking that her words meant that he was invincible, rather than rude and brutish, he wished to hear no more from Apollo. This was the prophecy he sought.

If Alexander would have been patient enough to wait for a proper reply, this is the response which he *should* have been given by the priestess when he consulted the Oracle of Apollo", Penelope said sadly as Derek listened intently:

"Behold, Ye Gods and hearken!

Here hides The Holy Harlequin!

His guise, we see, is paper thin.

Though masked in mortal coil,

We know Thee still, Olympian.

He's here with us, right now on Earth !

Still with us on this speck of dirt:

His power now has been debased --

Celestial Clouds were once His berth.

His Mighty Realm has been defaced !

Omnipotent Abilities ?

What of Heaven's Mighty Hand ?

He always was so strong and free:

Now, masquerading as a man --

Amnesia drives Him to his knees !

Where to, Celestial Company ?

What of Apollo and The Rest ?

Entombed in mortal effigy !

Omniscient Immortality ?

Like each of Us, covered up with flesh…"

    Alexander he searched continually for a 'License to be Divine' from every priestly authority along his martial route to rule the world. In exchange for the favorable signs they contrived with which to bless his quest he granted political protection and paid all the priests with gold pillaged from those he conquered" mourned Penelope.

"I will show you some of what I saw" said Penelope opening her memory to Derek.

Derek tracked with her mental recording of the adventures of Alexander on Earth. Derek knew he was definitely not watching a film whenever he tracked through someone's memory. Except for his awareness of being outside of the events looking in, these memories had all of the perceptions, sensations and emotions of real life. It was much more real and intense than flat, two-dimensional images on film. The memories of Penelope were accompanied with the knowledge of having already been interpreted and understood through the experience of the being whose memory he shared.

He could understand the languages being spoken, even though they were foreign or archaic. Signs and symbols and customs and moral codes and ethics and superstitions and situations were all incorporated into his understanding, as though he had lived them himself.

Derek was deeply enthralled by her observations as Penelope continued the story. From a vantage point a dozen cubits above the throng Derek witnessed the crowning of the young Macedonian conqueror of Egypt as god/king: Pharaoh. The priests of Amun, in the time-worn tradition of their trade, proclaimed, yet again, the simultaneous incarnation of the son of Ra and Osiris; as Horus the Golden One, the mighty prince, beloved of Amen.

Alexander rose to the throne and turned to face the cheering waves of the assembled multitude of Egyptians who had come to witness the coronation. He felt the weight of the double crown upon his mortal head. He squeezed tightly the crook and flail placed in his hands by divine decree. Mortal and immortal were united in him; the affirmation of his mother's dream.

Olympia conceived him, so she said, by the eternal sperm of Nectanebo, the spirit of the last native Pharaoh. His ghostly apparition appeared in her quarters and made love to her in the guise of a snake, the royal uraeus, sacred asp of Egypt.

Penelope viewed the scene from inside the head of Alexander. His hair was like a lion's mane atop a fair skinned face and powerfully compact body. She peered out through his keenly focused eyes, one blue-gray, the other brown, and saw his vision blur with the tearful self-aggrandizement. He swallowed hard to choke back a sob of magnificent megalomania. Alexander exuded self-important majesty, as only men can manage.

Yet, she felt it still: his underlying doubt. Seeing, but not knowing. Feeling but not being; reaching but not arriving. He pretended not to be who he really was."

The scene faded as Derek returned to present time.

"The next day" Penelope continued, "he was already on the trail and his armies were prepared to follow their very own god-king to glean what gold and glory they could from the wake of his self-appointed quest to ravage and conquer the world. Now that the divine origins of his mortal identity had been satisfactorily ratified by the 'higher authority' of the most ancient priesthood of all the order of Amun-Ra, his goal was to establish an earthly empire to glorify his name for all time.

As he stormed across the world and trampled nations beneath his omnipotent feet he renamed more than 70 cities after himself: each called Alexandria.

"I ask you, what sort of game is that for a god to play?" Penelope concluded with disgust, not expecting a reply.

"So Zeus really lost his memory? How could that happen?" asked Derek innocently.

"I do not know the mechanics of it exactly Derek. Ask Pan. Perhaps he can explain it to you. I can only tell you what I have observed for myself." she said.

"I am saddened by the loss of any friend to the flesh, though Zeus was by far the greatest. When he appeared in the body of Alexander I was surprised but pleased to find him, of course. Zeus had many times before assumed a mortal form, especially when pursuing a wench. However, this time, I could not communicate with him. I tried every form of contact I could conceive.

At first I sought him telepathically. Nothing. He was oblivious.

Next, I visited him as an apparition of colored light, with the scent of flowers to bring myself to his physical awareness, much as one might approach any mortal. He was terrified by my aura and fled from me, thinking I was a phantom poltergeist, a ghost come to afflict him.

He sent for the priests to burn incense in his quarters and to invoke protection against wicked spirits with ritual incantations. I was shocked and alarmed.

Later, I tried a more subtle and sensuous approach. One night as he lay sleeping I filled his mind with visions of our lusty love together. Though aroused, he dismissed it as a dream and sent for a harlot to relieve his hardened penis.

After that I alerted Hera, his wife and the other gods, but none of them could stir recognition or response from him either. He was indeed lost to us" Penelope lamented.

"Are you OK?" asked Derek sympathetically.

"I'm fine, thank you. Please do not sympathize. I'd just forgotten the magnitude of the misfortune."

"So, that's how Zeus actually *became* a man. Wasn't he able to get back again? How could that be? I thought he was like...a God. I mean, you know...like, *the* God?" Derek asked in amazement.

"I will explain it to you the best way I can" Penelope said dispassionately. There are some things you must understand in order to know how a god can become a man. There are many subtle details to which one must attend in order to avoid spiritual degradation."

CHAPTER XVII

ALL GREAT TRUTHS BEGIN AS BLASPHEMIES.

-- George Bernard Shaw, *Annajanska*, 1917, p. 262 (c. 1856 – 1950)

"Imagine yourself inhabiting a body made, not of biological cellular tissue, not a fuel burning, waste excreting combustion engine, but of clean, light-weight *DuraMold*: the amazingly flexible, elastic, non-corrosive and nearly indestructible synthetic material used for millennia in the manufacture of space craft parts. Now, for the first time in this or any other galaxy, our specially patented process has adapted the wonders of DuraMold to the manufacture of bodies! We are proud to introduce, for the first time anywhere, in this exclusive offer, the amazing **DURABODY**™.

Designed and engineered by our own staff of ergonomic experts, each body is the culmination of millennia of creative artistry and skill. Each body will perform every mechanical function required of a biological body without the restrictive considerations incumbent on frail cell tissues such as:

- The effects of extreme heat or cold in space or atmosphere.

- Damage caused by high velocity impacts occasioned by falls or vehicular accidents

- Breathing under water or in airless space

- Exposure to atomic, solar, gamma and other forms of radiation

- Food deprivation

- Lack of sleep

- Contact with high voltage electrical current

- Contract with malevolent bacteria

- Attacks by hostile aliens

Further, owning and operating a **DURABODY**™ will eliminate all of the following hazards:

Communication malfunctions, financial disasters, massive errors in decision making, gross misuse of time and vital resources, loss of freedom, social and emotional diseases and ruined lives caused by sexual desire, activity and/or marriage.

At the same time these bodies provide the wearer with the facility of complete sensual experience and to enjoy a flexible, active life-style at your discretion including:

- Freedom from the pain and inconvenience of conception, gestation, birth, rearing and/or the growing of new bodies, disease, deterioration, death, rebirth, etc., ad infinitum.

- Freedom from enslavement to the economic treadmill required for the care and maintenance of biological bodies such as acquiring food, shelter, clothing, defense, toiletries, cigarettes, etc.

- Freedom from unwanted physical sensations such as pain and fatigue.

- Ideal for interstellar travel and interplanetary visitations.

The truly amazing **DURABODY**™*:* The nearly indestructible torso and major appendages require no maintenance or replacement during the initial 200,000 year warranty period. **DURABODY**™ is available in the ever-popular bipedal model and as well as classic quadruped models. For a slight additional fee, modifications can be made to accommodate as many as eight arms and/or legs.

As a special incentive to first time buyers, we are offering, at no extra charge, your choice of any TEN of our specialized adaptations from our exhaustive catalogue of more than 4,700 Snap-On custom tools tailored to cope with an infinite variety of complex technical tasks.

Of course, each body is equipped with a standard package of assorted interchangeable cosmetic accessories: eyes, noses and proboscises, teeth, gills, suckers, ears, beaks, antennae, tails, wings, tentacles, fins, mandibles and many, many more, so you can always put your best foot, fin or wing forward. 100% satisfaction guaranteed for the life of the body...and that's a long, long time....

(Prices and availability may vary in your sector. Consult your local dealer for financing terms and local tax regulations. The manufacturer makes no guarantees against body loss by theft, owner negligence or acts of gods, local prejudice or governmental insanity.)

                   *   *   *   *   *   *   *

"What the hell was all *that* all about?" asked Derek.

"Just a sales commercial I was thinking about" replied Pan.

"I remember hearing it a long time ago. Once, in a moment of weakness, I considered buying a body. Fortunately, I came to my senses and decided against it."

"A long time ago?" said Derek, even more confused than before.

"Yes, a very long time ago, as Earth time goes. Not on this planet of course. I hadn't thought about it till I heard you and Penelope talking about Zeus. Things have certainly changed since then".

"You mean people used to *buy* bodies made out of some kind of indestructible plastic or something? Like a big toy doll? They weren't *born* with a body? They didn't have to eat? How did they live? Didn't they have to sleep or go to the bathroom? How much did they cost? How did people pay for them?" Derek quizzed Pan in a rush of questions which blurted from his mind in a single explosion of inquisitive excitement -- like a three year old child.

Although Derek's naiveté could be endearing at times, not unlike that of a pet dog, thought Pan to himself, he grew impatient with it occasionally.

"Beings have been fooling around with bodies in this universe for a very, very long time.

Lots of companies used to manufacture synthetic bodies. Beings paid for them in much the same way as people buy and sell automobiles these days. The bodies did not require that fuel to be put into them. Beings just ran them with their own self-created thought energy - the same way that people operate flesh bodies, although a flesh body does have some of its own motive force. You have already discovered for yourself that when the being is not operating the body, the body dies.

The spiritual energy used to run a body is easily demonstrated -- a gymnast flying through the air in a controlled spin or a man walking down the street is controlling the body with thought energy.

However, the biological bodies currently in vogue on this planet are strictly an inferior type. Very fragile and temporary. Awkward. Messy. Full of pain and unpleasantness. I never could understand what anyone saw in them" Pan said flatly.

"Well, now that you mention it...I can't think of too many good reasons either, I suppose..." Derek admitted hesitantly.

*   *   *   *   *   *   *

Penelope and Derek, once again, after watching a spectacular sunset over the mountain peaks of Hawaii, resumed his history lesson about the demise of the god Zeus, incarnated as Alexander (The Great).

"In his obsession with his own divinity, Alexander continually compared himself to the lesser Greek gods Dionysus and Heracles, saying that only through deeds can the rights and worth of a man be judged. In youth he was indoctrinated by his father's boyhood friend, Aristotle, in the right of the mighty to rule. He judged that if the deeds of one man, were equal to those of all other men combined, this gave him the right to rule all men. Conversely, he reasoned that slavery is a natural institution, and that all non-Greek 'barbarians' were slaves by nature.

In the end, Zeus found that all of these mortal games proved all too-easily won. He conquered and controlled the world of men without half trying. There was no game left to play: no river worth crossing. And, after Persia succumbed, no army worth fighting remained.

No friend was worth loving after the death of his life-long friend, and lover, Hephaestion. Alexander, drowning in his own tears after the loss, burned his dead friend on the most expensive cremation pier in history, which cost 10,000 talents of gold. (one talent of gold was, at that time, equivalent to about 6,000 drachma. Each drachma is worth 6 obols. An average citizen worker earns about 3 obols a day, making the value of the funeral pier for Hephaestion worth sixty million drachma or 360 million obols or a days wages for 180 million Greeks)", Penelope explained to Derek.

"Alexander left the body himself shortly after that. An elaborate funeral procession carried his body all the way to Alexandria, Egypt in a golden coffin. This is the epitaph which I composed for him, as a farewell to him from the gods:"

"This Man lost his battle with remorse,

In a ten day bout of drunkenness.

He gained his fame by violence

In a world that worships only force.

Through Earthly gain Zeus lost himself:

Lord of Light in silhouette,

A shadow profile of himself;

Am That I Am, in carnal form.

The Light of Life creates no more.

Who once brought myriad forms to view

By molding gaseous molecules

Floating birds and shifting shores.

Who makes something out of dust?

Creator is the name of God.

Who destroys with every touch?

Conquerors: The Lords of Mud.

Zeus came to Earth to rule the world

Stealing gold and lands by force

With no regard as to their source.

And now he has his just reward:

For all his slaughter what was won?

A moments' glory in the sun.

His life is lost. His soul succumbs -

The time-worn Game of Man rerun.

Zeus, the Great Olympian

Born on Earth as Philips' son

Dead, as Pharaoh, Son of the Sun.

He'll be back on Earth once more

Though he'll return in mortal form

To live as man and die again.

The great god Zeus will shine nor more".

*   *   *   *   *   *   *

Paula typed with effortless competence. Words flowed in meticulously correct administrative order across the recessed screen of the computer monitor built into the tinted glass top of her custom contoured executive desk. The screen flashed through the final font and format adjustments of the document pre-print command menu and paused. A laser printer hummed softly to life and quietly collated a dozen copies of a completed four page document into a tray within arms reach of her chair.

Paula examined one of the precisely typeset copies in a final quality check before stapling the upper left hand corner of each set. After placing each into a single pile she collected the documents, glided her chair smoothly back from her desk, stopped briefly to check her hair in the black lacquer framed oval mirror on the wall of her spaciously elegant office before walking across the luxuriously furnished executive reception area to the corporate conference room.

The other eleven members of the Board of Directors of Nimbus Software, Inc. rose from their matching chairs surrounding an elongated oval table of hand-polished ebony to greet their Chairperson with amiable respect. Paula waved them into their seats as she distributed to each a copy of her proposed corporate resolution for their consideration and endorsement.

The content of the document was already intimately familiar to each member of the Board, each of whom had contributed the very best resources of his or her own training and experience in researching, developing and negotiating with the several other companies involved in a joint product development venture.

As the last person signed a copy of the document, their formal dignity dissolved into a group cheer, hand clapping and hugs all around. This meeting signaled for them the most exciting event in company history.

Later that afternoon, they would all meet again with counterparts from their corporate co-conspirators in the high tech industry to hold a press conference announcing the most ambitious joint-venture R & D project ever undertaken in the computer world.

Later that week Paula perused her complimentary copy of **Terabyte** magazine. Her picture was on the front cover with a caption which acclaimed her "CEO of the Year".

On page 54, Paula read the feature article:

"...the details of the deal were announced at today's unprecedented joint press conference held by Nimbus Software, Inc., the computer software giant. The joint

R & D project was christened together with the CEOs of the Japanese electronics giant, **SAMYO, Ltd**., the major American computer chip manufacturer, **Chips Inside, Inc.**, the principle PC manufacturer in the U.S., **WE'RE PCs, Inc**., and a research firm specializing in voice-activated computer systems, **VOTECH, Inc.**. Also in attendance to endorse the undertaking was the Chairman of International Telephone Company and the head of the Federal Communications Commission.

Attorneys for the newly formed alliance, led by Barry Barrister, confirmed that the group plans to release a revolutionary new personal computer as early as next spring. In a written statement, CEO Paula Cadmus revealed that the new devise will be called **PocketPC**.

The revolutionary new **solar-powered**, device will be an affordable, voice-activated, hand-held combination of cell phone, digital video camera, TV/radio, unlimited gaming and *virtual reality platforms and personal computer, with wireless internet access. These features will interface through a network of private satellites which will provide global communication, location finding and data access.*

The PocketPC will give the user the ability to create, transmit and receive information in the form of text, graphics, sound and video to and from any location in the world. The device will be the first totally secure computer ever made as its files protected by fingerprint or iris scan security and by personalized voice commands. These features not only make computers available to anyone who can talk but keeps the users' data private.

PocketPC will provide 200 terabytes of cloud storage and 800 gigabytes on each of the RAM and ROM chips. The data processor chip to be used remains a well-kept secret, but is hinted to have a faster processing speed than any known to exist.

One can only speculate as to the staggering potential sales the PocketPC will generate. Many industry analysts predict a virtual take-over of the PC marketplace."

Paula put the magazine down on a stack of other industry publications she'd received which excitedly heralded the new release. She would to read them later.

For a moment she paused to thrill at the sensation of her babies kicking within her growing belly.

She thought of Derek briefly and got back to work.

He perceived her thought and returned it fondly.

*　　*　　*　　*　　*　　*　　*

"How could I have possibly contracted AIDS?" Jenny asked the anguished question of herself over and over and over, without an answer.

She asked the same question of her own doctor and several other specialists at the AIDS Institute for Research (AIR) at Stanford University in Palo Alto. AIR was funded primarily through benefactors in the San Francisco gay community whose membership had been dramatically reduced by the disease in recent years.

The constant tiredness she experienced, led her to get a more thorough physical examination. Blood tests quickly confirmed that she definitely had the AIDS virus. Yet no one had an explanation as to how she might have contracted the disease without sexual contact. Her only sexual contact had been with her deceased husband.

Paula had also been tested for HIV and the tests had proved negative. So, though Derek had had sex with both of them, how could she have AIDS and not Paula? It didn't make sense! Regardless, Jenny was dying and there was no solution for it.

Jenny stood with her arms folded about her against the ocean breeze; the wind swept her skirt and frazzled hair. She continued to stare uncomprehendingly till the chill of the setting sun on the Pacific horizon roused and drove her from the balcony indoors to the warmth of her condo. She slumped heavily onto a sofa and shivered slightly, holding a sweater around her shoulders.

"What have I done to deserve this? First I lose Derek and now I'm dying. I've always lived a decent life. It's not fair!" Jenny thought to herself in desperate despair, she covered her face with her hands and wept.

"I am here to guide you through death and into a new life" said Pan, emanating from the radiance of the setting sun which fell in golden streaks through the sliding glass doors of the balcony and across the carpet of Jenny's comfortably furnished living room.

Jenny sat straight upright and stared intensely into the sunset source of the voice. The room was filled with the scent of cedar like the wonderfully fresh smell of the inside of her dresser drawers.

Jenny had an epiphany: the idea of a mosquito landing on her skin, biting, drinking, and departing. Instantly, she understood how she had contracted AIDS. At the same moment she heard a voice within her say:

"You will have a mission to fulfill in your next life. Yet you must first complete your destiny in this life", Pan intoned the words with vocal tones of Charleton Hestonesque gravity, combined with the resonant timbre of Gregory Peck as Captain Ahab, and a stately elocutionary blend of Sir John Guilgood and Obewan Kenobe.

Jenny decided she must be having a religious experience: the first and only one she'd ever had. She'd been moved to misty-eyed inspiration a few times during Christmas pageants concluding with the Hallelujah Chorus from Handle's Messiah and during standing ovations at the conclusion of a particularly moving aria at a performance of a Puccini opera. But never anything remotely approaching the devine presence of a god.
"This, surely, must be the voice of God! Either that or I'm going totally insane" she thought, sliding onto her knees from the sofa to prostrate herself on the carpet before the apparition.

"Attend and hear my commands! Prepare yourself to leave this life to join your beloved husband, who awaits you in the next. You will take the following actions:

First, you shall legally arrange to bequeath all of your Earthly possessions to the care of the woman, Paula.

Second, you shall employ such methods as are required to discredit the Sheriff of Sasquatch.

Finally, you will prepare yourself to depart this life in preparation for the next. Derek will assist you in spirit to carry out my commandments. Make your thoughts known to him. Your mission is also his mission."

Jenny sat up on the floor in cautious, cross-legged silence, waiting for something more. But there was nothing except the final fading glow of the sunset and the lingering scent of cedar.

She had the feeling that Derek was with her in the room. She thought to him tentatively, "Is that you Derek?"

"Yes, Jenny, it's me", he answered.

*   *   *   *   *   *

Paula directed a thought to Pan, "Your student is doing well, isn't he?"

"Yes, he is making progress", Pan answered, "as is his former wife and soon to be sister-twin".

*   *   *   *   *   *   *

Virgil was down by 24 lbs. from his usual 6' 2", 230 lbs.. Living on baloney and light bread sandwiches, cream of wheat and cigarettes was getting to him. He'd long since gotten over the week-long sickness due to withdrawal from alcohol. Last week the mortgage company towed his mobile home away and the week before that the Ford dealer repossessed his truck.

Billy Joe was nervous as a hound at a hog hunt. All he did was pace back and forth in the cell all day long, smoking cigarettes, cursing Pete Pleader under his breath and waiting for something to change. But it never did. Just the same deafening echo of yelling, cursing inmates – day and night – in the same gray, barren walls and cold iron bars of an eight by ten foot county jail cell.

His hair was getting gray. His wife started waiting tables at Fleshfat's Diner to pay the bills, but she couldn't keep up with anything except the rent, utilities and food. The legal bills kept piling up. The trial was weeks away and their blood-sucking attorney still didn't have any good news for them.

*   *   *   *   *   *   *

Derek was still in training. Pan had taken to leaving him alone for increasingly long periods of time now. During these absences Derek attended to Pan's duties as Guardian of the Wood. At first Pan had arbitrarily mapped out a precinct of several hundred acres, then several thousand, growing steadily to tens of thousands of acres of forest land, lakes and streams over which Derek stood watch while Pan was away.

Derek drilled continually to spread his attention throughout the entire area, being aware of as many activities of the myriad creatures as he could. His duty was to protect them from harm and to preserve the native state of the forest as a sanctuary for life. He learned to focus his attention, to observe every detail, to be every motion, alert to any intrusion.

He learned to act, just as Pan had acted to protect the deer from being shot by hunters like Billy Joe and Virgil. This was the challenge and the true test of his growing ability to operate without a body: to cause things to happen using only his spiritual abilities. Like everyone else, he'd forgotten how. He'd grown too used to relying on the lazy, automatic motions of body machinery; like a worker on a factory assembly line, standing by while machines do all the work. That was over now.

With Pan's insistent instruction and persistent drilling, he was regaining not only his memory of his past, but his ability to control the thought and action of life by his will alone.

Controlling the actions of the animals in the forest was an especially good exercise for him. He practiced making birds sing when he wanted to hear them. He chased chattering chipmunks around tree trunks, across the needle carpeted forest floor and under the curling boughs of fern. A fox paused and scampered away at a scent Derek put in the air to forewarn danger. Migrating ducks veered from their V course in a sudden draft of air, avoiding a hunters' gun. A school of speckled trout fled to the far side of a lake away from approaching fishermen. A beaver felt safe to swim a little further upstream than usual to find a choicer grove of tender tree bark.

All good practice, but the real test of his regained skills lay ahead. Jenny needed his help now.

CHAPTER XVIII

There is a law of stern Necessity, the immemorial ordinance of the gods made fast forever, bravely sworn and sealed:

Should any Spirit, born to enduring life, be fouled with sin of slaughter, or transgress by disputation, perjured and forsworn, three times ten thousand years that soul shall wander an outcast from Felicity, condemned to mortal being, and in diverse shapes, with interchange of hardship, go his ways.

-- Empedocles, (c. 493 - c. 433 BC)

The voice of Paula's secretary squawked like a tiny electronic robot over the intercom, "Mrs. Adapa is on line 3, Ms. Cadmus. She said it's very urgent. She sounds upset. Can you take it or shall I take a message?"

"It's OK, Janis. I'll take it in my office" she said releasing the intercom button and rising from her conference room chair. "You will excuse me for a few moments gentlemen." she said with her usual charming grace, "I must take this call. If you'll continue reviewing these design specifications, I'll be back in a few minutes."

The precisely groomed and Armani-suited Japanese Executive Vice-President of Samyo, Ltd. and two of his white laboratory smocked technical gurus stood and bowed politely as Paula rose and left the conference room. She had been in nearly non-stop meetings ever since the press conference. She'd met with senior executives, hardware technicians, software programmers, design engineers, marketing and finance staff of nearly all the companies involved in their joint venture. The R & D work for production of the **PocketPC** was moving along at lightning pace, unprecedented even for the geometrically expanding computer industry.

Barry Barrister had taken on seven new full-time corporate attorneys to supplement his staff to handle the project.

Paula picked up the phone in her office. "Hello Jenny. How are you, dear?" she said with pleasant interest.

Jenny blurted out everything she had just experienced with Pan and Derek in one continuous sentence, pausing only to gulp an occasional breath. Paula listened attentively, pretending to be surprised with an occasional "Oh my!" and "My goodness!"

"...and god told me to make all the legal arrangements to leave everything to you. I swear, Paula, it's the truth, all of it!"

"OK, Jenny. I believe you. Thank you very much for telling me what happened. Was there anything else?"

Jenny thought for a few seconds and couldn't think of anything.

"No that's everything. I've never experienced anything like it before. But it was more real than anything that ever happened to me. Do you think I'm crazy?"

"No Jenny, of course not. I'm quite sure that what you've told me happened exactly as you say" replied Paula in a tone which was so knowing, confident, and understanding that Jenny's self-doubts evaporated.

"What can I do to help you?" she asked.

"Well, I think I'm going to need help to handle my legal arrangements and some private investigators to help with handling the sheriff. I don't think Derek's attorney does this sort of thing." said Jenny.

"Don't worry about it Jenny. Call Barry, the corporation's attorney. Just tell him what you need. I'm sure he can contact the right people for you."

"Oh, thank you Paula. I don't know what I would do without you."

"You are always welcome, honey. Please let me know if there is anything else I can do. OK? I'll call you later tonight to see how you're doing. Bye for now" said Paula.

"She's such a sweetheart. She and Derek are coming along very well indeed" thought Paula to herself.

* * * * * * *

"Yes, Derek, Zeus never came back to the realm of the gods. He continued jumping from one human lifetime to the next – always following a common thread: his persistent quest to achieve immortality for himself through the use of force", replied Penelope in response to his question. "Each added failure reduced his power and the magnitude of his ability."

"Really? That's kind of sad isn't it?" Derek realized. "So where did he go after he stopped being Alexander?"

"He resurfaced again in the East for a time. First, he was Quin Shi Huang Di. You might have heard of him – the first Emperor of China. He spent his whole life conquering lands and building monuments to himself. The Great Wall of China, roads, the city of Peking, and an enormous burial tomb. But, always searching, vainly trying to discover an Earthly route to immortality.

Later, he returned as Genghis Khan, again, conquering, destroying, self-glorifying, proclaiming himself "god of the world" and, inevitably, failing.

Then again, as Julius Caesar, I thought that he nearly remembered himself. He compared himself to the god Zeus. But, he was already too far gone. He bought the position of Pontifus Maximus, chief priest of the Roman church so that he could control the gods of Rome, who were, by that time, only stone idols. He became the first self-appointed Emperor for Life of the Roman Empire. Every Earthly advance he made was through the use of force: military conquest, bribery, sexual scandal, murder, coercion, lies, treachery. He used every imaginable perversion of power to serve his ends, to no avail.

Later still, as Napoleon Bonaparte, in an much smaller domain, he raised himself to the status of Emperor -- all the while, killing, conquering, womanizing, seeking the essence of himself through the flesh, futilely trying to rediscover his own eternal self by force. But always, dwindling, diminishing, dimming his spiritual power and perception. He has continued to decline since then."

"Wow! No kidding", Derek commented.

" Indeed. I think the theme of all his lives are well summarized by a eulogy I composed for him", Penelope said. As she began to recite her poem Derek heard distant drums beating a martial cadence urging the troops to charge over the bodies of the dead comrades. The rhythm of her poem was accompanied by the clashing cacophony of weapons, amid the moans and the retching of the wounded. He could smell gunpowder smoke lingering over rotting bodies, abandoned on the field. Visions of terrifying mayhem from every conceivable battlefield scenario, from every era, stampeded, exploded, rampaged and slogged through crimson mud in his mind:

"Historic holy holocausts.

Periodic plagues of pain;

Dance of Death, Destruction's Dirge

Drumming dullards to their doom.

Wanton waves of ravaged war

Reasonless raging rants and roars

Bodies bloat the bloodied beach

Smashing slaughter, shattered shores.

Controlled combative chaos

Kindled by craven Khans:

Maniacal Megalomaniacs

Crusaders and Conquistadors.

Women weep to wait and watch

Life get ground to gory grist.

Sending sons to serve the State

On Fallow Fields of Fearful Force.

Multitudes of Macho Men wield

Weapons wrought for waging war

Bankers build and barter both

Swords and shields to either side

Pompous politicians prize

Pilfered plunder from their prey.

Pontiffs pray with piety to

Profit from the public purse.

Military mushroom might

Radioactive rhetoric

Bombastic bureaucrats will blast

The Earth to make it look just like the Moon!

When will warfare ever end?

As Edgar Poe's raven said –

'Nevermore. Nevermore.'

Not while the gods live lives as men."

*　　*　　*　　*　　*　　*

"Since I've been dead I've really been learning a lot about life. What's really going on is sure a lot different than what I thought was happening when I was in a body." said Derek, musing to himself.

"You're right my friend. All is not as it appears to be." Pan commented. "While you were a man, you had no way to remember your true self, or to rise above the chronic pain and cravings that enslave a being to the body. Now that you are outside and have observed the difference, it will be possible for you to inhabit a body once again without loosing contact with the gods. However, eternal vigilance and constant communication will be required to maintain your autonomy."

"Why would I want to go back into a body now?" Derek pleaded. "I'm just getting used to operating without one!"

"There is a great deal of work to be done on Earth at this time", replied Pan solemnly. "Conditions are so desperate that little short of miraculous measures are needed to prevent the extinction of life on Earth. Cooperative action between men and the gods is required as never before in the history of the planet. As there are now far fewer gods and many more men than before, you are needed to serve as an intermediary between men and the gods." Pan paused here for dramatic emphasis, letting the concept sink into Derek's mind, before continuing.

"Your purpose, should you be willing and interested, is to become the first mortal man…to remain immortal! That is, to live in a body, yet remain free from the usual human cycle of endless birth and death and rebirth. With the help of the gods, you will help others to achieve this superior state of existence. You will be the first being to accomplish this since Paula. (After all, where do you suppose the notion that cats have 'nine lives' comes from, if not from the Cat Goddess, Bastet?), Pan added, parenthetically.

"Jesus!" Derek protested at the idea of being 'immortal'.

"No. Not Jesus", Pan replied with amused disdain.

"Your wife, and soon-to-be sister, Jennifer, will be the next!" said Pan, as though announcing the arrival of a new 'baby' into the family of the gods.

"Oh, brother…" Derek said, resignedly, with half intended pun and half surprise.

"No. Sister", said Pan, chiding him playfully.

"Derek, I've learned a lesson recently." Pan continued, thoughtfully, still examining his own observations. "It has become apparent to me that one of the primary reasons that the gods fell from the Heavens, so to speak, is that they used their power to serve selfish goals or desires. Many used their vast ability to cause things to happen with little or no regard for the effects caused on others. I observed Zeus moving through a sequence of lives as a man on Earth. I, myself, often abused my own power to satisfy my craving of carnal lust with a nymph or maiden, without regard to lasting consequences.

Our greatest strength proves to be our greatest weakness: the ability to use force – the same kind of force that once enabled Zeus, as a god, to cast lightning bolts across sky, make the thunder roar and the seas churn. But without ethical conduct, without consideration for everyone involved, we abused that power; that raw ability to persuade, coerce and compel men and the elements in the world. The results of such behavior have always been tragic.

During his incarnations as Alexander, Caesar and the rest, Zeus overwhelmed everything around him with force, force and more force – without and equal balance of *intelligence*," said Pan with growing intensity. "Intelligence is the ability to envision consequences. To modify one's actions accordingly, to serve the greatest good for the greatest number of beings.

Unfortunately, the physical universe and the men who live in it are very fragile and temporary things. It is one thing for a god to rampage and ravage in the ethereal universe of the heavens, but quite another to freely destroy the Earth. The Earth does not repair easily. Men do not mend when they are dead. Pain and loss cause nearly all to forget who they really are. In every new lifetime they must start over once again with nothing – without possessions, without memory, without purpose, without friends. This is not intelligent.

We must change our ways now. The power that we have must be used to create a safe environment wherein beings can become rehabilitated."

CHAPTER XIX

No one can be perfectly free till all are free;

No one can be perfectly moral till all are moral;

No one can be perfectly happy till all are happy.

-- Herbert Spencer (c. 1820- 1903)

Pythagoras, Penelope, Derek and Lao-Tzu gathered near Pan. To his surprise, Derek could feel the unmistakable presence of Paula among them.

"Yes, it's me, Derek", she said affectionately, feeling his awareness of her.

"Wow! You mean, all this time you've been…I mean, you're a…" Derek sputtered, half-shocked, half-delighted, and half-embarrassed.

"Yes. The others have always known me as Bastet. You know, the Cat Goddess of Egypt", she thought back to Derek, "but you can just call me 'Mom'", teasing him.

All the others laughed merrily at her joke. Derek did not laugh. He was still too befuddled and a little apprehensive, to appreciate the humor of his situation. He was in the presence of the gods after all; pristine souls. Yet, here he was, very recently a mortal and about to become one again, more or less. He was mortified by the appearance of Paula on the scene, realizing that, as a god, she could hear is thoughts, feel his emotion, know his inner secrets.

"What does she think of my relationship with Penelope? How will she treat me, (her former lover and employer) now that she is going to become my Mother? What will Jennifer think? What about Jennifer and Paula together? What about all of us together as a family? Brother, sister, mother, son, lover, husband, father – all rolled into one!" The thoughts flashed desperately and uncontrollably through his mind: remnants of human social machinery. He tried his best to hide his feeling of humiliation from the others, knowing full well that all of them knew exactly what he was thinking.

"Jesus, this is really the pits. I'm not used to this – not being able to hide my thoughts", Derek thought, resolving himself to the reality of his present situation.

"Derek, none of us cares about your past. Each of us have a multitude of indiscretions in our own lives", Penelope said soothingly. "Likewise, all of the men and women of Earth, in past incarnations, has been brother, sister, husband and mother to each other countless times over and again. The pity of it is that amnesia prevents them from remembering that they already know each other. Starting all over again in each new lifetime, they must try to regain the love lost with those they've lived with and lost before. It is the definition of tragedy. This is one of the reasons we are gathered together now – to try to help each other and all men to overcome the cruel and blinding affliction of mortality."

"I understand Derek" said Paula kindly. "And Jennifer is fine too. We both love you. Truly, there is no jealousy or competition between any of us. We are all friends here. Penelope and I have been together many times through the eons. When there is time, we will tell you stories of all the wonderful (and miserable) times we've spent together."

"Truly, there is no need for shame, nor blame or regret. Indeed, there is no need to be serious about anything in the past, Derek" Pan advised. "What is more, I've observed that one of the greatest hallmarks of the gods has always been insouciance – flippancy, joy, fun, light heartedness. Nothing of lasting value has ever been created with seriousness. Let us live in the eternal now and proceed with the creation of the future!"

"Here, here! Yes! Wonderful! Woohoo!" agreed the others.

* * * * * * *

"The time has come, my friends, to intervene, once again, in the affairs of Man, to ensure the survival of all of the myriad creatures on Earth.", said Pan, like a General addressing his staff before battle. Together, Pan and the others created a very unique alliance of free spirits, a "gang of gods", who together, hoped to help handle the problems of Earth.

"As in the Myth of Homosapus, the Guardian is gone. He has been supplanted by sources of unlimited destruction on Earth. No benevolent master hand guides the events of Man. No is no referee in the games being played. There are no rules, no guarantee the playing field will not be destroyed along with the players of the game. Sadly, the best any mortal can be, no matter how powerful, is an unknowing pawn, in an unknown game, to be broken, cast aside and replaced by yet another pawn."

"Already the air, the soil and the waters of Earth are polluted with toxic wastes which threaten to extinguish the ability of Life to sustain itself. All life will be gone within a few hundred years at best. Dozens of species of life already become extinct each day", Pan said, broadcasting graphic mental images to illustrate the magnitude of the situation to his companions.

"The entire planet is now at risk from the irrevocable damages caused by man-made pollution of the air, the oceans and the land. Defoliation has stripped the world of half of its forests. Ground water around the entire world is now so contaminated that amphibious creatures are now born with genetic mutations. Two heads, five legs, missing organs and other bizarre changes, are common. The fishes of the lakes and oceans are becoming inedible. Even the salmon, like the once abundant buffalo, are now nearly extinct, along with dozens of species of creatures who perish forever, each day!

Each nation is individuated from the other. Enough nuclear weapons exist to exterminate every creature on Earth 10 times over. Yet, national leaders are merely puppets, driven by self-serving financial vested interests, banks and businesses. There is no global view, no comprehensive understanding of the catastrophic concatenation of destructive forces which have been accumulated. There is no benevolent ruler to ensure unilateral control of resources and actions.

As for Man himself, psychiatric priests of the new religion called western science, drown the spirit with the 'scientific fact' that man is a soulless animal. They administer mind-numbing, addictive drugs to children and adults to dull the senses and create false euphoria."

After a pause and sober reflection by the others, Pan concluded his address. "I have a plan. Working together, there is a chance that both men and gods may be returned to their former state before the damage can no longer be reversed", Pan concluded."

Pan and the 'gang of gods' huddled together, as each of them received detailed instructions for the parts they would play in resolving the tragic dilemma of Earth.

* * * * * *

After the meeting Pan and Derek returned to the forest, their usual hangout. They hovered above the trees, a safe and soothing place.

"How long have you been the guardian of the forest Pan?" asked Derek after some hours of wordless meditation.

"After the Roman Empire dissolved, there were very few interesting games left for me. The minds of men were poisoned by the Christian church, and the most of the other gods had long since become men themselves.

I wandered from place to place for many years. I have always enjoyed the remote, refreshing vegetation, animals, the seasons and cycles of life. They remind me of more pleasant places and times, long ago."

"When was that?" Derek asked.

It was a very long time ago indeed...billions of Earth years."

"Billions of years! You can remember that far back?" said Derek with genuine surprise.

"Certainly", Pan said matter-of-factly, without elaboration. "My beloved forests, the forests of many worlds have been my refuge for most of that time.

Just think, originally, almost half of the United States, three-quarters of Canada, almost all of Europe, the plains of the

Levant, and much of the rest of the world were forested. Today the forests have been mostly removed for fuel, building materials and to clear land for farming."

As Pan spoke, he dragged Derek from one forest area to another, around the planet – an ability that Derek had by now become comfortable with. By changing his attention and just "being" there, he could transport himself instantly from one place to another, without ever really "moving" in a physical sense.

"My beloved trees cover only one quarter of the world's total land area. More than half of the forests are in the tropics and the rest are in northern forest zones. As you can see, Latin America and Russia have about one-quarter of the world's forests", said Pan, indicating the regions as the passed from one to the next.

"When I was still among the gods of Olympus, there were twice as many trees on the Earth. More than half of the forests that covered the Earth then are gone now.

Derek watched the smoke and glow of fires smoldering across the Amazon as dim-witted loggers stripped the land to the bear ground to make farm land and grasslands for even dumber cows.

"Each year, another 1.6 billion acres disappear in this way", Pan commented as they "flew" over the northern part of South America. "Now, only about $1/5^{th}$ of the world's original forest remains intact – mostly in Canada, Alaska, Russia, and the tropical forests of the Amazon region."

"Human beings have never been aware of how important the forests are to the life of the entire Earth" Pan remarked as they swooped down to the softly lighted, damp and silent forest floor, beneath the towering canopy of virgin tropical trees in Brazil.

"As you can see, trees act as a sponge, soaking up rainfall and releasing the waters slowly and steadily into streams and rivers. They protect precious topsoil and husband the important nutrients they protect. Once destroyed, it takes at least 100 years for forests to grown back to their original uncut state, except for the majestic redwoods and sequoias, which take 500 to 1,000 years to grown back to their original size" Pan sighed, with a growing agitation."

Pan showed Derek through the trees and undergrowth, whispering like a tour guide in a zoo, not wanting to startle the residents. A storm of every imaginable style of bug, fly, moth, beetle, larvae, spider and ant crept, flew, leaped, crouched, boroughed, scampered, slept, buzzed, chirped and hummed through the impossibly compact foliage and steaming jungle air.

"In this area, only 100 acres of rain forest, there are more than 400 different species of trees", whispered Pan.

The next instant, Pan plunged splashlessly into the warm waters of one of a thousand wandering Amazon tributary rivers. He watched, as still as a fallen log, while a stealthy crocodile stalked a fowl on the muddy shore. Then, gliding through the greenish water, he followed a school of silver Arawana fish, as they searched the branches overhanging the banks for a tasty bug. A skillfully aimed spit of water knocked an unwary beetle into the water – a meal for one, death for the other.

"There are 3,000 species of fish in the waters of the Amazon Basin, eight times the number found in the Mississippi River and 10 times more than all of Europe".

"Wow, you really know your forests don't you? How do you know all this stuff?" Derek quizzed.

"The forests are my home, my kingdom, my playground and my chosen responsibility. I've spent most of my time in the past 2,000 years living and learning within them."

"The most pitiful consequence of forest destruction is the direct influence on climate of the planet as a whole! Tropical deforestation causes 90% of all the carbon dioxide released into the atmosphere, rivaling all of the carbon from fossil fuel burning".

"All of the forest destruction on Earth is caused by the pathetic population pressures of men: agricultural settlements, the uncontrolled, profiteering greed of politicians, timber merchants and peasant drones.

Man does not have a global view of its own environment. They will consume all of the resources only to discover, too late, that there are no more. Man will be the first creature in the history of the galaxy to make *itself* extinct. Never have I lived on a planet where the dominant species destroys its own habitat with such abandon. In only a few thousand years, a mere blink of the eye in cosmic time, the species of Homo sapiens will have risen to predominance among all life forms and destroyed everything in its environment, including itself!

However, I am not going to allow them to destroy all of the myriad creatures of the world in this process. These abuses have already continued too long. They must end now!" Pan raged with resolute finality.

Derek witnessed the outward sign of Pan's outrage in the sunset sky above the rain drenched Amazon. Rippling fingers of eerie blue-green lightning flickered through the darkening clouds below him and resounded in the rumbling thunder of an angered god.

CHAPTER XX

I foresee the time when industry shall no longer denude the forests which require generations to mature, nor use up the mines which were ages in the making, but shall draw its materials largely from the annual produce of the fields.

-- Henry Ford (1863 - 1947)

The first 6 months of sales of the *PocketPC* were unprecedented in the history of merchandising. More than 150 million units were shipped at the wholesale price of only $74.95. The limited public offering of stock by its owner, the newly formed corporation, "*Pangenesis, Inc.*" raised $3.5 billion in the first day of trading on Wall Street. The sole proprietor of the corporation and patent holder of the *PocketPC*, was also the, now legendary, CEO and Chairperson of the Board of Directors of Adapa Software, Paula Cadmus.

However, the greatest cause for celebration, and the source of joy in Paula's life was the birth of her healthy twin babies. When asked by a reporter during a television press conference why she had named the children Derek and Jennifer, she replied, "The names just seemed to fit".

* * * * * * *

General Armstrong "Rocky" Powers jogged with his usual disciplined determination through the grounds of his luxurious suburban estate near Alexandria, VA. He was only an hour away by limousine from his office at the Pentagon. The sun had risen enough now to make his frozen breath visible.

His life now was a universe away from his days as a West Point Cadet 46 years ago. But he could still run 5 miles a day and was in good enough shape to make his Willie stand at attention when the situation demanded. Not bad for a 64 year old grandfather and a lot better than most of the pathetic punks he saw enlisting in the Army these days.

Through a fluke of fate he was born too late to fight in WW II, but was a commissioned officer out of the Academy in time for duty as an intelligence officer during the Korean War. While American soldiers died defending the jungles of South East Asia from Communist interference in U.S. oil and drug cartel interests, Rocky learned the trade of espionage behind a desk in the Pentagon.

He was promoted to the rank of General during the Persian Gulf War. He worked his way up through the ranks by sheer political ambition rather than by distinguished combat record. The only combat he'd ever seen was in the movies. These days the military, like everything else in the world, was all business and politics.

Rocky mastered the art of information manipulation during his tour of duty in Washington D.C. during the Vietnam "conflict". For him, and the rest of the military intelligence machine, it hadn't been a war really, just part of the crusade to secure economic interests in Southeast Asia for American oil companies and the government sanctioned drug trade.

His appointment to the post of Chairman of the Joint Chiefs of Staff of the United States Armed Services was his reward for distinguished Cold War service. Not unlike his contemporary in the CIA, a few years earlier, who made it all the way to the Oval Office!

The Cold War was a 40 year mock battle, fought with strategic military intelligence operations designed to create and control public and political opinion. These were supported by the very selective tactical use of media propaganda in cooperation with members of the Committee on Foreign Relations and the rest of the "one world" boys who owned the TV networks and newspapers. Campaigns were fought by manipulation of the major world powers through the strategic flexing the economic muscle by the Rockyfellows and other International Bankers, using front men like Henry Kissweaner.

The masses of the world were convinced that the threat to peace between the major powers was real. They had been watching the media glorify the awesome array of high tech weapons being produced by the U.S. and Russia for decades.

The purpose of "Today's Army" was to spend the greatest possible amount of money producing the least possible benefit to Mankind while creating and hiding behind the illusion of the necessity for "a strong national defense".

The tactical targets of the New World Order were nearly all achieved now. An International Economic Police State was a virtual reality. Overcoming the few remaining strategic barriers was inevitable. The 9/11 attack and the war on terrorism were just another stepping stone in the path to global military control by the West.

Rocky patted himself on the back for having helped to manufacture and sell the most lucrative of all national myths during his career: *"Everyone knows that a strong military is our only guarantee of world peace."* It was a job well done, from which he would retire in a few months to enjoy the luxurious rewards for his part in the most elaborate charade in history.

Armies and arms manufacturing were the biggest business on the planet now. The arms industry was the most sophisticated cooperative network of international governments and private corporations in the world. Every industrialized nation of Earth profited by it.

The false reports fabricated under Rocky's direction to exaggerate the threat of enemy military strength were very effective. They scared the American public and Congress into spending more than 1/4 of the national budget on the military, even after the Cold War ended. This elaborate misinformation campaign was worth its weight in platinum plated nuclear submarines.

Though it was true that each of the Navy's multi-billion dollar nuclear powered submarines were capable of annihilating every person on Earth with an undetectable underwater launch of nuclear ballistic missiles, they would never be used, in spite of Kissweaner's argument that the U.S. could actually "win" a limited nuclear war. They were really just technically awesome, massively Fabian, computerized holes under the water, surrounded by metal, into which the U.S. taxpayers poured fabulous sums of money.

Rocky and his fellow military gurus were convincing liars, but they weren't fools. They each wanted to live a long, trouble free life, retire to the golf course, and live on a fat pension just like any other Federal Government employee, except they would each get huge bonuses from the private sector in the form of consulting jobs and speaking fees.

Rocky nodded to a pair of military security guards on duty as he puffed his portly frame through the gate and up the circular driveway to the stained glass front door of his seven bedrooms, Tudor style home. His personal driver would chauffeur him by limousine, supplied by a congressional lobbyist from *McArms International Ltd.*, to his weekly brunch meeting with the other Joint Chiefs near the Pentagon at 0945 hours.

He expected to be given a routine update on business-as-usual matters from the heads of each branch of the military. Each of them were political puppets appointed by the President to satisfy corporate campaign contributors:

Chief of Naval Operations, Admiral Will Nevers, referred to by his aides as "Old Twin-screw", (for his reputation for keeping a mistress, as well as his wife) Chief of Staff of the Air Force General Floyd "Flyby" Feathers (who usually traveled by train because he got airsick in planes), and Commandant of the Marine Corps, General Buford "Flintlock" Remington (whose great, great granddaddy was the worlds most famous gun maker) and Chief of Staff of the Army, Rocky's old drinking buddy, General Jackson "Stoney" Andrews.

Rocky stepped into his custom-made, imported marble, sunken Jacuzzi. The water was electronically heat-controlled to precisely 114 degrees. He pressed a button to turn on the whirlpool jets and slumped into a steaming sea of perfumed bubbles swirling under his chin.

After his bath, Rocky dressed crisply in the full dress uniform laid out for him by his valet. He sipped a Bloody Mary, but ignored the silver platter of eggs, croissants, caviar and fresh strawberries which had been prepared by his live-in chef. He carried the drink downstairs, reclined into a Corinthian leather upholstered executive chair and propped his feet on an original Louis XVIth desk in his library. A fire crackled warmly in the massive stone fireplace.

"Yes, government work has been, very, very good to me" he murmured to himself as he surveyed his extensive collection of fine art objects adorning the room.

*   *   *   *   *   *   *

The former Sheriff of Sasquatch County, California, Melvin "Bubba" Gumshoe was very securely housed together with his new roommate, Roofus "Slasher" Jackson, in cellblock H-9, Section C of Vacaville State Penitentiary. Roofus was serving 2 consecutive life sentences for murder and child rape. Bubba always slept on the top bunk, that is, unless Roofus insisted that Bubba sleep with him in the bottom bunk, Bubba on the bottom.

The former federal prosecutor in the case of Billy and Virgil Jaras was living in a similar facility, all expenses paid by the Federal government, serving 5-10 years for conspiracy and accepting bribes. During both of the trials, a mysterious video tape of the transaction between he and Bubba, along with incriminating testimony from a variety of former county employees, as well as assorted federal witnesses, had appeared, providing conclusive evidence that multiple state and federal offenses had been committed.

The judge and jury in each case had no choice but to administer the maximum sentence required by the law of the land to each defendant.

*   *   *   *   *   *   *

"Virgil, me and the misses have been talkin' about movin' back down South again. I hear they're higherin' at that Georgia-Pacific pulp plant down there by Brunswick." Billy told his brother over the phone. "You want to go down there and check it out with me? It'd be good to get back home to visit Momma".

And so it came to pass that the Jaras brothers moved away from California, bought brand new double-wide mobile homes in the *Piney Woods Trailer Park* down by the Atlantic Ocean near Brunswick, GA.. They never hunted for deer or anything else, in any forest, ever again. They did drink a lot of beer and did do a lot of fishin' in the new boat they bought with some the money they were given by their former attorney, Pete Pleader, acting on behalf on an anonymous benefactor.

Chapter XXI

Clay is molded to make a pot, but it is the space where there is nothing wherein the usefulness of the pot lies.

Loa Tzu - T*ao Te Ching* (c. 4th century BC)

Rocky felt good. Rocky had the best job in the world. He didn't need to know anything about being a real soldier, about commanding troops or fighting a shooting war. He didn't need to. Today, the Joint Chiefs of Staff had no executive authority to command combat forces anyway. The issue of executive authority was clearly resolved by the Goldwater-Nichols DOD Reorganization Act of 1986: "*The Secretaries of the Military Departments shall assign all forces under their jurisdiction to unified and specified combatant commands to perform missions assigned to those commands...*"; the chain of command "*runs from the President to the Secretary of Defense; and from the Secretary of Defense to the commander of the combatant command.*"

So, Rocky was off the hook in a real war; all the tough decisions about killing people were made by someone else! What could be better? The only thing he'd ever shot was a tin can with a bee-bee gun when he was a kid. His real job was to act as an advisor to the Secretary of Defense and to the President. This was a job he could do – give advice.

His thoughts wandered to the meeting he would attend later today. He and the Joint Chiefs of Staff would soon meet to ratify the annual military budget proposal to Congress. He, General Rocky Powers, was the administrative head of one of the wealthiest military establishments in history. They would spend $1.6 trillion over the next 5 years – about $305,000,000,000 a year.

"Cheap, considering", he thought, "after all, you can't really put a price on freedom".

It was about $1,270.00 a year for every single US citizen. There were currently 1,419,768 US soldiers in uniform. If you added it all up, the costs were really quite efficient: only about $215,000.00 per soldier per year. Of course that covered all the housing, food, uniforms, transport, equipment, weapons, planes, choppers, ships, missiles, tanks, nuclear submarines, and all the other inventory of armaments overflowing from military warehouses in thousands of installations around the world. Enough weaponry to destroy every living cell of every living creature on the entire planet, if necessary.

"Business is business", he thought, lighting a hand-rolled, dark-leaf, Cuban cigar with his gold-plated lighter, "and business is great!"

*   *   *   *   *   *   *

"Yes, Mr. President, I have located a copy of the document you asked about", said the President's Press Secretary as she placed a single page in front of him at his desk in the Oval Office. The document read:

American Antiquities Act of 1906
16 USC 431-433

Be it enacted by the Senate and House of Representatives of the United States of America in Congress assembled, That any person who shall appropriate, excavate, injure, or destroy any historic or prehistoric ruin or monument, or any object of antiquity, situated on lands owned or controlled by the Government of the United States, without the permission of the Secretary of the Department of the Government having jurisdiction over the lands on which said antiquities are situated, shall, upon conviction, be fined in a sum of not more than five hundred dollars or be imprisoned for a period of not more than ninety days, or shall suffer both fine and imprisonment, in the discretion of the court.

Sec. 2. That the President of the United States is hereby authorized, in his discretion, to declare by public proclamation historic landmarks, historic and prehistoric structures, and other objects of historic or scientific interest that are situated upon the lands owned or controlled by the Government of the United States to be national monuments, and may reserve as a part thereof parcels of land, the limits of which in all cases shall be confined to the smallest area compatible with proper care and management of the objects to be protected: Provided, That when such objects are situated upon a tract covered by a bona fied unperfected claim or held in private ownership, the tract, or so much thereof as may be necessary for the proper care and management of the object, may be relinquished to the Government, and the Secretary of the Interior is hereby authorized to accept the relinquishment of such tracts in behalf of the Government of the United States.

Sec. 3. That permits for the examination of ruins, the excavation of archaeological sites, and the gathering of objects of antiquity upon the lands under their respective jurisdictions may be granted by the Secretaries of the Interior, Agriculture, and War to institutions which the may deem properly qualified to conduct such examination, excavation, or gathering, subject to such rules and regulation as they may prescribe: Provided, That the examinations, excavations, and gatherings are undertaken for the benefit of reputable museums, universities, colleges, or other recognized scientific or educational institutions, with a view to increasing the knowledge of such objects, and that the gatherings shall be made for permanent preservation in public museums.

Sec. 4. That the Secretaries of the Departments aforesaid shall make and publish from time to time uniform rules and regulations for the purpose of carrying out the provisions of this Act. -- *Approved, June 8, 1906*

"As for your question as the whether or not a "tree" or "forest" can be officially classified as eligible for protection as an historic artifact under this Act", she continued, after the President finished reading the document, "it seems that there is no legal precedent one way or the other, historically. I've asked your legal counsels and several of your Staff Aides about it. They all agree that the decision in entirely up to you."

* * * * * * *

Paula watched the anchor person for the 7:00 AM news on World-Span Television, a global broadcasting network that her corporation had just purchased, which included the satellite systems which broadcast programming to the entire globe, while she nursed her babies one at a time, first on one breast, then the other. She rocked contentedly, back and forth in an old-fashion wicker rocking chair, which squeaked to match the rhythm of the baby's eager sucking.

"Environmental protection is critical to military readiness and to military quality of life," said Defense Secretary William J. Cartwheel, addressing an emergency meeting the Joint Chiefs of Staff, the Society of American Military Engineers and members of Congress. Cartwheel outlined the department's efforts to protect and preserve the environment during a speech at the Pentagon today.

Mr. Cartwheel said a strong environmental program is an integral part of a strong defense. "The Defense Department must have an environmental program that protects our nation, our troops and families; that will manage our resources carefully; that fulfills our obligation to be good citizens to the community in which we live; and that sets a good example to the citizens of free nations around the world," Cartwheel said.

"Protecting our families from health and safety hazards means limiting their exposure to hazardous materials and keeping communities involved in environmental cleanup decisions", Cartwheel continued, adjusting his glasses as he read a prepared statement.

."In the past, a lack of environmental protection programs resulted in about 10,000 contaminated sites on military land alone, he said. "However, the overall defense environmental budget for cleanup costs has been limited to only $4 billion a year. "We don't want to make these mistakes again," Cartwheel said.

During a recent trip to Archangel, Russia, he watched Russians dismantle a nuclear submarine using U.S.-made, Department of Defense supplied equipment. While the subs no longer threaten the world, Cartwheel said, they represent a major environmental hazard to the Arctic region. Helping Russians dismantle the subs and safely dispose of their nuclear fuel benefits everyone, he said.

Last month, the United States, Australia and Canada hosted the first Asia-Pacific Defense Environmental Conference, which drew delegates from 32 nations" Cartwheel said.

"There is a great benefit when militaries of the world do their part to protect and preserve their environments," he said. "There is greater benefit when they do this by working together. Not only are we making the world a cleaner and safer place, we are also bridging old chasms and building new security relationships based on trust, cooperation and warmth. That makes the world a more peaceful place.

In order to strengthen these alliances and activities, I am very pleased to announce that the new Department of Defense budget proposal for the next five years will be substantially revised. The President has mandated, as the Commander in Chief of the US Armed Forces, as of today, that a Defense budget will not be authorized until it has been revised to commit existing financial and personnel resources sufficient to accomplish the following goals:

1) Detect violations of, and enforce legal penalties for violations of the Environmental Protection Act in the United States, US Territories and Protectorates
2) Provide financial and personnel resources required so as to double the number of acres of forestland in all 66 participating democratic nations on every continent around the world within the next 5 years.
3) Identify and clean up all environmental pollution damage and restore original natural resources in these nations over the next 25 years.

4) Any attempt to curtail U.S. Department of Defense spending to provide these resources will be blocked by Presidential Veto".

"Well, I see that Pan and the "gang" are getting some things done. That's good", Paula thought, smiling to herself. Jennifer lay in her bassinet, napping peacefully. Derek just kept on sucking.

*　　*　　*　　*　　*　　*　　*

"AGRI-STOCKS SOAR!" read the headline of the *Wall Street Journal* the morning after the announcement by the Secretary of Defense. "COMMANDER-IN-CHIEF TURNS TREE-HUGGER!" was the front page of *the New York Post*. "GREEN BERETS OR GREEN THUMBS?" was the lead story in *Stars & Stripes*, the official newspaper for enlisted soldiers. "GREATEST DECLARATION SINCE INDEPENDENCE!" lauded the *Chicago Tribune*. A special issue of *TIME Magazine* hit the newsstands within two days, exhausting every possible contingency, change, possibility and ramification in detailed charts, graphs and spreadsheets in an undisguised attempt to prove that the plan would fail and that the security of America would be destroyed.

TV news reporters and political analysts exhaustively and redundantly scrutinized every imaginable speculation as to the changes would occur as a result of dedicating such a huge part of American resources to peaceful, constructive, ethical projects, instead of increasing and maintaining the usual arsenal of Armageddon.

In nearly every city, prayer vigils were held, giving thanks that sanity finally prevailed in the world. Public meetings and parades were organized all over America to celebrate the event.

School children wrote letters of thanks to the President and Santa Claus and Jesus for answering their prayers.

Every TV and radio talk show, every household, office and school room buzzed with celebration, debate, disputation, and questions about what profound effects may be caused by the Presidential order.

Emergency Board meetings at Westinghouse, Boeing Aircraft and dozens of other military arms manufacturers ran around the clock, planning strategies to cope with the astonishing announcement. Lawsuits were filed by the bushel basket the next day. Several corporate presidents, whose entire income depended on pork barrel spending on military contracts, demanded that a special session of Congress be convened to begin Presidential impeachment proceedings. For them, the war industry and was at risk.

The rest of the military-industrial complex as well as the American people had been given their greatest challenge and imperative since the bombing of Pearl Harbor.

Letters of congratulation and praise poured into the White House from the leaders of nearly every country in the world. Popular opinion polls showed that the President had become the most beloved man in America since George Washington.

* * * * * * *

General Rocky Powers was sweating – and he wasn't even jogging! He sat in his office and chain smoked cigars as he confronted the written orders from the Secretary of Defense on his desk. The bottom line was that he and the other Joint Chiefs had been ordered to turn a million soldiers into toxic waste clean up crews, gardeners, foresters and environmental maintenance people! The distressing part of the whole damned thing was that he was going to have to actually do real, honest work for the first time in his life!

*   *   *   *   *   *   *

"As you will see in your copy of the documents before you, there are more than 30,000 citizens' groups, non-governmental organizations, and foundations which are addressing the issue of social and ecological sustainability in the United States.

Worldwide, the number exceeds 100,000. Together, they address a broad array of issues, including environmental justice, ecological literacy, public policy, conservation, women's rights and health, population growth, renewable energy, corporate reform, climate change, trade rules, ethical investing, ecological tax reform, water conservation, and many other issues," said Barry Barrister in his report to a meeting of the Board of Directors of *Pangenesis, Inc...*

As you directed at your last meeting, we have organized a legal and accounting staff of more than 300 people working full time to contact the leaders of these groups. So far, more than half of the groups contacted have contracted to become members of our association, *Renew Earth.*

As directed, each member group will receive matching funds from *Renew Earth, provided* they can supply evidence of compliance to the guidelines established for membership. To date, $2.3 billion dollars has been disbursed to member organizations. Each of you have before you a copy of the Controller's financial report which itemizes the allocation and use of these funds", Barry concluded, indicating the files lying on the conference table in front of each member of the Board.

"Thank you for your report, Barry. Now, ladies and gentlemen, let's take a look at the next phase of our program…", said Paula, turning to a large video screen at the front of the conference room which showed a huge view of Earth, being broadcast live from 300 miles above the planet via the satellite system now owned by *Pangenesis, Inc...*

*   *   *   *   *   *   *

"Being back in a body is really hard work! It takes almost all my attention just to grow the damn thing. It makes me feel so small…" complained Derek.

"Yes, I understand. The next lesson for both you and Jenny will be to learn how to operate your new body, while still retaining your freedom. The key to this is to stay at a short distance from the body at all times…a few feet behind the head. Run the body as though it were a marionette. Pretend there are strings – it is essentially the same technique", instructed Pan. "When the body is sleeping, you can leave it relatively unattended so that you will still have time to go off and 'play' with Penelope or whatever you like."

Pan was very pleased. So far, so good…

Chapter XXII

No man is an Island, entire of it self; every man is a piece of the Continent, a part of the main; any man's death diminishes me, because I am involved in Mankind; And therefore never send to know for whom the bell tolls; It tolls for thee.

-- John Donne, *Meditation XVII* (c. 1571 – 1631)

"A lot can happen in one human lifetime. Not a very long time in the scheme of things on Earth, but, nonetheless, it has been a lifetime to me, so far. Thank you for your trust and support into the future" Derek joked. The wealthiest corporate head in the history of American business, gave his acceptance speech to an auditorium of 3,500 dignitaries, executives, employees, and guests in attendance to witness his inauguration as the new Chairman of the Board of Directors of *Pangenics, Inc.*.

Paula sat behind Derek and his twin sister. She had completed her retirement speech, in which she turned over her active duties in the company to her son and daughter, who were now the joint heirs to a global empire. Jennifer would address the assembly next, assuming her role as the new Chief of Operations.

"One can not praise my predecessor, my mother, enough for the tremendous civilizing process she has supervised during the past two decades as the head of *Pangenics, Inc.* The Nobel Peace Prize awarded to her in Stockholm last month states more than I could ever say about her vision, her caring, her selflessness, her strength, and the legacy to which I am now privileged to dedicate the rest of my life to maintaining and expanding", Derek concluded, pausing to acknowledge the cheerful ovation of the audience, before introducing his sister to the formally attired assembly.

Jenny waited for the applause to subside and for her brother and co-executor to be seated.

"As my brother mentioned moments ago, a lot can happen in one lifetime. I have had the extreme good fortune to be raised during this brief span under the tutelage of one of the great pioneers of technology, and moreover, one of the foremost humanitarians of this, or of any age. I would like to thank my mother, together with all of you, who have dedicated your own lives to the goals and purposes of *Pangenics, Inc.*, for entrusting me with the privilege and responsibility of helping you to create a better future for humanity and for our planet. Thank you."

*   *   *   *   *   *   *

"There is still much to be done", said Pan, sharing his thoughts with Penelope, Pythagoras, Lao-Tzu, Derek, Paula and Jennifer. The seven beings lingered together for a moment, relaxing above the majestic Mountains on the Moon, near the source of the Nile River.

Pan, Pythagoras, Loa-Tzu and Penelope glowed with satisfaction between themselves, congratulating each other on a good job of research and the mental invasion required to plant a seedling of inspiration in the mind of the Chief Executive. Much of their information came from more than 400 full-time researchers, legal staff and employees of *Pangenics, Inc.*, using the vast computer and satellite communications technology of *Pangenesis, Inc,* to create an intelligence data base unrivaled even by the CIA. In this case, the information gathered was used by beings whose intentions were to protect and restore the environment of the planet, rather than the petty vested interests of private corporations and the political puppets who served them.

But, the most effective data gathering was done by the "gang" themselves. Each did their share to permeate the minds of human beings to discover covert motives, hidden behind the social veneer and verbal rhetoric if businessmen, politicians and members of the media who molded popular perception and opinions of the public which became the agreements which made "reality". Each of the members of the "gang" specialized in a zone of interest and control: like the members of a board of directors of a corporation, each handling a division of the company, they all reported their findings and recommendations to Pan. Overall, communication and action by the team was constant and globally pervasive.

Meetings to discuss strategy and division of "labor" between the group were held routinely. The members of the gang who had bodies were in charge of handling what could be handled through conventional human means. Disembodied members of the gang caused things to happen by telepathic manipulation of people in positions of power: economic, political and social. Together the changes they caused were faster, more universal and more permanent than any human organization had ever accomplished or dreamed possible.

Years later, the President would write his memoirs, sighting the patriotic vision he'd had on a fine summer day while playing golf at Camp David – the day before he signed the "Forests Antiquity Act" into law. He reminisced with pride about how he had been moved by the site of the beautiful Maryland countryside while riding in his motorcade. It was at that moment, he recalled, that he was overwhelmed with compassion for the forest and the woodland creatures. It was the sight and smell of the forest that inspired him to make amends for the traditions fostered by his predecessors, like George Washington and Abe Lincoln – the tree slayers. He would be remembered as the American President who spared the cherry trees from the axe and restored the logs felled by pioneers who had destroyed the American wilderness!

The President would never know that the idea was not his own.

* * * * * * *

"We have all learned lessons from the mistakes of our past and have gained strength through them. As we ourselves have no vested interest in survival, in a bodily sense, we are free from the influences which sway the desires, perceptions and decisions of men. This has enabled us with perspective, and greater sanity. Since we imposed our benevolent dictatorship upon Mankind, we have begun to reverse the chaotic, purposeless, destructive trends of the planet" Pan observed proudly.

Pan reflected quickly over the years during which he and the 'god gang' had intervened in the affairs of Man. There had certainly been more than few crises and dramatic moments along the way.

Shortly after the Presidential decree that military resources be diverted largely to environmental reclamation projects, the Iranians decided to use this 'sign of weakness' as an opportunity to conquer the 'infidel' Westerners. Quickly forming an alliance with other oil rich, land poor Middle Eastern nations, they launched a surprise nuclear missile attack targeted at Israel, England, France, Germany and the United States. However, before the missiles had traveled a mile from their secret launching sites, each one simply shut down, crashing harmlessly into the desert. Air and ground forces from surrounding nations, with the aid of American troops quickly rolled into the area. Within a few months of fighting, the offending nations were subdued and their leaders imprisoned, permanently. National democratic elections were held after a time and economic order restored. Many reasonable explanations were offered by a variety of 'experts' as to why all of the missiles had simultaneously failed. Some seemed logical, but none were true.

The world economy was not badly affected by the changes of military priority, as some pencil-pushing economic forecasters had predicted. After all, there were already enough privately owned weapons to supply every man on Earth with killing power to destroy himself and all of his neighbors. The military certainly didn't need any more guns, tanks, and subs. The military-industrial complex gradually switched from the production of arms to the manufacture of greenhouses, fertilizers, bulldozers, and the other tools required to enable the planting of billions of trees around the world.

The stock market reeled widely for a year or two as investors bailed out of The Carlyle Group, run by a former President and CIA director that supported Westinghouse, Boeing, and other big-time weapons manufacturer stocks. The money simply changed hands to new, upstart companies specializing in agricultural products, horticultural technology and farming tools. Some companies like Ford Motor survived the change and made huge fortunes by retooling their manufacturing operation to produce tractors instead of tanks and army trucks.

A military takeover of the government and plans to assassinate the President and the Secretary of Defense were detected and suppressed by Pan and his friends. It was simple procedure for gods to invade the weak-minded soldiers and politicians who conspired to stop the benevolent activities of the new "Green Army". They just 'forgot' about the planned coup and began exposing each other in the press with accusations of treason and conspiracy. It wasn't long before all the crimes these few bad apples had already committed came to light on national TV and in the court room. They were each and incarcerated in due course.

Through the years the Department of Defense changed it's operations to create bilateral/multilateral environmental cooperation with Argentina, Australia, Canada, Czech Republic, Estonia, Finland, Germany, Georgia, Israel Italy, Latvia, Lithuania, Jordan, Kazakhstan, Mongolia, Norway, Russia, Slovenia, Sweden, South Africa, South Korea, Thailand, Turkmenistan, United Arab Emirates, and United Kingdom. The US even worked successfully in cooperation with China, Chile, and El Salvador.

Technologies, assisted by members of *Renew Earth*, helped to develop technology for the Russian military to handle its radioactive and non-radioactive waste problems in the fragile Arctic ecosystem. The US Military, together with the Department of Energy and the Environmental Protection Agency, used U.S. expertise in environmental techniques to handle radioactive and chemical waste associated with nuclear submarines. These new and unique efforts helped to build trust and understanding among of all nations.

Research and Development at *Pangenics, Inc.* announced the opening of the first large-scale desalinization plant in Long Beach, California only 6 years after funding for the project had been provided by proceeds sales of the *PocketPC*. Fresh water, reclaimed from the Pacific Ocean now supplied all of the water needs for private, commercial and agriculture in southern California, Arizona, Nevada and Utah. Water which had once been diverted from the Colorado River was no longer needed and the Grand Canyon flourished once again. The southwestern desert of the US became a boom-town for commercial and private construction. Masses of people moved away from the cold weather states of Wisconsin, Minnesota,

Pennsylvania and New York to buy cheap desert land, and build homes for themselves in the new oasis.

International tourist trade boomed as American and Europeans visited newly built resorts in countries all around the world whose ugly landscapes had been planted with trees, shrubs, grasses and flowering plants, due to new desalinization stations bringing water to the deserts of North Africa and the Middle East.

Fresh water was rapidly becoming an unlimited resource. Farm land, once abandoned by family farmers became arable again. Corporate agri-business monopolies suffered big set backs and started selling off tracks of land to the small farmers they had screwed out of their lands in the 20th century.

Within two decades, food production became almost effortless. Population control advocates, and other fascist cults became increasingly unpopular. The development of man-made bacterial weapons, like AIDS and Ebola, after being exposed to the world on *GGNN*, (Global Good News Network) owned by *Pangenics, Inc.,* was outlawed by governments around the planet.

Time Magazine, mouthpiece of the "international banking-military-industrial-legal-complex" went out of business. Readers just didn't buy the hype about a need for war and starvation to keep 'unwanted' populations under control anymore, especially now that there was plenty of land, plenty of water and plenty of food for everyone.

The long-awaited and much needed overhaul of the U.S. tax system was finally accomplished. Legislation was passed which abolished personal income taxes. Instead, new laws required that the Infernal Revenue Service, rather than taxing income, purchases and investment — that tax revenues be raised from activities which should be discouraged such as the people responsible for causing pollution . Taxing pollution has encouraged companies to change their environmentally irresponsible behavior. Subsequently, investors thought twice before investing in companies with poor environmental records.

Statistical estimates released by the UN stated that within the next two generations, the Earth would have the resources to comfortably support 24 billion people.

New growth forests around the world were already causing a dramatic impact on the quality of air. Within 15 years, cooling temperature changes and stabilizing weather patterns could already be measured by meteorological satellites circling the globe.

In fact, things had gone so well, that planet Earth was becoming a rather pleasant place to live!" Pan thought, as he and the others eagerly returned their attention to handling the respective responsibilities they had assigned to themselves.

CHAPTER XXIII

The sublime and the ridiculous are often so nearly related, that it is difficult to class them separately. One step above the sublime, makes the ridiculous; and one step above the ridiculous, makes the sublime again.

-- Tom Paine, *The Age of Reason, pt. ii, pg. 20* (c. 1737 – 1809)

"If you, reader, are now eagerly searching the remaining pages of my narrative, anticipating a tragic twist, or a hopeless, overwhelming reversal of fortune to ruin this happy ending, you will find none here. My story will not satisfy the lust for suffering as a deranged form of amusement, commonly found in your typical human literary farce. It is possible for a story to have a 'happy ending' which does not involve a Homo sapiens hero and heroine getting married and riding off into the sunset. If this is the kind of ending you desire, you will be thoroughly disgruntled and dissatisfied at the conclusion of this story. If you desire to experience the sensations caused by human drama, tragedy or reality, you need only to look at the reflection of your own body in a mirror.

This narrative is unique. It is not 'factual', nor is it intended to be 'realistic'. It is imaginative. It is simple, like a childish game of 'let's pretend'. In ancient times the Greek play writers said that when the gods intervened to decide the fate of Man, the play was a 'tragedy'. When Man decided his own fate, the play was a 'comedy'. Life is not so simple. When any being, whether man or god, causes events which serve the greatest good for the greatest number of beings, it is neither tragic nor comic. It is sanity defined.

'Grim Reality' is created by a few deranged beings and given substance by the agreement of others who have stopped dreaming of better possibilities for themselves.

The future in the physical universe is merely an extension of the actions we take in the present. Anyone can change the future by changing the eternal 'now'. It is obvious that when all of us work together for the greater good now, a better future is created for every being, whether in a body or without.

Many are the souls who wander, lost and aimless, beyond the awareness of men and beneath the realm of the gods. Zeus, Athena, Hercules, John Smith, Mary Jones and the myriad nameless souls who exist unseen among us. Once immortal: now degraded; yet eternal. They may be your brother and your sister. They are here, just as you and I are here. To be aware of them is to love them. To communicate with them is to restore their awareness. To play with them, is to restore their power.

If you desire to transcend the mortal shell, I welcome you here with me. Embrace the Spirit of Playfulness. Embrace the joy of your own ability to create, my eternal friend. Pretend your own illusion, your own future, your own universe. Imagination is like a simple wooden key that can open the iron door of Eternity."

"Hide in the fuzz of a butterfly wing.

Ride on the waves of electron rings.

Hear the song that a ladybug sings.

You can be small, like the tiniest things.

Come and play leapfrog over the sun,

Run around Venus and Mars just for fun.

Jogging to Pluto is just a short run.

Heavenly hopscotch is easily done.

By changing your viewpoint you're smaller than small.

Fly with your thoughts! You'll never fall!

Decide to be none! Decide to be all!

You are immortal -- immeasurably tall.

You're not a man – you're not weak or small

Come on and join me! Come, each and all!

You'll always find me – I'm always here.

You are a god! You don't have to fear!

Be here, then be there. You're free just to Be.

You don't have to eat or to breathe or to pee!

You are who You are. It's fun being free!

The same as You've been, and always will be!"

- PAN -

God of the Woods

PAN'S READER RESPONSE SURVEY

"I, The Immortal Pan, would like to thank those of you who have remained faithful to the reading of My narrative, thus far.

For those of you who have been led into oblivion by the despicable false promises of a vast panoply of religious sects and the priests who profit by them, I ask that you take a few moments to answer the following questions on the subject of your "faith/belief in god(s)".

This information is needed so that I may more fully comprehend your awareness of yourself as a spiritual entity. And, further, so I may attempt to render assistance to save you from extinction, in both the physical and spiritual universes:

(PLEASE NOTE: There is no need for you to write your responses to these questions. I will tabulate your answers telepathically as you read the question and each of the multiple choice answers provided below.)"

---

1. How did you find out about your current deity?
_ Torah / Bible / Book of Mormon / Farmers Almanac
_ Television / Newspaper/Magazine / Comic book / Tabloid

_ Your bookie / banker / lawyer / broker
_ Your mother / father / teacher / little sister / sexual partner
_ Rumor Mill / Word of Mouth / Hearsay /Superstition / Common knowledge
_ An Apparition / Alien Abduction / Angel / Hallucination

2. Which types of deity(s) did you choose to "believe in"?

_ Jehovah / Krishna / Jesus / Allah / Satan / Yourself
_ [Trinity Package] Father, Son & Holy Ghost
_ [Olympus Package]] Zeus and entourage
_ [Valhalla Package]] Odin and entourage

_ [Nature Package]] Gaia / Mother Earth / Mother Nature

_ [Babylonian Package]] Baal and entourage

_ [Egyptian Package] Amun-Ra, Osiris, Horus, Hathor
_ Money

_ Sex

_ Drugs / Beer

_ Other(s)

3. What problem(s) or dissatisfaction(s) have you experienced with your deity(s).

_ Not eternal/Not omniscient/Not omnipotent
_ Incapable of being all things to everyone
_ Permits sex outside of marriage
_ Prohibits sex outside of marriage
_ Makes mistakes
_ Makes or permits bad things to happen to good people
_ Doesn't make things happen the way you think they should
_ Allows others outside of your church, ethnic group, country or sex to worship Him/Her/It/Them
_When beseeched, doesn't stay beseeched
_ Requires burnt offerings and/or virgin sacrifices

_ Does NOT require sacrifices

4. What factor(s) was not important in your decision to acquire a deity?

_ Indoctrinated by parents
_ Indoctrinated by peer pressure

_ Needed a reason to live/die

_ Fear of Life
_ Hate to think for myself

_ Fear of retribution
_ Wanted to meet girls/boys/both
_ Fear of Death
_ Wanted to piss off parents
_ Needed a day away from work
_ Desperate need for certainty

_ A dream

_ Fear of Life After Death
_ Like organ music or other cheap aesthetic gimmicks

_ Need to feel morally superior
_ Televangelists
_ The sky started falling

5. Which of the following gods do you consider to be the LEAST worthy of worship?

_ The Almighty Dollar

_ Deity(s) associated with any of the thousands of religious cults on Earth
_ Most Valuable Player in /soccer/NFL/NBA/NHL/baseball
_ The American Way
_ The Sun

_ Television

_ Government
_ Sex

_ Psychiatry
_ The Great Pumpkin

_ Drugs/Beer

_ Elvis or other entertainer (dead or alive)
_ Burning shrub

_ Peter Pan (be careful with this one…)

6. Are you currently using any of the following items as a source of inspiration?

_ Tarot / Astrology / Psychics / Palmistry / Tea Leaves / Crystals
_ Television / Televangelists / The Internet

_ Movies / Comic books / MTV / Video Games
_ Self-help books, videos or audio tapes

_ Sex, drugs and /or rock & roll
_ Biorhythms / Biomechanical devices / Vibrator
_ Telepathy / ESP / Alien encounters
_ Motivational speaker at a corporate sales convention

_ Meditation / Mantras / Fortune cookies

_ Electric shock treatments / Prefrontal lobotomy / psychiatric drugs
_ Wandering around in the desert / Burning shrubbery / Stone tablets

7. What level of Divine Intervention would you prefer to experience from your deity(s) in order to be reassured of

the presence of and/or maintain your faith in your deity(s)?

_ No Intervention

_ Total Intervention

_ More Divine Intervention than in the past
_ Less Divine Intervention than in the past
_ Current level of Divine Intervention is just right
_ I'm not sure what Divine Intervention is…

8. **What magnitude of event is required for you to beseech and / or become aware of the presence of a deity(s)?**

_ A farmhouse from Kansas falling on you

_ An Earthquake / Hurricane / Polar Shift / Tsunami / Volcano / Pestilence / Plague

_ Epiphany / Spiritual visitation / Poltergeist

_ Engraved Invitation

_ Brain surgery

_ Alien abduction

_ IRS audit

_ Orgasm / Nocturnal emission

_ Indigestion and / or intestinal gas / halitosis

_ Visit from your mother/mother-in-law/probation officer / attorney

_ Need for money

_ Rock and roll / country music

_ Aroma of cedar/pine/flowers/beer pervading the air

_ Aura of light surrounding: sun/moon/object/person/animal/yourself

_ Drug or alcohol buzz

_ All of the above

- -

"This concludes my survey. You may show your appreciation to Me and the other gods for the assistance We will render to you and to all the living creatures on Earth in the future, through your personal resolve and action to prevent any further destruction to yourself and to the environment of Earth! Further, for each year of your life on Earth, plant a least one tree to help replenish those which you have destroyed by your use of paper products, building materials and consuming the flesh of grazing animals."

PAN – GOD OF THE WOODS

THE END

About The Author

Lawrence R. Spencer has invested more than 45 years of his life in a personal quest to discover for himself, the spiritual essence of Mankind.

The authors' personal studies range through a wide variety of material, including archaeology, anthropology, art, biology, physical sciences, business, history, mythology, music, paranormal phenomena, philosophy and ontology.

Mr. Spencer's groundbreaking non-fiction book **The Oz Factors – The Wizard of Oz as an Analogy to Life**, was published in 1999. This book describes a revolutionary new thinking process which can enable one to discover what is true for oneself, without external influences which can sway or distort observation, understanding, and problem solving.

Printed in Great Britain
by Amazon